Totally Bound Publishing books by K.M. Mahoney:

Odd Man In
In Teddy's Arms
The Lonely Heart

A Dragon's Treasure
Cody's Dragon

I0663180

A Dragon's Treasure

CODY'S DRAGON

K.M. MAHONEY

Cody's Dragon
ISBN # 978-1-78184-739-8
©Copyright K.M. Mahoney 2014
Cover Art by Posh Gosh ©Copyright January 2014
Interior text design by Claire Siemaszkiewicz
Totally Bound Publishing

CODY'S DRAGON

Dedication

For those who dream of dragons.

Prologue

Kirit shoved the last shirt into his pack and fastened it tightly.

"Are you certain you want to do this?" Nyx lounged against the bedpost, arms folded, face solemn.

"I believe I've answered that question often enough over the past week that you shouldn't need to hear it again."

"Tell me anyway."

Kirit slung the bag over his shoulder and glowered at Nyx. "Don't you have anything better to do with your time?"

Nyx shrugged. "No. Since the Ardreth surrendered, it's been deadly dull around here."

"You need a hobby. Or, better still, you can come with me."

Nyx snorted, falling into step beside Kirit as they left the room. "No, thank you," he drawled, wrinkling his nose in distaste. "I, at least, have enough sense to realize there's nothing of value on the other side of the Veil."

"Tell that to Merrick." The nobleman, one of the king's advisors, had returned from his last trip to Earth with a new bride. It had, in fact, inspired Kirit's current scheme.

"Merrick isn't Draak," Nyx replied simply.

"I'll take my chances."

They arrived at a split in the hallway, where two long corridors stretched into the gloom, dimly lit by sputtering candles.

In silence, they entered opposite sides of the passageway. Nyx paused just before the shadows swallowed his lean form.

"Call if you need us," he ordered.

"I won't." Kirit's reply echoed off the walls, his stride not hesitating in its path.

Nyx shook his head. "Stubborn bastard."

Chapter One

Kirit's boots hit the pavement with a dull thud. He paused a moment and surveyed his surroundings with narrowed eyes.

Nothing unusual caught his attention from where he stood, hidden between two buildings. He didn't really expect it to. Old habits were hard to break, though.

He shifted his pack into a more secure position before diving into the crowded walkway. He would have to pick one of the busiest times of day to arrive— bad timing all around. At least the weather was still warm, and he wasn't forced to wade through knee-high snow. Denver was a bitch in the winter.

Kirit ate up the distance with long-legged strides, people unconsciously clearing a path for him. He knew his sheer size, along with his harshly carved features, didn't invite any pleasantries.

It took Kirit less than ten minutes to cover the blocks to his destination. He ascended a rickety staircase, which clung to the outside of the brick building with precarious tenacity. The metal door squealed loudly when he opened it, revealing a dim and narrow hall.

Halfway along, he rapped firmly on the door marked 1207.

"Who's there?" A voice called from the other side.

"Kirit. Open up."

Locks clicked. Kirit counted six. That was, in his opinion, a bit unnecessary. Harper wasn't exactly helpless on his own.

The door swung open to show a short, stocky man standing there. He had well-tanned skin and a spiked mess of blue-tipped brown hair. "What're you doing here?"

"That's a marvelous way to greet someone. Are you going to let me in?"

"Will you go away if I don't?" Harper stepped aside to let Kirit enter his tiny apartment.

Once inside, Kirit dropped his pack to the floor next to his feet, not bothering to look around. He'd been here often enough and there wasn't much to see.

"Want a beer?" Harper disappeared into the tiny closet he called a kitchen.

"Hardly."

"Snob."

"Absolutely."

Harper reappeared seconds later, popping the lid off a bottle. He let it fall to the floor, obviously unconcerned when it bounced off the cracked ceramic tile and rolled under the olive-green couch. "So, what brings a high and mighty Draak to the human realm?"

"I'm on a hunt."

Harper's expression sharpened with interest. He let the bottle in his hand dangle at his side for a moment. "Dragon, Fae, or—"

"Not that kind of hunt."

"Oh." Harper returned his attention to his drink.

"I'm on a mate hunt."

"Good for you."

"In this realm."

Harper choked, spraying his last mouthful of beer across the room. The distance was impressive—Kirit had to sidestep to avoid being hit.

"Sorry," Harper said. "I think my hearing's going."

"Your hearing is fine. It's the rest of you that's...going."

"Yeah, yeah. Tell me something I don't know. But you're going right alongside me. A mate? On this side? Are you nuts?"

"It worked for Merrick."

"Merrick isn't Draak."

"Everyone keeps saying that. I'm sick of being alone. My mate is clearly not behind the Veil, and I'm not interested in waiting for the next generation to grow up. I didn't come here for a lecture. I've heard it all. Dozens of times."

Harper looked resigned. "Fine. Why did you come, then? Where do I fit into this grand scheme of yours?"

"I need connections. Information. What is the best way to meet the most number of people in the least amount of time?"

"Sheesh, you don't ask for much, do you?"

Kirit crossed his arms and raised one dark eyebrow.

"Do you realize how many people live in this frickin' city?" Harper pointed out.

"Shall I give you a precise number or an estimate?"

"Shut up." Harper groaned. He grabbed another beer before plopping onto the couch. The ragged piece of furniture echoed Harper's groan, creaking ominously under his weight. "Make yourself comfortable," he said, waving with his bottle. "This will take a while. Oh, and grab something to write with. You can make a list."

Kirit did as directed, settling himself gingerly on a chair which was slightly newer than the couch, but even uglier. "You may begin," he directed.

Harper growled. "Fucking dragon."

Kirit gave the witch an extremely toothy smile. "That's the ultimate goal."

"Next time, I'm not opening the door," Harper declared.

* * * *

Cody wasn't having a very successful night. Normally, the pounding of the music and the flashing lights energized him. Tonight? He just wanted to hide in one of the many pockets of shadows. Alone. He realized he was scowling and quickly wiped the expression away—the goal was to be approached, not scare off potential…dates. The fact that he didn't feel like being social shouldn't matter so much. There was rent and bills to pay, and new clothes to buy.

Jay-Jay passed by, lean hips swinging to the beat of the music. He was instantly pulled onto the dance floor by an older gentleman. Jay-Jay flashed Cody a triumphant smile.

Cody scowled again. Normally, Cody could ignore the little jerk, but he was irritable tonight. Extremely, inexplicably so. He plunked his glass down on the table and stood.

"I'm going home," Cody declared loudly. He got a few glances, but no one seemed to care all that much.

Definitely time to call it a night.

Cody was halfway across the packed building when a tingle washed over. He stopped and looked around. There were eyes watching him, but he ignored them, trying to identify the source of the itch at the back of his neck. *Now, where is — Oh, holy crap!*

Someone smacked into his back, sending Cody staggering. He moved out of the line of fire, but couldn't stop his gaze from constantly wandering back to the man sitting at the bar.

Cody didn't know him. That in itself was a little unusual. He'd been around and knew most of the regular weeknight visitors to Macland's. This guy, though...oh, he would have remembered this one. Huge, broad and buff, he was an intriguing sight. He wasn't a biker — no tattoos. He wasn't a construction worker — not tan enough. And he most definitely wasn't in the military, not with that thick black hair, pulled into a braid that almost reached his waist.

Cody licked his lips. Oh, man, did he ever want himself a piece of that. A large piece, preferably the one showcased in those tight jeans.

A bright flash of color registered in his peripheral vision. Cody saw Jay-Jay making a beeline for the bar. For his man.

"Oh, no, you don't, bitch." Cody moved to intercept Jay. Normally, he didn't bother with Jay-Jay's little competition, but this one was his.

Cody was almost to the bar, the big guy in his sights, when someone grabbed him. Vicious fingers dug hard into his arm. Cody probably should have panicked, but all he could do was think, *that's gonna leave bruises, damn it.*

"We need to have a little talk."

Cody already knew who he would see when he turned his head. "Hello, Johnnie-boy. What brings you to this part of town?"

"Don't play with me. Let's go have a little chat, you and me."

"I'm kind of busy right...now..." *Well, shit.* In the brief minute that Cody's attention had been diverted, the hunk of gorgeous man had left. He caught a glimpse of Jay-Jay at the bar, looking disappointed. Cody could sympathize.

"Fine." Cody yanked his arm free. "We'll talk. But I don't give freebies. And you're buying me a drink."

With the way he was feeling? Johnnie was buying him two drinks. At least.

Looked like he was working tonight, after all.

Chapter Two

Kirit dropped onto the bed with a heartfelt sigh. He rubbed his forehead, ears still ringing. Why in the name of the gods did humans find it necessary to deafen themselves with their music? His ears were probably permanently damaged after three days spent doing what Harper called 'trolling' the clubs—and why it was called that he'd never know, as there were so far no trolls involved.

Kirit fell backward onto the itchy comforter and abandoned the ineffectual head massage to fling his arm over his eyes. Those hurt, too. He was coming very close to conceding defeat. Perhaps a mate was out there for him, perhaps not. But it was clear he wasn't going to be successful this way. Conversation was nigh well impossible at the places Harper had suggested.

"Three days isn't so long," he muttered into his arm. "Too soon to give up."

Maybe he should have told Harper about his little handicap. That might have simplified matters. But damn it, it was embarrassing.

Most Draak identified a potential mate initially by their scent. A mate would smell like the most magnificent flowers, more appealing than anything ever encountered. The second indicator came with close contact. Not sexual, although supposedly that would be enough to make all past partners pale in comparison. No, it was more far-reaching than sex. Draak were irritable creatures on their best days, belligerent and grumpy with those outside of their kind. And often within, as well. A mate, however, put them at ease and softened their rough personalities.

Unfortunately for Kirit, he was being forced to rely entirely on the second sign. Well over two decades ago, during a battle with a roving band of…whatever the hell they had been, he had taken an extremely fierce and painful blow directly to the face. His nose still bent to the side a little where the bone had shattered. The healers had been able to put his face back together, but they hadn't been able to fix the internal damage. Namely, they hadn't been able to restore his sense of smell to what it once was.

Hence why prowling bars and clubs was not a very effective hunting technique. He needed interaction, conversation—and wasn't that an awful thought? They were elements extremely difficult to come by in the establishments on Harper's list. Every person, man and woman, seemed to want to drag Kirit into a dark corner. Or the so-called 'restroom'. Humans were strangely enamored with restrooms.

The sudden crash of an orchestra had him rolling over reluctantly. He yanked the cell phone he'd purchased upon arrival from the back pocket of his jeans.

"What do you want?"

"We need to work on your manners."

Kirit sat up fully. "Harper, you thrice-cursed bastard, where have you been? I stopped at your home around one o'clock and it was empty."

"I was working," came the indignant reply.

"At one in the morning?"

"Oh, that 'one'. No, I was...otherwise occupied."

"Harper, I swear by the gods, if you were out having sex with some—"

"Not that kind of occupied, more's the pity. Speaking of which, how's your hunt proceeding?"

Kirit growled.

"That bad, huh?"

"Worse."

"Sorry, man. I'm thinking maybe we should give the clubs a break, try the coffee shops, maybe a couple of bookstores. I've never done this before, you know. I'm winging it here."

"You're doing what?"

Harper sighed. When he spoke next, his voice was soft. And was that a touch of compassion? Nah, couldn't be. "Kirit, who's to say you even have a mate in Denver? If there is a human mate prospect for you, the odds are extremely slim that you'll ever find them. Perhaps you would be better off going back through the Veil and waiting for the next generation, after all."

"I... Hell. It's only been three days. I promised myself at least a week, and I intend to follow my plan."

Harper mumbled something which sounded a lot like, "Goddamned anal, rigid bastard."

Kirit chose to ignore the comment. After all, profanity aside, the witch was only being truthful. "It's late and I'm going to bed. Call me at a decent hour. Late afternoon will do nicely. I'm not used to these strange hours you humans keep."

"Not all—"

Kirit snapped the phone closed. He dropped it over the side of the bed, not caring where it landed. Then he flopped over and fell asleep in his clothes.

He awoke several hours later feeling distinctly grimy. He smelled like cigarette smoke and alcohol.

Kirit dragged himself out of bed with a low groan. He felt several millennia old. His head weighed fifty pounds and his stomach churned—and all on only one beer the night before. Or was it this morning? Damn, he was all turned around.

He stripped off his clothes on the way to the bathroom, leaving a trail on the dull blue carpet. It took the water an eternity to warm, but he finally stepped into the heavy spray with a sigh. Oh, that was heaven.

Kirit braced his arms on the cold tiles and let the water pour over his head, hoping the stresses of the last three days would run down the drain with the dingy water. It didn't work, but he was starting to feel a little better. Well, cleaner, anyway.

He stood there for several long minutes and just breathed, the drops pounding against the tension in his shoulders. His normal morning erection was making itself known, but Kirit did his best to glare it into submission. He simply couldn't summon the energy for pleasuring himself.

It was close to three in the afternoon by the time Kirit felt civilized enough to socialize without trying to eat anyone. Kirit sat at the Starbucks a few blocks from his hotel and stirred a straw around in circles, staring at the table top while he waited for Harper to arrive.

Kirit wanted to go home. He missed the clear water, the rolling green hills and the pale, cool reflection of

Chelios and Mequa—the twin moons that often lit the sky as brightly as the sun. He missed his small lair tucked into the mountains surrounding the capital. Hell, he even missed those damn Fae. More than once, he'd wondered whether he was being a stubborn idiot and if he should just give up and go back through the Veil.

Two things stopped him. First of all, he hated giving up. Hated, hated it. He wasn't the type to quit—was, in fact, quite well-known for his stubbornness. He also was not eager to prove all the naysayers right.

And he was lonely. By the moons, he was so very lonely. Draak were, by nature, solitary creatures. Oh, they fought well as a group, formed strong ties with their own kind. But at the end of the day, they retreated to their own lairs. The single exception was their mate, a person—or creature—all for them. And Kirit wanted that, with a desperation that grew more prominent every day. He wanted someone to curl up with at night, someone to soothe his anger and hold him after battle.

He wanted someone to love. Human or Fae. Male, female, or something in between. It didn't matter. Kirit just wanted a mate.

Harper slapped Kirit heartily on the shoulder in greeting, startling him from his contemplation. Kirit drew back his lips and snarled at the witch.

"Well, I see someone is in a cheerful mood."

"Count yourself fortunate," Kirit said. "An hour ago and I would have bitten you."

Harper backed away with satisfying alacrity. Yes, indeed, that made him feel better. Kirit had been so preoccupied of late. He had started to worry about losing his edge. It was nice to know he could still be fierce when called upon.

Harper pushed Kirit aside to slide into the booth next to him. All right, so maybe he wasn't as intimidating as he would like.

"What must I do to make you leave?"

"You're the one who came to me," Harper pointed out.

Kirit found his reasonable attitude irritating. "I take it back. I still may bite you."

"Oooh, kinky."

Kirit snarled again. Harper chuckled. Kirit almost dumped his coffee onto Harper's head, but decided the caffeine was too precious to waste. But Harper's drink, now that had possibilities.

Unfortunately, Harper ordered one of those iced drinks. Not nearly as satisfying to dump—it would just come out in a big lump. Kirit resigned himself to putting thoughts of retribution aside until later. He really would bite the witch, but the entire Denver coven would most likely cry vengeance. Not to mention it would annoy the king. Seamus frowned on little things like murder and dismemberment. At least, he did off the battlefield. Put a sword in the Fae's hand and he could lop off limbs with the best of them. Or the worst, if you wanted to look at it that way.

"Earth to Kirit," Harper snapped. "How the hell am I supposed to help if you keep zoning out on me?"

Kirit growled once more.

"Stop that." The witch actually hit Kirit in the arm. "I'm doing you a favor here. The least you can do is be polite."

"I don't do polite."

"Try."

Maybe Seamus would overlook it. Just this once…

"What are you thinking about *now*?" Harper demanded.

"Eating you."

Unfortunately, Harper didn't take him seriously. "We need a new strategy. You don't say."

"Maybe you should start wandering the streets. I thought you'd look silly walking around aimlessly with your nose in the air, but desperate times and all that."

Gods curse it, he was going to have to tell the man.

"It won't work," he said to the thick, gloppy remains in the bottom of his cup. He wanted another one.

"Why not?"

"Because."

"Because why?" Harper encouraged. He was probably trying to look patient, but the grinding sound coming from his jaw rather ruined the expression.

"I have to talk to them."

"Kirit!"

"I can't smell," he mumbled.

"Come again?"

"You heard me the first time." Kirit bared his teeth. "But so there are no misunderstandings... I have a deficient sense of smell."

"Well, hell."

Kirit's sentiments exactly.

"So how were you planning on finding a mate if you can't scent them?"

Kirit shrugged. Very well, so he hadn't precisely walked into this with a solid plan. That was why he'd gone to Harper. Kirit just wanted a mate. Was that really too much to ask?

Harper rubbed his forehead. "Give me a moment."

"Gladly."

Kirit went back to the counter and ordered another mocha. It was one of the few things he missed about the human world when at home—the coffee concoctions, with the bitter espresso strong enough that he could taste it. In Faerie, they had chocolate, and they had a coffee-like substance, but it wasn't the same.

When he returned, Harper looked far less irritated. Kirit didn't think the expression of sympathy was an improvement.

"Let me talk to a few members of my coven," Harper said. "We might be able to piece together some sort of searching spell to at least narrow down the field, so to speak."

"Don't you think that's been tried before? It's never worked."

"You never had me before," Harper replied. It wasn't a boast, but a simple statement of fact. And as much as the witch grated on his last nerve, Kirit would be the first to admit that the man's power was impressive. They might call Harper a weather witch, but his abilities went far beyond conjuring a thunderstorm.

Harper stood with a decisive air. "Give me a day or two. In the meantime, hang out here. You never know. You might meet someone interesting."

Harper grinned and turned to go. He only took a few steps before coming back. "Listen," he said, more serious than Kirit had ever seen him. "I wouldn't worry too much about it. Fate works pretty well for the most part. You'll find your mate, and likely without any help from me. Just be patient."

"Harper," Kirit said around a heavy sigh. "I've *been* patient. For decades."

Harper squeezed his shoulder. "Then a few more days won't matter."

Chapter Three

The coffee shop finally kicked Kirit out at ten that night. The sky was dark but the streets were still bright, although not many people wandered them at this hour. Kirit shrugged on his leather jacket and zipped it up. There was a chilly bite to the air, an advance herald of the coming winter. Hopefully, he would be long gone by the time the weather turned cold in earnest. He hated the cold. And mate or no mate, he wasn't sticking around for the snow. Snow was icy and wet and just...*yech.*

Kirit hunched his shoulders and shoved his hands deep into the pockets, wrinkling his nose when his fists encountered fuzz and something sticky. He would have to check later. Few things were worse than unidentified sticky objects where he couldn't see them.

Kirit walked with swift strides, eager to return to the warmth of his hotel room. Despite Harper's parting words, he had made a decision while drinking his fourth cup of coffee. No more nightclubs. They weren't working. He would just wait until he heard from the witch. Hopefully, there would be some sort of solution from that direction and he would never have to go into a dance club again. He liked that thought. A lot. Crowded, noisy rooms with a plethora of smoke and flashing lights weren't exactly to a Draak's liking.

He was only two blocks from his hotel when a small sound made him pause. His nose twitched. He might not be able to smell worth a damn, but that certainly didn't stop his body from trying. He narrowed his eyes, peering into the darkened alley as best he could.

It was a tiny sound, no more than the rustling of cloth, perhaps soft breathing, but something about it awakened all his senses. Curiosity pulled Kirit forward, off the brightly lit sidewalk and into the dim confines of the walkway between buildings. That was all right. Draak had good night vision. Better hearing, but shadows hardly posed a deterrent.

Kirit walked toward the sound, nose still twitching madly. He found the small figure tucked next to an overflowing dumpster. He imagined the stench was awful, but the male didn't seem to mind. Dressed in a pair of jeans with holes in the knees and a thin black T-shirt, the young one was slumped against the wall, seemingly without a care in the world. He had a floppy mass of dark hair, and Kirit very much wanted to know what color his eyes were.

"What are you doing back here?" Kirit asked with genuine curiosity. It did seem to be an odd place to wait.

The man jerked, startled, and almost lost his balance. Kirit caught himself before reaching instinctively for the slight figure.

"I'm not hurting anything," came the sullen reply.

"I didn't say you were."

"I'm taking the night off. Go away."

Kirit wrinkled his brow. "Taking the night? Taking it where?"

"Dude, what are you on? Never mind, don't wanna know." The kid shoved away from the wall, scowling belligerently. "Why don't you just toddle off to wherever you were going?"

Kirit didn't know precisely what 'toddle' meant, but he could make a guess. "No," he said. "I'm supposed to be here." He didn't know where the words came from, but they rang with truth. Anyone from his world learned pretty early in life not to argue with that particular feeling.

Instead of the harsh retort he expected, the sentence got a quiet, "Oh." The smaller man looked around furtively, stepped closer, and lowered his voice. "Look, I don't know what Johnnie told you, but he's full of shit."

"I don't know anyone named Johnnie," Kirit told him. Unless you counted Johnny Two-Fingers, the cave troll. But he didn't think the kid was talking about a cave troll.

"Sure you don't."

A rustle from the far end of the alley had the man jumping and glancing around nervously. "We can't stand around and talk all night," he said. "Listen, it's cool. I guess I can put in a little time tonight. One hundred and fifty bucks. You wear a rubber and nothing kinky."

"I still don't know what you're talking about." He'd understood about every other word in that short speech. And he was waiting for something. What, Kirit didn't know. But he was supposed to be in this alley, at this moment. Something momentous was approaching.

He took a step closer to the young one. "What is your name, youngling?" he asked gently.

"Young what?"

Kirit didn't respond, tilting his head and waiting patiently.

A loud crash, and the male whirled. In the dim light, Kirit saw him tremble. "Oh, damn," he whispered.

Then he tried to dart past Kirit. Kirit grabbed him around the upper arm to halt his flight. The force of the youngling's momentum swung him around in a half circle, and Kirit had to swivel himself to keep his hold. "Hold still," he ordered.

"Damn it, man, let go!"

"Not yet."

He felt good under Kirit's hand, skin soft and pale in the moonlight.

"Let go, let go!" The attitude had vanished, replaced by pure panic. He kept tugging futilely.

Kirit wasn't in any mood to let his prey go.

"Please," the small figure urged. "Johnnie's gonna think I was working off the books in his territory and he'll be really pissed. Like really, really."

"He'll get over it."

"No, he won't. Johnnie's a bastard at the best of times. When he's mad…"

The pale face held an expression of fear. Kirit couldn't stop the growl that rumbled free. "I won't let him hurt you," he promised.

The man stared, speechless, and met Kirit's gaze for the first time. Large green eyes blinked up at him.

Oh. Oh, look at those eyes. So pretty.

The whole world tilted on its side as he stared into those eyes. *Well, what do you know?* If Kirit was lucky, maybe he wouldn't need that spell of Harper's, after all. Of course, only time would tell, and Kirit was rarely lucky. But that momentous feeling wasn't showing any signs of going away.

"Come," Kirit said. He tugged on the arm in his grasp, dragging his captive in the direction of the street.

The small man seemed to...deflate. Then he straightened, running his free hand through spikes of light brown hair, obviously trying to recapture his cocky attitude. Kirit couldn't stop looking, not at the slender, toned body or the narrow, almost pretty, features. And most especially, those brilliant green eyes.

The man remained quiet as they walked, but he kept glancing backwards. Just as they reached the welcoming haze of the streetlights, two hulking figures took shape at the far end of the alley.

"Oh, shit." The man took off running. Unfortunately for him, Kirit hadn't let go and didn't have any intention of doing so. The jerk nearly yanked him off his feet.

"This way." Kirit could remove the problem, if necessary, but he would rather not. He wasn't sure it would be possible without revealing a bit more of his nature than he would like. They appeared to be very large men. Of course, that didn't mean they could fight worth a damn.

Still, Kirit had other plans for the night than engaging in fights. Most of them were unlikely to come to fruition and involved him, a flat surface, and the squirming individual he was presently dragging down the sidewalk.

He figured a cold shower was the more likely scenario in his near future, but a dragon could always fantasize.

"Where are you taking me?"

"To my hotel."

"Oh." To Kirit's surprise, the boy stopped fighting him. "Why didn't you say so?"

The attitude was back, but now that the light was better, Kirit noted other emotions underneath. Such an interesting blend of cocky and vulnerable. He found the prospect of digging through the layers to get to the real personality enticing.

He still didn't know the boy's name. *Ah, well. One issue at a time.* Safe and warm first. Questions second.

They made it to the hotel without any further problems, but Kirit didn't relax until he had the door to his suite firmly locked behind them. He still hadn't the slightest idea what he was doing, but he felt better now that he had his companion in a safe, secured area. Where he couldn't run away.

"Name," he demanded.

The kid paused in his aimless wander around the room. "Cody," he said after several seconds.

"Cody." Kirit tasted the sound on his tongue, nodding. Unusual, not something he'd heard before, but he liked it.

A shirt hit the floor, and Kirit's jaw followed it. Before he could react, he was staring at a stark naked man. His mouth watered at the sight of all that creamy skin. *No*, he told himself firmly. He reached down and adjusted himself, adding a squeeze for good measure. *Bad cock. Not yet.*

"What are you doing?" he asked. His voice came out hoarse and a little unsteady.

Cody raised one eyebrow. "What do you think? Money up front. Let's get on with it." Cody held out his hand, snapping his fingers impatiently.

"Get on with what?"

28

"Sheesh, did you leave your brain in the alley? Sex, what else?"

Kirit had to sit down on the edge of the bed. Well, he hadn't seen that coming. Maybe he should come to this side more often, if he was going to be that oblivious. Now that he re-ran their conversation, things made a lot more sense.

Kirit let out a low growl. "Put your clothes back on." Even as the words emerged, he wanted to call them back. *All that pretty skin...* "I didn't bring you here for...that."

Cody planted his hands on his slim hips, seemingly oblivious to his state of undress, green eyes flashing with ire. "They why did you bring me here?"

"Damned if I know!"

The kid snatched up his clothes. "Right. Nice to meet you. See ya around."

"Hold!" Kirit roared, jumping to his feet. "I said no sex. I did *not* say you could leave."

"Dude, I'm not staying here."

Clutching his clothes to his chest, Cody ran. But not for the front door, which Kirit had moved to block. No, Cody ran for the bathroom. Kirit heard the lock engage just before he reached the door.

Damn it.

Oh, well. At least the youngling couldn't leave.

Kirit ordered something to eat from room service. He was hungry, and if Cody's slender build was any indicator, he must be, too.

Then, Kirit changed into a pair of sweats and flipped on the television while he waited for the food. He kept half his attention on some mindless show, the other half searching for any sounds from the bathroom. It was very quiet. He would have checked, but they were on the fifth floor. Cody wasn't leaving, not until Kirit let him.

Now, Kirit just had to figure out what he was going to do with the man. Besides the obvious, that was.

Chapter Four

Cody rested his forehead on his knees with a low groan of annoyance. The tile was cold on his butt and back, where he had wedged himself between the toilet and the bathtub. He should put his clothes back on.

How do I get myself into these situations? Honestly, it was so ridiculous it was almost funny. *I should've learned by now.* A hot guy came along, his dick took control, and the next thing you knew, he was hiding naked in a hotel bathroom.

"God, I'm an idiot." Cody banged his head against the wall a few times. Maybe it would pound some sense into his underworked brain.

It was just...that guy. Cody had been tense and on edge ever since the confrontation with Johnnie the night before, jumping at sounds. He'd felt like a complete wimp, and not himself at all. Then, along came the guy he'd been drooling over — there was no mistaking that hair — and Cody had followed along like a needy puppy.

Why are the gorgeous ones always weird?

Cody chewed on his lip, straining to hear any sounds from the world outside his temporary shelter. There was the gentle rustle of cloth through the thin walls. A thump. A garbled curse.

He dropped his head back onto his knees. *What on earth am I going to do?* The big guy was between him and the door, but he couldn't stay in the bathroom forever. He'd starve.

There's something wrong with that logic. Cody was too tired to reason it out, though. His head was throbbing —*probably from banging it on the wall, idiot*— and he could feel a migraine lurking at the edges of his consciousness.

A soft knock made him jerk, slamming the back of his head into the wall again, hard. Spots danced on his eyelids.

"I have food, if you're hungry."

Cody opened his mouth to refuse, but his stomach had annoying timing. It chose that moment to growl angrily. Only then did it occur to him that he hadn't eaten since yesterday morning. No wonder he was getting a migraine. He'd been too stressed to be hungry, and was paying for it now.

"I'm not going to hurt you," the big guy called through the door. Frustration edged the words.

Cody groaned. He wriggled free from his spot and yanked on his jeans. He didn't think the guy was lying, but he was willing to chance it. After all, it wasn't like he had much choice. He had to emerge eventually —he might as well try to get a meal out of the deal.

Besides, if the man was going to hurt him, he could have done it long before now. Hell, with those shoulders, the bathroom door wouldn't hold up for long against a concentrated assault.

Cody pulled his shirt down, took a deep breath then unlocked the door. He opened it slowly.

The man on the other side cocked his head, boring into him with those odd, pale eyes. Cody tried to summon his trademark cocky smile, but it wouldn't come. Damn, the guy was big. Huge. Massive. And he pulled at Cody more than anyone he had ever met.

Give over, who are you trying to fool? Cody knew damn well his earlier offer hadn't been about money. He'd let this guy at his ass and enjoy every second of it. *Those hands...* He couldn't quite suppress a shudder.

The man saw it and scowled before turning away. "Help yourself," he said shortly, jerking his head in the direction of the small table.

Holy cow. Cody's jaw dropped. The tiny surface was completely covered in food. He counted at least six burgers and three steaks.

"Are you having guests?" Cody asked dryly.

The big guy shrugged, looking almost sheepish. It should have been a weird expression on someone built like a house, but it wasn't. In fact, it made him look rather...adorable.

Cody pushed the thought aside and reached for a burger. *Oh, yeah.* It wasn't one of the fast food kinds, but an actual burger with thick meat and a bun not soaked in grease. He took a big bite.

"You never told me your name," he mumbled around a full mouth.

"Kirit Mokenslayne."

"Huh. Anybody ever told you that's a really strange name?"

"Several times. But it's the only one I have."

Cody finished off the last of his burger, sucking the juice from his fingers. Now that his focus wasn't occupied with food, he was having a hard time not staring at Kirit. Wide shoulders topped a well-built chest, pecs clearly defined. His stomach muscles were cut into an honest-to-God six-pack, waist and hips lean and narrow. His chest was smooth, with a light trail of dark hair disappearing under the low-riding waistband of his sweats. And that hair. It was even more stunning close up. Pulled back into a tight braid, it trailed well past his waist in a fat mass of black. The style only accentuated Kirit's long and narrow features. His face wasn't classically handsome by any stretch, but with a body like that, who cared?

Damn. He looked like the starring figure in every one of Cody's wet dreams since puberty. Cody had seen more naked men than he cared to recall, but none of them had looked like this. Damn, again.

"Are you sure you don't want sex?" Cody offered hopefully. "No charge."

Kirit muttered something. Was it wishful thinking, or did he actually say, 'Don't tempt me'?

"Sit," Kirit ordered.

Cody plopped onto the bed and gave his best sexy, come-hither look. Now that he had some food in his stomach and a chance to get another good look at the big guy, his worry seemed to have evaporated.

He wanted this man and, one way or another, he intended to have him.

Hell, maybe he'd even do something unprecedented and keep Kirit for more than a few hours.

Kirit tried very hard not to pounce on the sexy man in his bed. The smoldering look in those pretty eyes was about to shatter his control. But he needed to talk first, find out if Cody was really his.

Every instinct Kirit possessed was screaming, 'This man is the one!' But Kirit wanted to be certain before he treated Cody like an all-you-can-eat buffet—another thing about this side he really liked. Because once Kirit had Cody, he didn't think he'd want to give him up. Better to be certain.

"What were you doing in that alley?" Kirit asked.

"What do you think?"

Kirit shook his head. "You told me you weren't working. I don't believe hanging out in dark alleys next to trash repositories is what most humans do with their free time." Kirit winced belatedly at his slip, but thankfully it slipped by Cody unnoticed.

Cody shrugged, looking toward the window as if trying to see through the closed curtains. "It's quiet back there."

"Who were the men?"

Cody chewed on his lip. Kirit couldn't help himself—he reached out and gently rubbed that tempting mouth.

The first touch shot straight to Kirit's gut. His muscles tightened, balls heavy and cock throbbing. Cody's gaze dropped to where the soft material of Kirit's pants was doing little to hide his arousal.

"Do you really want to talk? Wouldn't you rather I take care of that for you?" Cody waved a hand at Kirit's crotch.

"No. Yes. I mean...talking," Kirit stammered, feeling like an idiot. "We're talking. First. Now."

A grin pulled at Cody's lips. There was something about the big guy. Something...endearing. And that wasn't a word Cody usually used to describe guys. Not in his world.

Maybe it was time for a new one.

Cody rose onto his knees. "Come on, big guy," he cajoled. "I'll tell you anything you want to know. Later." To his surprise, Cody meant it. He didn't usually spend much time talking to johns, and he rarely told them the truth. But he would for Kirit.

Kirit groaned, a low, deep sound that rumbled from the back of his throat.

Cody could tell he was going to have to be proactive. Otherwise, it might take them all night to get to the good stuff.

With a wicked grin, he launched himself across the small space separating them. Kirit caught him in an automatic move, his arms folding around Cody's waist. Cody yanked his head down, capturing surprisingly lush lips in a soul-searing kiss.

And that's another thing I don't do with johns, Cody noted in a far corner of his brain. Kissing was special, not something he shared with any of the men who paid him.

Kirit met his kiss with equal passion, the fierce gentleness melting the hard knot that normally held residence in Cody's stomach. There was passion there, almost unchecked, but Kirit still handled him with care. No split lips or harsh clashing of teeth—just the gentle, moist pressure of lips and tongue.

Cody clung harder, trying to climb Kirit like a jungle gym.

"Bed," he ordered, trailing kisses across the lean cheeks and pointed chin, relishing the slight scrape of stubble. He wrapped his hands around the long, silky braid, tugging firmly. Kirit obliged with another kiss, walking them backwards until he could drop Cody onto the mattress. Cody bounced a couple of times, light laughter bursting free. It surprised him, that outward sign of amusement, but he did like the pleased expression the sound brought to Kirit's face.

The sound of Cody's laughter seemed to make Kirit's whole spirit lighter. In that instant, all doubts vanished. He didn't need to talk any more to know — Cody was his. His man. His lover. His mate. Draak were notoriously possessive, and he wasn't giving up his find for anything. He would, in fact, happily kill anyone who tried to take Cody away.

His. All his.

Worries tried to niggle their way in. He still had to convince Cody. Explain what he was. Where he came from. All those details. There was a reason they didn't usually hunt mates on this side. It was far too complicated.

Those were problems for later, though. Right now, he was going to play with his new mate. Love Cody until all the other man could do was scream Kirit's name.

Oh, yes. He had a plan. A very good plan.

Kirit dropped on top of his lover, careful to brace his weight on his arms. *No crushing the mate.*

"Hello," he said, looking down with a smile.

"Hi," Cody said, smiling back. "I'm wearing too many clothes."

"You are," Kirit agreed. "I can remedy that."

"Please do."

For the second time that night, the sleek body was bared to his hungry gaze. This time, he could look his fill. He took a long moment just staring. Cody was much smaller than Kirit's own powerful frame, but his muscles were well-defined and his chest a thing of utter beauty. The skin was smooth and hairless, except for around the groin. Cody's cock, red and swollen, rose from a bed of thick brown curls.

Damn. The gods had truly blessed him.

Kirit ran his palms up Cody's arms and over his shoulders. "So pretty," he said.

"Guys aren't pretty." The protest would have been more effective if not delivered so breathlessly, or if Cody hadn't arched into the light caresses. He wrapped his fists in Kirit's hair again and tugged. "More," Cody demanded.

"Anything you wish." Kirit took a quick kiss before trailing his lips down Cody's neck, over the collarbone, and finally to his destination. He closed them around one puckered nipple and sucked.

"Kirit!"

The tugging became fiercer, almost painful. Kirit growled around his prize, digging his fingers into Cody's hips. The need in Cody's voice awakened something deep and primitive in him.

Damn. Kirit had wanted to savor this first time, but he didn't think it was going to happen.

Kirit nipped and licked every inch of skin he could reach as Cody writhed and moaned underneath him. Kirit ached with arousal. His fangs kept trying to descend. He could feel the telltale itch and pulse under his skin as his body fought the urge to change.

Kirit closed his fingers around Cody's leaking cock. With the noises Cody was making, and the way he bucked into the touch—Cody was near the breaking point.

"Now, Kirit, now, please."

"I won't hurt you," Kirit said. "Preparation first."

"Oh, God. I won't survive preparation!" Cody wailed.

He didn't think Cody would, either, a fact of which Kirit was extremely proud. Kirit slid one spit-slicked finger inside Cody's body. The instant he brushed Cody's prostate, Cody lost control with an ear-splitting shout. Cum shot from him in a hot stream, coating both their bodies and mingling with their sweat.

Kirit watched his lover with awe. He'd never seen a more beautiful sight in his life than that passion-flushed face.

Kirit ran his tongue along Cody's stomach, cleaning off the sweat, savoring the sweet and salty taste of his mate.

"Wait," Cody protested, struggling suddenly. "It might not be safe."

"Hmmm?"

"I get around." Cody flushed a dull red. "I use protection, but there's deadly crap out there, yeah?"

Kirit growled at the thought of his Cody with other men, but he didn't stop his gentle ministrations. There were some definite advantages to not being human. Few diseases communicated across species—the blasted persistency of the cold aside—and he'd never been more glad of that than at this moment. He wasn't going to give up learning the intimate taste of his new mate.

He just wished it was more vivid. Stupid lack of smell. It dulled the taste of everything. But Cody was still his new favorite snack. Oh, yes. Better even than flavored mochas. Maybe even better than steak.

"Kirit!" Cody protested again.

Kirit gave one last long lick and rose until he could touch noses with his Cody. "Mine," he stated.

Cody scowled, but gave up. He slid down on the bed, lifting his legs and draping them around Kirit's waist. He wiggled enticingly.

"Gonna fuck me now?" he teased.

Kirit growled again at Cody's words. And damn, but that was like the sexiest sound in the world.

"I'm going to love you," Kirit corrected.

The words hit Cody with the force of a fist to his gut, and with about as much pleasure. He turned his head away. "Don't," he requested.

"Get used to it. Mine."

The big guy really liked that word. Cody was practical, though.

Oh, all right, he wasn't practical at all, but he tried. And if there was one thing he did know, it was hook-ups. Kirit might say the most amazing things now, but they'd still go their separate ways in the morning, and in a couple of days Cody would be no more than a — hopefully — pleasant memory.

Cody was going to do his best to make it more than pleasant. He wanted his memory to be the kind that caused big smiles and daydreams. The kind of memory that remained hot and arousing long after the physical sensations faded.

He used his legs to pull their lower bodies more tightly together then rubbed his rapidly re-hardening cock against Kirit's washboard stomach. "I need again," he whispered into Kirit's ear.

Kirit pulled away and unwound Cody. Cody whimpered in protest.

Kirit sat back on his heels and just about fell off the bed trying to snag a nearby duffle-type bag. He rummaged around before returning triumphantly with a large tube of lube. Watching him try to pry the lid off, with accompanying frustrated curses, was more than a little amusing.

The lid came free, a stream of lube gushing out with it. Kirit gave a yell of triumph and wasted no time slicking up his cock.

Cody got his first good look at Kirit's fully engorged penis. His eyes widened. He reached out his finger and ran it along the longer than average length. "Damn," he said.

"No worrying, love," Kirit assured him. "I will fit."

"I know you will. You're going to feel amazing."

"I certainly am."

Well, the man didn't lack for confidence, that was for sure.

Cody wanted badly to explore, to trace those prominent veins with his fingers and tongue. The large, heavy balls called out to him with equal temptation, but Kirit didn't give him time to play.

That was okay, too. They had the rest of the night.

Kirit squirted a generous dollop of lube onto his fingers before tossing away the container. He knelt between Cody's spread legs. Cody happily obliged by splaying wider and bracing his hands on those wide shoulders. Kirit circled Cody's hole with well-greased fingers, teasing the skin and dipping in slightly before pulling back. Cody thrust his hips, pushing into the touch, begging with his body for more contact.

Kirit obliged by sliding one finger past the tight ring of muscle and deep into Cody's body.

Cody realized he was thrusting uncontrollably again. He was so hard, it was difficult to believe he'd come only moments before. He hooked his ankles over Kirit's shoulder, sparing a brief bit of gratitude that he was still so flexible. He heard a voice chanting, "Now, now."

Oh, that's me.

The chant seemed to snap the last of Kirit's control. He plunged three fingers deep, even as he apologized for the burn. Cody couldn't hold back a shout at the sudden stretch, but he didn't pull away.

That seemed to be all the encouragement Kirit needed. He yanked out his fingers and lined up his cock with one hand. With a steady pressure, Kirit pushed forward, groaning Cody's name. Cody pulled him into a kiss, nearly bending himself double in the process.

"Let go," Cody ordered.

Kirit did precisely that, throwing back his head and roaring. Cody watched in fascination as his face contorted with pleasure. He started a pounding rhythm, dislodging Cody's legs. Cody wrapped his arms around Kirit's neck and held on.

Cody wanted to be more proactive, wanted to participate, but in the end, all he could do was cling and accept the fucking of his life. Each powerful thrust slid him along the sheets until Cody was forced to remove one hand from Kirit to brace against the headboard. Kirit was muttering words that held no meaning for Cody. He didn't think it was English.

Kirit's eyes were blazing, the pupils dark with need. *Strange, I don't remember his eyes being that blue before.*

"Close," Kirit ground out between clenched teeth which, for some strange reason, looked a little sharp all of a sudden. "So close."

Me, too. Cody summoned up enough presence of mind to squeeze his ass cheeks together. The sudden constriction was enough to push Kirit over the edge. His roar shook the walls as his whole body tensed.

With a low moan, Kirit leaned over and sank those sharp teeth deep into the flesh between Cody's shoulder and neck, using his lips and teeth to suck up a mark. The position mashed Cody's cock between their bodies.

The pressure was enough to set Cody off again. His climax had him seeing stars as he screamed. The waves of pleasure seemed to wash over him for endless minutes.

Slowly, so slowly, he came back to the world around him. Kirit was still buried balls-deep, sucking gently on Cody's skin.

Cody lifted tired arms, rubbing up and down the strongly muscled back. "Wow."

The word was barely louder than a whisper. His brain cells were fried, his lungs burned, and his throat ached. Cody didn't even want to contemplate leaving this bed. Not for a couple of days.

Kirit pulled away from the mark he had left. He gave the bleeding wound one last affectionate lick.

"Rest, mate," he told the exhausted man in his embrace.

"Hmmm." Cody's arms fell away, eyes closing as he drifted to sleep.

Kirit pressed a kiss to Cody's forehead, smoothing out the last lingering lines with his lips. He reluctantly slid his cock out of Cody's ass and heaved himself off the bed. He made his way to the bathroom on unsteady legs.

Returning with a wet cloth, he studied his ravished mate with pure satisfaction. Limp limbs sprawled over the destroyed bed coverings, brown hair spiky and damp with sweat. A soft snore triggered a smile from Kirit. His mate was so cute.

He figured Cody would protest that description, but it was true. The man *was* cute. And all Kirit's.

Kirit climbed onto the bed, feeling a surge of pride as he spotted the cum leaking from Cody's ass and dripping down his legs. Kirit almost hated to wash it away. If he didn't, though, Cody would wake up sticky. It wouldn't do for his mate to be uncomfortable.

He cleaned Cody up with gentle strokes, careful not to disturb Cody's sleep. Kirit gave himself a cursory wash then covered himself with a towel.

Cody might be worn out, but Kirit felt energized. And hungry.

It was a good thing he'd ordered those steaks.

Chapter Five

Cody woke up in an unfamiliar bed with a sore ass. Not necessarily an unusual occurrence. The smile on his face, now *that* was new.

He rolled over and came flush up against a large, hot body. Cody allowed himself a brief moment to cuddle close. Then he reluctantly moved away and slipped from the bed.

Last night had been amazing, but it was time to go. A lot of guys didn't mind falling asleep next to him, but they rarely wanted to wake up the same way. Cody gathered his scattered clothes and tried to ignore the loss already burning in his chest. If only things were different. If he was a different person, had a different life.

A quick search turned up his pants, and Cody yanked them on. He winced at the twinge in his ass, sore muscles clenching in protest. Damn, Kirit was big. Not only that, but he knew what to do with that oversized cock, too. Cody couldn't remember sex ever feeling like that. And, in general, he *liked* sex. Couldn't do what he did and not like it. Cody didn't really have many regrets. He had a decent life. He made some money to put aside, set his own hours. Pretty good for a guy without a high school diploma and with no other prospects. Or at least, it had been a decent life. Until Johnnie.

Cody pushed those thoughts aside, as he'd been doing for weeks now. He'd have to deal eventually, but not yet. Not until after he'd gotten home. And maybe taken some time to relive a few memories.

He was almost to the door when a rustle came from the bed. Cody froze in his tracks, barely breathing, feeling torn. *Do I want Kirit to stay asleep or not?*

A low grumble emanated from the pile of covers. "Why are you always trying to leave?" Kirit complained in a sleep-roughened voice.

"I thought—"

"Get your lovely little ass back in this bed," Kirit ordered. "I'll feed you breakfast later."

Cody grinned and shed his clothes, practically bouncing onto the mattress. "Someone wakes up grumpy," he teased.

"Only when I wake up alone. Rule number one— morning sex is a requirement. You aren't allowed to leave the bed before I do."

"I'm not so good with rules."

Eyes dark with lust peered over the edge of the comforter. "Not even good ones?"

"Well, maybe good ones." And that was definitely a good rule. Not only did it hold the promise of fantastic sex, it meant Kirit wanted him to stick around for a while.

Cody shoved the logical side of his brain aside with practiced ease. It wanted to catalogue all the potential problems. Cody just wanted to enjoy the moment.

He propped himself on top of Kirit's wide chest, staring into those penetrating eyes. "Hi," he said.

"Hi," Kirit said back.

The abbreviated greeting sounded funny coming from Kirit, with his tendency towards overly proper speech. It was adorable.

And there was that word again. Cody pulled out his best wicked smile and moved in for a quick kiss. When Kirit would have taken it deeper, Cody pulled away. He began to wiggle his way down that massive body, lips never leaving Kirit's skin. He slid his tongue over the cut muscles until he reached that lovely little trail of hair. Cody simply had to follow it.

Kirit shouted, body arching violently, as Cody followed his path to the end. He buried his nose in the nest of curls, flicking his tongue out for a taste. Kirit smelled fantastic. Like man and sex, with the faintest hint of cinnamon. Kind of reminded Cody of autumn.

Settling in to enjoy his treat, Cody latched onto a patch of skin on the larger man's hips and sucked up a nice mark before moving to the other side to give Kirit a matching set.

"Cody," Kirit said, already breathing heavily. "Quit playing."

"Who's playing?" Cody used his best innocent tone, which was pretty damn good, if he did say so himself. "I'm exploring."

"Explore later."

"Really? Because I was going to explore *this* next."

Cody sucked the tip of that fat cock into his mouth, teasing the head with rapid flicks of his tongue.

"Never mind. Explore all you wish."

"Thank you. I believe I will."

He dove back down and went to work in earnest. He licked and sucked, his efforts earning a long series of groans, moan, growls and assorted curses. *Oh, yeah.* That was just what he wanted.

"Cody!"

Third time's the charm. Or, at last, the third yell meant Kirit was getting desperate enough that Cody could move to phase two. He pulled back and surveyed his handiwork. Kirit's cock shone wet with spit and pre-cum, pulsing an angry red, veins prominent. Kirit's stomach muscles were clenched, balls drawn up tightly against his body.

"Enough exploring." Kirit sounded as desperate as he looked.

"You know, I do think you're right."

Time for the good stuff. Cody swallowed Kirit down whole, until the hard shaft slid into his throat and his nose mashed into that patch of curls again. Cody moaned as the salty taste hit his tongue.

Cody hollowed his cheeks, pulling strongly, bobbing off to take a deep breath before going down again. He couldn't keep from moving, humping Kirit with shameless abandon. Cody loved sucking cock. Loved, loved it. He loved the taste, the smell, the sounds a man made when someone was going down on him.

Cody's moans soon joined Kirit's. He rode the big man, relishing the scrape of hair against the sensitive skin of his balls, rubbing his dick firmly into the solid flesh beneath him.

"Cody! Cody, damn it. Close. Oh, gods, love. Right there. Harder."

Kirit was babbling now, a rapid string of encouragement and passion. Cody tightened his grip on Kirit's hips and sucked one more time, sliding almost all the way off before plunging down with slow, deliberate movements. It was hard to concentrate with the explosions going off in his own body, but Cody managed. He was determined to give Kirit the best blowjob of the man's life.

The thick shaft slid into his throat and he held Kirit there for long seconds, breathing through his nose, before swallowing. Kirit bucked, his roar deafening. The taut muscles under Cody's body tightened, giving him just enough warning to pull back a bit. Warm spunk hit his tongue and Cody continued to swallow, sucking Kirit through his release and beyond.

Cody rubbed frantically against Kirit. Then his own balls drew up painfully, his climax tearing through his spine and nearly taking the top of his head off. Sparks danced behind his eyelids and Cody sucked harder on the rapidly softening cock in his mouth, using it to anchor him in his body when the pleasure threatened to drag him away.

Slowly, Cody's climax faded. The world came back into focus. Cody became aware of Kirit's harsh breathing, the sticky cum binding them together. He licked his lips, savoring the taste lingering in his mouth.

Cody never swallowed. Ever. But...yeah. Maybe he was being stupid, but this was Kirit. His Kirit. And Cody was going to live in his little fantasy for a while longer.

Cody laid his head on Kirit's hard stomach, letting the gentle motion of breathing soothe him. Kirit smoothed Cody's hair with tender caresses.

Nothing lasts forever. It was while Cody lay there, basking in the afterglow, that reality started to intrude. *Damn it. Don't I at least get to enjoy myself for a little while?*

But no. His busy mind wouldn't let him.

Cody sighed and rolled over until he could look at the limp form of his lover. Kirit hummed and continued to stroke Cody's hair. Cody relished the touch.

Then he sat up. "I should go," he said, looking towards the window. "I've got things to do."

He tried to sound casual, but it was hard. He bit his lip, holding back the words that wanted to come out. *How long will you be around? Can I see you again?*

You're a whore, Cody, he scolded himself. *No guy wants to attach himself to a rent boy.*

"Very well," Kirit said in a sated rumble. "Give me a few moments to recover and we can leave."

"We?" Cody's mouth fell open. "Oh, no, man. I mean *I* need to leave. You know?"

Kirit growled and sat up. "No, I don't know."

"Oh, forget it." Cody climbed off the bed. "I'm going to take a shower."

He stomped to the bathroom, not quite sure why he was so angry. Cody turned the water on, letting it run to warm up, and checked his appearance in the mirror. See if he needed a shave.

He didn't. As usual.

He leaned closer to the reflective surface. *Is that...?*

"You bit me!" he bellowed.

Kirit's large bulk appeared to block the doorway. "I did."

"Dude! Not cool!"

Hickeys were one thing, but this was a freakin' bite. Like break the skin, draw blood, noticeably-obvious-teeth-marks bite.

Kirit at least had the decency to look slightly ashamed of himself. "It will heal."

"Of course it will. That's not the point. But what do I do in the meantime?" Cody leaned toward the mirror again. "It's like the size of a freakin' handprint! People are gonna notice that." Another thought hit him, and he could feel the color drain away. A blow job without a condom was one thing. Hell, even the sex last night was different. Maybe he was being an idiot, and more than a little irrational. But this was an exchange of blood. His blood. Into Kirit. And he hadn't been tested in almost a month.

"What if you get sick?" he wailed. "What if *I* get sick?"

Kirit rolled his eyes. "Not this again."

"You're not listening. This is serious. You bit me!"

"Calm down," Kirit said, an uneasy expression taking over his sharp features.

Cody did not want to be placated right now. Okay, so maybe he was exaggerating a bit. And definitely starting to repeat himself — a sure sign that complete loss of control wasn't far behind. The bite was big, but it wasn't *that* big. Still, it paid in his business to try and avoid any obvious marks. Particularly ones that could be interpreted as possessive. No john wanted to worry about a hulking boyfriend in the background.

Cody turned on the water and splashed his face, trying to slow down his rapid breathing. He didn't know why his temper was on such a quick trigger this morning. He was usually a very easy-going type of person. *I can't possibly be this worried over Kirit. Can I?*

No, he told himself firmly. *I am not getting attached.*

A large hand settled with hesitance on Cody's shoulder. When Cody stayed silent, Kirit squeezed gently.

"I do not understand why you are so concerned," Kirit said.

"Me neither," Cody admitted. "Maybe I just need to eat."

In the mirror, Cody could see relief settle on Kirit's face. "Food. I can provide food."

The big guy gave him another small squeeze then left the bathroom. "Come along, little one," he called from the other room. "I'll feed you, and then you will no longer be irritable."

Cody smothered a small laugh, thinking Kirit wouldn't understand his amusement. It was just funny as heck. Kirit could snap Cody's neck with very little effort, but he seemed genuinely relieved to have an active solution to a problem he didn't understand.

Cody climbed into the shower, scrubbing at his eyes. He'd let Kirit feed him and figure out what to do after that. One thing was certain—walking away from Kirit was going to be hard. Much harder than it should be.

* * * *

He was freaking Cody out. Kirit knew it, but he couldn't stop himself. He kept thinking that if he took his eyes off Cody, even for a moment, his mate would disappear. Kirit just wasn't this lucky. Ever. Amazing events happened to other people, not a grumpy dragon with a bad habit of biting those who annoyed him.

When Kirit stepped on Cody's heels for the fourth time in as many blocks, his mate whirled, eyes angry and cheeks flushed.

"What is with you?" Cody demanded. "You can go away now."

Kirit shook his head.

"Fine. If you're going to follow me, could you please do it from a distance?" Cody tapped an impatient rhythm on the sidewalk with his foot.

"No," Kirit replied.

Cody gave an impressive growl, sounding amazingly like one of the Draak himself. *Oh, yes.* His new mate would fit in quite well. Kirit couldn't manage to wipe the stupid grin from his face. Which was another thing that didn't happen to him. Smiling.

Cody threw up his hands. "Fine. But if you step on me one more time, I'm going to kick you."

"You'll only hurt yourself," Kirit pointed out.

Cody stomped away, muttering, "Coffee. I need more coffee."

Kirit wasn't certain caffeine was the best of ideas. His mate had already consumed three cups with their breakfast. He opened his mouth to say so, then thought better of it.

He trailed behind his mate again, knowing he was being ridiculous but unable to stop himself. *I am so very glad my clutch cannot see me right now.* All of them—particularly Chaos—would be beside themselves with amusement. *Oh, how the mighty have fallen.*

Yet he still followed Cody, dignity forgotten, first to the coffee shop, then around the corner to a market, where he watched his new mate poke at fruit. Cody purchased some brightly colored boxes. Kirit bought some chocolate for himself and munched as he followed Cody back out of the store.

Cody was doing an impressive job of ignoring the large, silent presence at his back. Kirit didn't mind. He was nothing if not persistent. He would wear his mate down eventually.

"Where are we going next?" Kirit asked.

"I'm going home," Cody stated without turning around. "And you're going to go away."

"No, I'll come with you."

"Nope. Don't think so."

Maybe if Cody had sounded firm, or annoyed, Kirit would have given him some time and space. *Maybe.*

Very well, most likely not. However, Cody didn't seem as if he expected Kirit to listen. So, Kirit didn't.

Their wandering finally halted at a dull grey building. Several stories tall, squat and dirty, the sight made Kirit's nose wrinkle.

"This is not a fit place for you," he told Cody.

"There's nothing wrong with it." Cody reached the doors and stopped, finally turning to face Kirit. "Okay. I'm home now. See? Safe and sound. You can go find someone else to follow now."

"I only wish to follow you."

Cody frowned. "Look, big guy. It was great. Really. But I've got things to do—alone—and I'm sure you do, too."

Kirit was torn. His instincts screamed at him to remain with his mate, but logic said to back off. Plus, he needed to go speak with Harper, and he needed to contact home. They would be wondering when he was returning, and the last thing Kirit needed was someone coming after him. That would immensely complicate an already complicated situation.

"I suppose," he said slowly.

"Great!" With a bright smile that looked fake, Cody slipped through the glass door. It clicked shut before Kirit could react. He tugged, but the door wouldn't open. He shrugged and turned to go.

A locked door wasn't much of a challenge. Kirit would go speak to Harper and give Cody some time to adjust. Then he would be back for his new treasure.

Yes, indeed. Cody would make a most excellent addition to Kirit's hoard. Not that he would tell Cody that—humans tended to take exception with being referred to as possessions.

Kirit was vibrating with pent-up energy. He would have walked to calm down, but he hadn't the slightest idea where he was. Resigned, he backtracked to a main road and waved until a taxi stopped. After that, it was a matter of minutes to arrive back at Harper's apartment building.

Harper opened the door at Kirit's summons, then stood there staring. Kirit figured it was the smile. He could feel the unfamiliar expression stretching his cheeks.

"Holy shit, you lucky bastard," Harper said. "You actually succeeded."

"I usually do."

"No, you don't. And to find your mate? Here? You do realize the odds of that are like fifty bajillion to one?"

"I don't think that's a real number," Kirit felt compelled to point out.

"Damn, do you dragons always have to be so literal?"

"Yes."

"Rhetorical, my man."

"I'm not a man."

Harper narrowed his eyes, the expression downright evil. "I wonder if your new mate would mind too much if I fried you with a bolt of lightning."

Kirit smirked. He couldn't help it. He was, overall, in an exceptionally good mood.

"So, when do you go back to Faerie?"

And just that like, the good mood evaporated. Kirit spent a moment contemplating his boots.

"All right, let me have it." Harper sounded resigned. "How much have you told him?"

"I…that is to say…none of it?"

"Good Glory Hound, Kirit!"

"I thought you could do it." Gods above, Kirit could actually feel a dull flush in his cheeks. He couldn't remember the last time he'd felt embarrassed enough to blush.

This mating business was difficult.

"Me?" Harper gaped. "Why the hell should I do it? He's *your* mate."

"Can we take this inside?" Kirit was growing tired of standing in the hallway. Besides, this wasn't really the type of discussion they should risk someone overhearing.

"No."

"But—"

"No."

"Will you at least speak with him?"

"He's your mate," Harper repeated.

"But you're human," Kirit protested. "I thought perhaps you could…relate, or something."

"Oh, for the love of all that is holy, stop being such a big baby. Suck it up and go talk to him."

"Suck what up?"

Harper groaned and thumped his head on the open door. "What did I ever do to deserve this?" he mumbled.

Chapter Six

Cody felt like a voyeur. *This is ridiculous. Really.*

He flicked the curtains to one side and leaned, peering out of the window while doing his best to remain hidden.

"This may be a stupid question, but what are you doing?"

Cody didn't take his eyes from the narrow view of the street below. "What does it look like I'm doing?"

"I can't even being to guess," Jay-Jay replied.

"He's out there, I know he is."

"You do realize how paranoid you sound right now, don't you?"

"It's not paranoia if it's the truth."

Cody let the curtains fall back into place, darkening the shadows in his small loft. With a sigh, he plopped down on the couch next to Jay. He rested his back against the arm of the sofa and situated his feet in his friend's lap. Jay grunted but didn't make Cody move.

"So tell me again why we're hiding here on a Friday night instead of working the clubs?"

"You don't have to hang with me," Cody pointed out.

"True."

Jay didn't make any effort to get up. Neither did Cody. They sat there in a weird silence. It felt heavy, significant. Like something important was going to happen soon.

Or maybe that was just the paranoia talking.

If Cody was going to be completely honest, he wouldn't go out even if he wasn't trying to avoid Kirit. It was crazy and more than a little annoying, but ever since that night with the big oaf, he hadn't been able to work. It felt…disloyal, or something. Like he was cheating. Which was utterly ridiculous, since they most certainly weren't dating. It had only been one night.

So why couldn't Cody get the guy out of his head?"

A loud series of knocks interrupted Cody's daze. He jerked, only then realizing he'd almost fallen asleep. He blamed that on Kirit, too. He seemed to have developed a slight problem with insomnia lately. And the dreams were getting stranger every night, full of fire and mountains and men in kilts. It made him wonder what, exactly, he had gotten himself into.

As the knocks continued, Cody's fingers went again to the side of his neck. The scabs from Kirit's bite were rough under his fingers. In his mind, he could see the man's smile.

And the man's fangs.

Jay shoved Cody's feet off his lap and stood.

"Don't open it!" Cody ordered.

Jay made sure Cody could see him roll his eyes. "Please, it's most likely just Aaron. I told him we were here tonight."

Cody ducked behind the couch. Jay gave him a disgusted look, and Cody had to admit he felt more than a little stupid. He didn't come out of hiding, though.

Jay unfastened the locks and swung open the door. "Hey, man, was wondering where— Oh, you're not Aaron."

"Nope. Gonna let me in anyway?"

"Depends." Jay blocked the door with his body like a good friend should. Which was weird in itself, since Jay really wasn't all that good of a friend, in any sense of the word 'good'. "Codes, some short dude is here to see you."

"I am not short." The man's indignant interjection was roundly ignored.

Cody stood, since that was most definitely not Kirit. The voice was all wrong, and no one could possibly, by any stretch of the imagination, consider Kirit short.

Plus, he doubted the big guy would wait for an invitation to come in. He seemed impatient like that.

"Yeah, let him in."

Jay-Jay stepped aside to admit...well, a short dude. Five foot six at most, a bit on the pudgy side, the guy looked perfectly harmless.

Until you saw his eyes. They were a deep, stormy gray and Cody could swear they flashed with tiny streaks of light.

"Oh, shit, that's all I need," Cody complained. He'd seen eyes like that before, on a night he preferred not to think about. But that was years ago, and he couldn't think of anything he had done lately to draw the attention of a witch.

Except meeting Kirit. *Damn him, anyway.*

"Good, you know what I am," the witch declared. "That simplifies things."

"Huh? Codes, what is he talking about?"

Shit. Jay-Jay. What was he going to do about Jay-Jay? Somehow, Cody didn't think this was going to be a conversation Jay was ready to hear.

"Look, Jay, why don't you go hit a few places, see if you can find where Aaron disappeared to? I've got this."

"Sure, man? 'Cause I'm cool with sticking around if you need me." The last bit was accompanied with a significant look at their visitor.

"Yeah, I'm fine. Go on."

Jay looked mildly curious, but not very concerned. The guy was a little on the shallow side and had a competitive streak that tended to get in the way of any real friendship. Cody still hadn't forgotten that first night, when Jay-Jay tried to make a play for his man.

No, not yours. Jay can have him. You don't want him, remember?

That argument made him feel nauseous. *Damn it, what is with me lately?*

"I'm Harper, by the way," the witch offered as the door closed behind Jay-Jay.

Cody ignored the introduction and went to grab a couple of sodas from the refrigerator. He took the drinks back to the living room, which took all of three steps. He handed one to Harper as he passed on his way back to the couch.

"Sit," Cody said. "Let's get this over with."

Cody popped open his can of Coke and stared at Harper, who had settled into the battered recliner set at an angle to the couch. Cody didn't think he was going to like what Harper had to say.

Harper put his unopened drink aside and leaned forward, resting his chin on his hands. He studied Cody with the intensity of a scientist with a rare bug.

Cody couldn't help squirming. "What?"

"What do you know?" Harper asked. "Give me a baseline here."

"I get around." Cody shrugged. "You see things in my line of work. I once met a guy with green hair. Thought it was a dye job, but most guys don't dye their crotch."

"Dryad. Careful around them. They've got nasty tempers and a bad habit of turning people into trees."

"Really? 'Cause I can think of a few people who would make fantastic trees."

Harper laughed. "Oh, I like you. Kirit did well."

"So, this *is* about the big guy." Not that Cody had thought otherwise.

"The big guy?" The lines around Harper's eyes deepened in amusement. "Yes, he is certainly that."

Harper shook his head, sobering. "So, how much did the 'big guy' explain?"

Cody arched one brow and gave his best sardonic grin.

Harper rubbed his forehead. Cody could sympathize.

"Right," Harper said with exasperation. "Start from the beginning."

"I know he's not exactly human," Cody offered, feeling sorry for the guy. "The fangs were kind of a dead giveaway. Plus, he gets a little scaly during moments of...high passion."

"I really didn't need to know that."

"Hey, you asked."

"I did not."

"Did, too. You asked what I knew. I told you. It's not my fault if Kirit's control slips when he's coming like a—"

"Oh, for the love of the gods, stop!" Harper slapped his hands over his eyes, which Cody totally didn't understand. Cody waited until he peeked to smirk.

"You two are perfect for each other." Harper didn't sound like he thought that was a good thing. "All right, here goes. Kirit is from a race called the Draak, very unique and rare. He's a warrior and a member of the King of the Fae's personal army."

"What, like, fairies?" Cody's skepticism rang clear in the words, but... *Really? Fairies?*

"Whatever you do, don't call Seamus a fairy," Harper advised. "It makes him extremely cranky."

Magnificent. Thirty seconds into this conversation, and I'm already lost.

"Look," Cody said. "I wasn't exactly at the top of my class. Better use small words, because I have no idea what you're talking about. And who the hell is Seamus?"

Harper blew out a breath of frustration. "Okay, forget that part. I'm going for the Cliff Notes version here, so just be patient, all right? There is a Veil, a magical boundary separating this world from the other, Faerie."

Cody blinked. *How did we get from Tinkerbell to a veil?*

Harper just kept barreling ahead, oblivious to the fact that his audience was still wandering behind him, figuratively speaking. "There are two main species in the Faerie court. Dozens of species overall, but the nobility is what we're concerned with now. There's the Fae, or the ruling class, of which Seamus is the...top dog, shall we say. The Draak are next in the hierarchy, like the Earls and Dukes of British society. They're also the muscle, the elite warriors of their world—although, I certainly wouldn't want to provoke a Fae. However, you really, really don't want to mess with the Draak. They're not exactly known for patience. Or even tempers. And they bite. Hard. Kirit, as I said, is Draak. Quite a stereotypical one, in point of fact."

"Okay, got that part, but what exactly *is* a Draak?" He had an inkling, but was really kind of hoping to be wrong.

"Kirit is a dragon."

Shit, he wasn't. "Dragon. As in big, scaly, breathes fire?"

"Yep."

"Okay." Cody drew the word out, not quite sure how he was feeling about all this. *Good God, I slept with a dragon! Although, I shouldn't be surprised. Scales and fangs, kinda fits.* "He looked pretty damn human to me. Ya know, for a dragon."

"Yes, well, big and scaly wouldn't exactly blend into the crowd in Denver. Most Draak prefer their secondary form when out in public, even in Faerie. Something about doors not being made big enough for dragons."

This has to be, hands down, the most bizarre conversation I've ever had.

"Dragon. Okay." Cody took a deep breath, trying to process. Then he shoved it aside. He'd deal with the whole dragon thing later. *In the meantime…* "So, why the hell is he stalking me?"

"The legends about dragons aren't entirely inaccurate. They do, in general, have an annoying habit of hoarding and a childlike attraction to anything pretty and shiny."

"So, what, he thinks I'm pretty and wants to add me to his collection?" *Because that is so not happening.* He wasn't anyone's possession, dragon or not.

"Not quite. While dragons are fond of treasure in general, they're not greedy. They're more the anti-social, irritable, possessive type." Harper said the last bit as an aside. Cody wondered if he meant all dragons, or if he was referring to one dragon in particular. "There's an exception, though, to all of the above. Both the Fae and the Draak tend to latch on to one person. They have some leeway, but a mate is someone who is well-matched to them. If you ask them, they'd describe it as a person fate has declared to be a good fit for them. I think it has more to do with genetics. See, there's this—"

"Let me guess." Cody had the feeling if he let Harper get going, they'd be there all day, and Cody would end up even more confused and quite possibly with a migraine to boot. "I've read my share of romance novels. Now you're going to tell me I'm his one true mate and we're supposed to live happily ever after."

"No, that's bullshit."

"Sheesh, don't sugarcoat it, man."

Harper ignored him, focused on his explanation. The guy would make a great professor, albeit one that put his classes to sleep on a regular basis. "There's no such thing as a 'one true mate', but rather many potential mates. A Draak can usually tell by scent if someone is compatible and able to fit with them for the long-term. Occasionally, they will find someone who's such a perfect match they're considered a Treasure, but that's neither here nor there. You're a potential mate for Kirit and, since he hasn't found another one in centuries, he's not about to let you go."

"So, I'm stuck with—wait, did you say *centuries*?"

"Time works differently on the other side of the Veil," Harper replied with a dismissive wave. It didn't really make Cody feel any better. And now he had more questions.

Cody closed his eyes, feeling the beginnings of that migraine. In deference to the pain waiting for its chance to strike, he decided more explanations were better left for later.

"I really didn't need this," he said to no one in particular.

"Tough luck," Harper said with what was probably supposed to be an attempt at commiseration. It would have worked better if he didn't sound so cheerful.

"What now? I'm supposed to move Kirit in here and spend the rest of my life tripping over him?" Because his apartment was so not big enough for him and one oversized dragon.

"I think that's something you should ask Kirit."

Chapter Seven

Harper let the door bang closed behind him. He shoved his hands in the pockets of his coat and took a deep breath.

If he didn't have to do that ever again, it would make him a very happy witch.

"You can come out now," Harper called to the empty street. He could feel that damn dragon hovering, just out of sight.

Kirit emerged from the shadows with the creepy stealth dragons were so good at. If Harper could only go back in time…

I would tell that thrice-cursed Seamus to shove it when he came to me for help.

That's what had started this whole thing. At first, Harper had been flattered when the Fae king had contacted him. Seamus wanted someone to assist his people when they moved between realms, and it had been neat to have someone with that much power put so much trust in Harper.

Little did Harper know he'd get stuck with the dragons all the time. Why couldn't he get a nice, temperamental ogre or something? Those he could fry without worrying about consequences. Made for a much simpler life.

"What did he say?"

Harper jerked his attention back to Kirit. He snorted and shook his head, shoving his hands deeper into his pockets. The wind was cold tonight. "He took it better than expected. You don't blend as well as you think you do. Anyway, I'm done. Next move is yours."

"Move? So I should—"

"God save me from literal dragons!" Harper couldn't hold back the outburst. He stopped, inhaled deeply. *Gods, I'm tired.* "Look, just track him down and talk. You can manage that, can't you? I know it will be a challenge, but charm him. Get him to go back home with you. I've done my part, and then some. You're on your own."

Harper brushed past Kirit. He could feel the dragon's gaze boring into his back as he walked away.

He'd been a cranky asshole, and he knew it. *Jealousy is a bitch.*

At least if the dragon went back home, Harper wouldn't have to watch the sickening display of a dragon obsessed. It only made him long for what he didn't have. Wouldn't have.

Seamus owes me big time.

Cody rounded the corner and smacked into a wall. He made a small sound of pain, staggering back and rubbing at his throbbing nose.

"Watch it, will you?" he complained. He opened his eyes, already knowing what he was going to find.

Yep. Called it.

Kirit stood there, staring at him with laser-like focus. It was a bit disconcerting.

"A little warning would have been nice," Cody continued, although he wasn't sure what he was complaining about anymore. *Damn, those eyes...*

Kirit reached out with one giant hand and stroked Cody's cheek. "You look very pretty today, my mate."

Cody scowled. "I am *not* pretty."

The annoying dragon just smiled indulgently. "Come, it is nearing midday. I would feed you."

Cody growled in annoyance when Kirit grabbed his arm. He couldn't break the hold as Kirit half-dragged, half-escorted him along the sidewalk. "Why are you always trying to feed me?"

"You are skinny," Kirit declared as if he were merely stating the obvious.

"I'm not skinny, I'm slender." And Cody had never had any complaints before. He tugged some more, but it was futile. Cody wasn't getting away until the big guy let him.

"Harper visited you." The words were a statement, not a question.

Of course he knows about the visit, he's been hovering in the street for days.

"He did," Cody confirmed anyway. "He's weird. And confusing."

Kirit nodded his agreement. "True. But he is trustworthy. He explained about the Draak?"

"Shh, not so loud," Cody admonished, looking around at the...all right, so they were almost alone on the sidewalk. Downtown Denver was often crowded in the afternoon, but it had started to snow again, keeping many people indoors. Cody kind of liked the snow, though, which was a good thing since he hated public transportation. *All those people, shoved together...ick.* With no car, he spent a lot of time walking, no matter the weather.

Kirit guided Cody through the door of a small Italian restaurant. The scents of garlic and tomato hit Cody hard, making his stomach rumble. He hadn't realized he was hungry, but now that he thought about it, a huge plate of spaghetti sounded marvelous.

They settled into a booth in the back. Kirit waited until the waitress had left, taking their drink orders and leaving menus, before he spoke again.

"So, Harper explained?"

"Sort of. I mean, I already knew you weren't quite human, but I didn't know *what* you were."

Kirit cocked his head, looking at Cody with curiosity in his pale eyes. "Harper said I did not hide well. How did you know?"

"Dude, I had my tongue in your mouth." Cody smirked. "Hate to break it to you, but most guys don't have fangs. And you get all scaly when you come, did you know that?"

Kirit blushed a bright red. It was utterly adorable— *damn, there's that word again.*

Cody grinned, suddenly feeling much better about the whole situation. And he was decidedly *not* examining the fact that he felt better in Kirit's presence than he had all week. "Your tongue is slightly forked, too," he said instead.

Cody hadn't thought it possible, but the blush deepened. *Oh, that is awesome.*

He would have continued to tease, but their server returned at that moment, forestalling Cody's fun. Cody ordered for both of them, since Kirit seemed slightly confused by the menu.

They sat in silence for several minutes afterwards. Cody watched Kirit with curious eyes. Kirit, on the other hand, stared at Cody with an uncomfortable amount of heat. Cody squirmed, arousal hitting him hard and sudden. He couldn't remember the last time someone had affected him like this — if they ever had. Sex had become, sad to say, commonplace. It took more and more to get him worked up as time passed. At least, until Kirit. The big guy seemed to be able to do it with one look.

"Stop it," Cody ordered.

"Stop what?"

Cody opened his mouth, then closed it again. He wasn't sure how to answer that without either sounding idiotic or sharing more information than he wanted others to be privy to.

"Never mind." Cody absently played with his silverware, trying to put his thoughts into some sort of order. The silence continued to grow. It was heavy with anticipation and more than a little lust.

"Give me a reason," Cody demanded into the silence.

Kirit tilted his head in a curious gesture, one that was decidedly *not* human. Humans didn't look so...flexible, when they did that.

"Give me a reason to give up my entire world, literally, to come with you," Cody clarified.

Kirit's eyes glinted with a wicked light.

"Sex doesn't count."

Kirit pouted.

"Sorry, but even though we're kind of explosive in bed, I need a better reason than that."

Kirit's expression firmed and he sat up straighter, taking the question seriously. "Don't underestimate the power inherent in the erotic," he said. "Beyond that, however, the other side of the Veil is like nothing you have seen. It is the world as it existed millennia ago, before so-called civilization took hold. I won't discount some of the advantages of modern life, but there is a beauty to Faerie that cannot be found here. It's far from a paradise—people are people, regardless of the world. But there, in my home, you will be cherished and safe. I can promise you a different kind of life, a better life."

Cody didn't know Kirit could say that much at one time. He couldn't summon a smart remark. The speech had been strangely poetic.

"I just don't know," Cody admitted, chewing thoughtfully on his lower lip. *God, it's tempting. So tempting. But...* "It's not that I don't like you, or that your world doesn't appeal to me. But what you're asking, it's huge."

Kirit tilted his head again. "I know."

He didn't try to justify himself further, which Cody found himself grateful for. He tended to be perverse that way—if someone tried too hard to convince Cody of something, he had a bad habit of doing the opposite out of spite.

Maybe they weren't a bad match, at that.

Their food had arrived while Kirit was talking. Cody went through the motions, eating on automatic pilot, mind racing in circles. He wanted to give Kirit an answer. It felt wrong to leave the poor guy hanging in limbo. But Cody just couldn't rush into this. He wasn't ready to say no, but he wasn't ready to say yes, either.

"When do you need an answer?" he asked.

Cody turned Kirit's words over, looking at them from all directions. He was drawn to Kirit, as he'd never been to anyone else. The sex was amazing. His life here wasn't exactly fantastic. And Faerie sounded gorgeous. Primitive, but gorgeous.

Then a horrible thought occurred to him.

"Do you at least have running water in Faerie?"

"I have a waterfall," Kirit offered.

"Okay, that might be a deal breaker." He really needed his morning shower. And he was *not* using an outhouse. That was just nasty.

"There are other benefits, and it's a very nice waterfall."

"Benefits?" Cody snorted. "You do realize that, once again, we're back to the sex?"

Kirit shrugged. "It's my best argument."

"Well, it's gonna have to be some damn good sex to make up for a lack of indoor plumbing," Cody said. "I've never even been camping."

"Oh, it is *very* good sex." He looked at Cody hopefully.

Cody could see the question in his eyes, buried within a boatload of desire.

Shoving his plate away, Cody chuckled quietly. "All right, big guy, you can come back to my apartment tonight. I'll let you do your best to convince me of the 'benefits' in Faerie."

One night won't suck me in any deeper in, right?

Kirit's leer was downright wicked, full of promise and lust. Cody mentally rolled his eyes at himself.

Who are you kidding? You're already in deep.

Chapter Eight

Most people would find the throbbing music and flashing lights painful. For Cody, it was comforting, particularly after last night's discussion. What did he know about fantasy worlds and forever after? Was that really what he wanted?

He'd been unable to knock the thoughts out of his head, and he wanted to. Desperately.

This is your world, he told himself firmly. This, right here, a place full of sweaty bodies and quick hook-ups. And, above all, the attitude that only right now, this minute, mattered. The future wasn't important, the past irrelevant. There was only the present and the endless search for instant gratification.

But it doesn't make you happy anymore.

Cody shoved the insistent little voice into the back of his mind. He flung his head back and rocked his hips, trying to let the music carry him away the way it usually did. He could feel the pounding beat under his feet and the stares of the people around him. Admiring stares, mostly.

He was hot, and he knew it. Relied on it, as a matter of fact. Vain? Sure. But Cody had no illusions about himself. He wasn't smart or talented or any number of other things people prided themselves on. His dark hair, bright green eyes, and perfectly toned figure was his meal ticket.

Cody wasn't the least bit ashamed of it, either. How he made his living. The pay was a hell of a lot better than any nine-to-five job he could get with his limited education—that was for sure. He liked the sex, liked dressing up and being the center of attention. He snagged one, maybe two guys a night. Worked four or five days a week.

It was a good life. Or it had been, until stupid Johnnie had moved into the neighborhood. No way did Cody plan to go to work for some weasely little pimp. He'd held Johnnie off so far. He could do it indefinitely. Maybe.

Now might be a good time to make a change.

And there went the voice again.

"Hey, man, guy at table six has his eye on you. Gonna make a move?"

Cody shook his head at Aaron's question, keeping his eyes closed and continuing to dance. He was off the clock tonight. No working the room, no pickups, he was simply here to blow off some steam. And think.

All right, so the middle of a packed club was a weird place to make life-altering decisions, but Cody always thought better surrounded by the trappings of his life. Shallow though they may be.

An image of glittering eyes floated through his mind. Strange eyes, really. Kirit might try to blend in, but he failed miserably. No amount of denim and leather was going to mask the almost alien appearance. It was a miracle no one else had noticed.

So what was it about the guy that had him invading every single one of Cody's thoughts? Kirit wasn't even that great to look at. He was tall and bulky, with a body worth drooling over, and that hair...but the rest of him? His face was long and angled, chin pointed, nose a sharp blade over thin lips. Now that Cody knew what to look for, he could see the dragon in Kirit's features, especially the slanted, narrow eyes that weren't any color he'd ever seen before. They reminded Cody of a diamond, pale and shimmering, reflecting the colors around in glittering facets that made Cody think of ice and sharp, painful objects.

Except when those same cold eyes looked at Cody, they softened. Melted. The almost-white warmed to a pale eggshell blue, looking at him with such awe...

"Cody? Cody!"

Cody shook his head again, but Aaron was determined not to be ignored. He grabbed Cody's arm and pulled him to the edge of the dance floor, brushing past Jay-Jay. There were small booths tucked around the edges of the room, and Aaron found an empty one. Out of the way, it wasn't popular, mainly because it didn't have a very good view of the dance floor. The slight isolation lessened the noise, though, and gave them a little space.

"What's wrong with you tonight?" Aaron asked.

"Sorry, just distracted," Cody replied.

"I've seen you distracted. This isn't it."

Cody mustered up his best smile. "I'm cool, Aaron, swear. Just trying to work some stuff out."

His closest friend knew him too well. Aaron clearly didn't buy the excuse. "Does your 'stuff' have anything to do with the guy with the death stare?"

"Huh?"

Cody followed Aaron's gesture and groaned aloud, although he really should have expected it. After all, Kirit had followed Cody everywhere in the last few days. Why would tonight be any different?

Cody winced when the crowd parted slightly and he caught a better look at the big guy. Oh, yeah, that was a total death stare. It wasn't aimed at Cody, though, but at the mass of writhing bodies around him. Cody was so used to it that he barely noticed the hands people slid over his hips or patted on his ass in passing.

Not so Kirit. Forget kicking ass and taking names, the big dragon looked ready to start maiming. *Shit.*

"You need a distraction?" Aaron asked with genuine concern. "I'm sure a couple of the guys would be happy to cause a scene while you slip out."

"Nah, just ignore him. Kirit is harmless." Maybe. Sometimes.

To you.

Cody studied Kirit, then Aaron. "Can I ask you something?"

"Mmm." Aaron's attention was mostly on the room around them. Cody's question grabbed his full attention, though.

"If you had a chance for a different life, would you take it?"

Aaron studied Cody with an odd expression for several long seconds. "Yeah," he said finally. "I probably would."

They sat there in silence for a time, studying the crowd with the same practiced focus. Even when Cody wasn't working, he realized he still automatically categorized and sifted. Which guys were looking for a hookup, which ones would pay for it. Which ones would beat the crap out of him, during or after.

"We're not getting any younger, Codes." Aaron's words startled Cody. He turned to see an unusually solemn look in his friend's eyes. "I know we like to pretend we're immortal, but the truth is, we can't do this forever. No matter how much we might try to pretend otherwise. I've made plans. Have you?"

Shit. When did Aaron turn so introspective?

Cody was forced to admit he hadn't planned ahead. He'd allowed himself to get caught up in the world around him. When was the last time he'd thought about the future?

Too long. Maybe because he hadn't been able to see a future. Until one big, cranky dragon refused to go away.

"You getting out, babe?" Cody asked Aaron, trying to take some of the pressure off himself for a minute. Damn it, that whole contemplation thing wasn't working out like he'd hoped.

"Been thinking about it," Aaron admitted. "Ever since Johnnie moved in, especially. I'm getting tired, yeah?"

"Yeah," Cody replied. This was the first time Aaron had put the feelings into words, but Cody had seen the restlessness for a while now. He'd been experiencing some of it himself.

"Codes? What are you still doing here?"

Cody swung his head sharply to stare at Aaron's all-too-knowing eyes. He opened his mouth a few times, but nothing came out. *Huh.* He couldn't remember the last time that happened. He always had a comeback ready and waiting.

"It's not that simple, Aaron." This wasn't a matter of moving across the city, or even across the country. This was…big. Scary.

A body slammed into their table. Cody jumped before turning a glare on a laughing Jay-Jay.

"Watch it, man."

"Sorry." Jay grinned, busy shaking his ass at a blond, preppy boy nearby. "Come on, dance with me." He yanked on Aaron's arm.

Cody knew why. Two good-looking boys together drew a hell of a lot more attention than one.

"Go on," he told Aaron. "I'm gonna sit here and think some more."

Aaron paused. "Good luck."

Watching him go, Cody tried to decipher the expression in Aaron's eyes. Then it struck him.

Aaron didn't think he'd see Cody again. And Cody kind of thought Aaron might be right.

Chapter Nine

Cody took a deep breath and adjusted the strap on his backpack. The cab driver was getting impatient, so he dragged the rest of his bags out of the backseat and paid the man.

This was it, the big moment. He'd gone back and forth for days, but really, he had mostly been stalling.

In the end, it came down to one thing—was being with Kirit worth the risk of the unknown? Strangely enough, his answer was 'yes' every time. After all, what did he have on Earth that was so great? Sure, he had friends, things, but nothing he couldn't let go of with surprising ease. He didn't own much, and he wasn't actually all that close to any of his friends, not even Aaron. They talked and hung out, but in the end, they were co-workers. The stiff competition they engaged in kept the ties from strengthening.

Cody took another deep breath. Grabbing all his luggage required some juggling—besides his backpack, he had a nice big suitcase on rollers and two duffle bags. He sort of balanced everything and dragged it up the stairs. He found the right entrance and lifted his hand to knock, then stopped. He stared at the fake wood in front of him. *Moment of truth.* If he went inside, there was no going back.

The door creaked open before Cody could take that final step, revealing a scowling face.

"Well, you gonna stand there all day or come in?"

Cody rolled his eyes and pushed past the cranky witch. "Someone didn't get their coffee yet today, I see."

"Of course not," Harper snapped, slamming the door closed behind Cody. "It's the ass-crack of dawn."

Cody smirked, dropping his bags next to the couch. In all honesty, he'd normally be sound asleep right now, but he'd never actually gone to bed last night. After he'd talked to Aaron, he'd sat there for a while, drinking some but mostly soaking up the atmosphere. Then, he'd gone home and packed. So now here he stood, at the lovely hour of five-thirty in the morning.

"Is Kirit here?" Cody asked.

"Why the hell would dragon-boy be here?"

Cody laughed. "Go get your coffee, witch. He'll show up soon enough, I would imagine."

He usually did.

As if on cue, a loud series of pounds rattled the door violently in its frame.

"You can get that," Harper said. "I need caffeine. Especially if I'm going to deal with a thrice-cursed Draak."

Cody laughed again — he was in a surprisingly good mood — and opened the door. It was something of a relief, making his decision. He looked up into those glittering eyes which were swiftly becoming so familiar. "Hey there, big guy."

"Cody."

Is that a smile? Indeed, I do believe it is. Kirit's narrow lips titled at the corners as he reached out, cupping Cody's cheek with his palm. Cody covered Kirit's hand with his own, frowning slightly at the cold skin under his touch.

"You feeling okay?" he asked, tugging Kirit into the small apartment.

"Of course."

Cody almost rolled his eyes at the tone in Kirit's voice. The stupid guy sounded almost reverent as he stared at Cody. Cody only stopped the irritated gesture because…well, it kind of gave him a warm, fluttery feeling.

"Kirit needs to go back to Faerie."

Cody grimaced, having completely forgotten about Harper's presence. "Say what?"

"He's a lizard," Harper explained. "Cold-blooded. He's not built for the snow."

"I am not a lizard," Kirit objected irritably. "I can handle the snow quite well. I do, after all, live in the mountains."

Harper smirked. "Whatever you say, dragon-boy."

"That's why I'm here," Cody reminded the pair before they could continue their bickering. "So, how do we do this?"

"You will return with me? Truly?"

Cody patted Kirit's chest—it was the highest part of the man he could reach. "I said I would, didn't I? Now hush and let the witch talk."

"That's really impressive," Harper said when Kirit closed his mouth. "I kind of wish I was coming along. The Draak aren't going to know what to do with you."

Cody scowled at Harper, who he was finding more irritating by the second. Thankfully, Harper pulled himself back on track without any guidance.

"All right, grab your stuff. We have to head downtown." Then Harper looked askance at the pile of luggage. "You know, you really don't need all that stuff."

"I'm not leaving my clothes behind," Cody said.

"Your club clothes won't exactly fit in at Seamus' court," Harper replied dryly.

"Court? What court?"

Harper took a deep breath. "Look, you won't need it all, okay? They have a different style of dress over there, and I'm sure Kirit would be more than happy to provide what you need."

Cody argued, but in the end he gave in. While an amused Kirit watched, Cody rifled through his things until he had re-packed everything into one of the large duffle bags. He secured a promise from Harper to hang onto his stuff—he figured if he needed it, Harper could get it to him somehow.

This isn't a one-way trip, he reminded himself. *You can come back if you absolutely have to.*

Cody didn't protest when Kirit took his bag. He tried to push aside his nerves and followed the two magical beings out into the dark night.

The instant they stepped outside it started to snow. Cody wondered if he should take that as a sign.

* * * *

Nearly an hour later, Kirit watched Cody stare with visible trepidation at their destination. This was really happening. His mate was here, and they were both going home. *What is it humans do? Something about pinching?* No matter, until Kirit had his new mate home and safe, he wasn't going to be able to bring himself to believe in this.

"I must be nuts," Cody mumbled. They stood outside in the lightly falling snow, in an older section of town. The gracefully aging building before them had a sign in the front window, 'Demon's Apothecary'. Said window was an extended bay, with a pile of cushions on a window seat visible on the other side of the elegant script. The building itself was wood-fronted, and a throwback to earlier days. Kirit remembered seeing buildings like this in some of those western movies Chaos was so fond of.

They bypassed the wide set of brick steps and went around the side of the building. Harper led them down the narrow alley, stopping at a small, innocuous entry halfway along. He inserted a huge brass key and unlocked the door. He pushed the wooden panel open, then pocketed the key.

Cody took a deep breath, stepping up to the entrance. Harper stopped Cody to give him a quick hug. Cody made a face.

"Take care of the big guy," Harper said, ignoring Cody's discomfort. "He needs you."

"I kind of got that," Cody admitted. "Why else would I be doing something this crazy?"

"Should I be offended?" Kirit asked, but wasn't surprised when his question went ignored.

"It's not crazy," Harper said. "Not everyone is lucky enough to find someone. Just trust yourself, trust Kirit, and don't let the Draak intimidate you."

"Are they all as big as he is?"

"I'm not big," Kirit said. "You're small."

One witch and one human turned disbelieving gazes towards Kirit.

"You do realize he's taller than I am?" Harper pointed out.

With a sense of surprise, Kirit realized Harper was correct. While the witch could be considered short, Cody outpaced him by at least three inches. That would make Kirit's new mate around five foot eleven, perhaps one hundred and eighty pounds. If memory served, about average for a human male, if on the skinny end.

He certainly felt tiny to Kirit.

Harper scowled. "Okay, enough stalling," he told Cody sternly. "Go. And if you ever need anything, you know where to find me."

Cody smiled nervously. "Something tells me I won't be back anytime soon."

"Damn straight," Kirit said with a proud smirk. He'd heard a human use that phrase and found it quite evocative.

Cody rolled his eyes and Harper sighed.

"I can't wait to have my life back," Harper said. "Good luck."

With that final admonishment, he turned and disappeared into the snow, which suddenly swirled in a manic, completely unnatural way.

Cody's quirked his lips. "He does have a touch of the dramatic in him, doesn't he?"

The snow trailed after Harper, vanishing round the corner with him. Kirit had to give the man credit—he certainly knew how to make an exit.

Kirit dismissed the witch from his thoughts and closed his hand tightly around Cody's upper arm. He ushered his new mate through the door and along a narrow hallway. The dim glow from old-fashioned oil lamps lit their way, guiding them towards the back of the building.

Gods, but Kirit hated magic sometimes. The journey felt endless, and far too long for such a tiny shop. Now that the moment had come, his spine was itching and he had this irritating feeling of urgency. He wanted Cody safe on the other side, now. Kirit couldn't help worrying that something was going to happen to mess up his plan. He simply wasn't this fortunate. Ever.

"Slow down," Cody protested.

"When we're on the other side," Kirit promised. Now where the hell was that stupid portal? And did this hallway ever end?

Cody tripped, only Kirit's tight grip keeping him upright. "Dude, I'm going to break something."

"No, you won't."

Okay, so that was probably true. Kirit seemed to be kind of obsessive about protecting Cody. From everything. They might not know each other that well, but it hadn't taken long for that particular character trait of Kirit's to become obvious.

Cody was eventually going to get the flu, and Kirit was going to fall apart. Cody had visions of emergency room visits—did they have emergency rooms in Faerie?—and Kirit terrorizing all the local doctors. Yeah. Good thing Cody had packed his vitamins.

The hallway dead-ended in a small room, wooden floors giving way to smooth cement. There was nothing in the room except a broom, leaning against the wall on their right. That, and a doorframe directly across from them. It was kind of creepy, at least as creepy as an empty doorway could be.

The scene was actually kind of disappointing. Cody had been expecting...well, he didn't really know *what* he'd been expecting. Maybe a glowing, shimmering curtain or something. Instead, he got this opening, no door, just an open frame. And beyond, a thick, heavy darkness.

"Go on," Kirit urged.

"Maybe you should go first," Cody replied. Something about that emptiness freaked him out and made his gut knot up with tension.

"It is perfectly safe."

"I don't—"

Kirit planted one big hand between Cody's shoulder blades and shoved. Cody yelped, taking an automatic step forward then regain his balance.

The darkness swallowed him whole.

Chapter Ten

"I didn't sign up for this." Cody lifted one foot and scowled at the gunk dripping off the sole of his tennis shoe. He took a step, a loud squelch accompanying the movement. By the third step, he was stuck. Again.

Cody pulled, cursing when his foot slipped. Damn it, he was *not* going to lose a shoe in this goddamn mess.

"Kirit!"

Cody waited, but his bellow didn't bring any response. He took a deep breath and tried again.

"Yes, my mate?"

"Aak!" Cody tried to whirl, forgetting that his feet were mired in the thrice-cursed swamp. He yelped again, arms flailing, as he tipped forward. *Oh, damn.* That nasty bog was rushing up to meet his face, and it was *not* going to taste good.

He collided nose-first with something hard, sending a shooting pain through his face.

"Goddammit." His heartfelt curse was swallowed up by fabric. Cody struggled to free himself. Since he still couldn't move his feet, it appeared to be an insurmountable challenge.

"Is there a problem?"

Cody looked up into Kirit's amused grin and completely lost his temper.

"I swear, Kirit, if you don't get me out of this fucking swamp, I'm going to kill you!"

"Then you would be all by yourself. And lost," Kirit pointed out with infuriating logic.

"Yes, but you would be dead, and I would be satisfied."

Kirit chuckled.

Sheesh. Nice to know his concerns were being taken so seriously.

"My feet are stuck," Cody groused.

"So I see."

A long pause followed, where the only sounds came from the gurgling of the water and a few creepy noises that he most emphatically did not want to identify.

"Well?" Cody asked. "Are you going to do something about this?"

"What would you like me to do?"

"You're my mate. Get me *un*stuck."

If Kirit laughed again, Cody would not be responsible for his actions. At the moment, he yearned desperately for the city. Dirty alleys, snow and all.

"Hold still."

"Where do you think I'm going to go with half a bog stuck to my feet?"

"Hush."

That command made Cody want to babble, just to be contrary. "Fucking swamp. You never told me there would be a swamp. I've gone over every conversation we've had, which is admittedly not that many. But nowhere was there a mention of a foot-sucking swamp. I would have remembered that."

Kirit glared.

"That's helpful."

Kirit grunted.

"Oh, do tell me more."

Kirit bent, grabbed Cody around the waist, and pulled.

"Holy—" One second he was stuck in the mud, the next Cody was airborne. He would have been happier about it, except his shoes were still earth-bound.

"Oh, no," Cody said. "I am *not* wandering around this place with no shoes. My socks will get all gross."

"Your socks are already…gross."

"Must you always be so literal?"

Kirit shrugged. Since Cody was clinging to the big dragon's shoulders, the motion almost sent him flying.

"You dump me in this swamp and I swear to God, Kirit, I really *will* kill you."

A low laugh—not Kirit's—emanated from behind a nearby moss-draped tree.

"Let me guess. Another one of you." Cody huffed and flopped forwards. The position now had him draped over one of Kirit's shoulders, limbs dangling. Of course, it also gave him an excellent view of Kirit's very fine arse.

At least there were some perks to this horrible adventure. Cody slid his hands down Kirit's back, grabbed two nice handfuls, and squeezed.

Kirit smacked Cody on his own arse, hard. "Behave," Kirit scolded.

"Oh, I am behaving."

"If this is you behaving—"

"It is. After all, I could do this." Cody squirmed, shifted his weight, and slipped his fingers under the waistband of Kirit's trousers.

"Cody!"

Another low chuckle abruptly reminded Cody that they had an audience. He pulled his hand free and braced himself before pushing his upper body up so he could see.

A large, dark-haired man stood in the shadows, leaning against a tree. His green eyes were piercing and utterly fascinating. If Cody squinted, it looked like his pupils were kind of odd-shaped. Almost like a snake's.

"Hi," Cody said with a grin.

"Hi." The big guy smiled back and added the most adorable wave.

"I'm Cody."

"Cody." The man nodded, as if in approval. "I am—"

"For the love of Draconis, we're not at a soiree."

"Nice word," the stranger drawled.

"Nyx!"

"Kirit likes to yell." Cody gave the other Draak—Nyx—a conspiratorial smile.

"Cody!"

"See what I mean?"

Is it odd that I think that growl is hot? Cody had to squirm in an attempt to adjust his position—his cock was hardening and pressing against Kirit's shoulder. It was *not* comfortable.

Nyx shoved away from his tree and slogged over to them. Cody noted with irritation that he walked through the muck with no problems. Of course, the nice, stompy boots probably helped.

"I have the shoes," Nxy declared a few moments later.

Kirit began walking.

"Give me my shoes and put me down," Cody demanded.

Nyx chuckled. Kirit ignored him, then grunted.

Cody might have *accidentally* kicked him in the chest.

The two men kept walking. Cody settled in for the ride. It was bumpy and awkward and Kirit's shoulder felt bonier by the second.

"So," Nyx said.

"Don't answer that," Kirit ordered.

"I haven't asked the question yet," Nyx pointed out.

"Keep it to yourself.

Nyx dropped back to grin at Cody and proceeded to ignore Kirit's advice.

"So, where did Kirit find you?"

"Denver, Colorado."

"Earth?"

"You don't need to sound so surprised. Sheesh, you'd think he found me on Mars or something."

Nyx opened his mouth.

"If you're going to tell me Martians are real, don't," Cody advised. "I don't want to know."

"I like you, Cody of Denver, Colorado." Nyx grinned wickedly.

"Thanks. I think."

Nyx moved back out of Cody's sight and they continued to travel along. Water kept dripping on Cody's head, he felt all sticky from the humidity and so far, he wasn't liking Faerie very much. He was being a complaining bitch, and he knew it, but damn it, he was miserable.

If Cody understood the process—which he quite possibly didn't—the portal from Faerie to Earth was limited. There were only a couple of specific places where you could come out. You had to use those same places to return, but the spell could drop you anywhere you wanted in Faerie. That's where Cody's understanding broke down.

Kirit could make the portal go anywhere, and he chose here? What the hell was the man thinking?

Cody asked that very question.

"I was thinking," Kirit replied grumpily, "that I didn't want to climb a mountain."

"What does that mean?"

"Oh, tell the hatchling the truth," Nyx scolded with far too much amusement. "You screwed up the transport spell again."

"You what?" Cody screeched, then winced. *Oh, no, that sound wasn't embarrassing at all.*

Kirit growled and spat something in a foreign language. Nyx snickered, and Cody smacked Kirit on the back.

"What does that— Holy shit!"

Cody's feet hit the ground with a hard thud. He staggered, trying to catch his balance after his unceremonious deposit.

"Your shoes."

Cody took the offered running shoes from Nyx, looking around. The swamp stretched along in his vision, murky and creepy. The squat trees were wreathed with the same mist that swirled on the ground, and he could still hear eerie noises from the dark depths. Cody shuddered and turned in a circle.

Oh, much better. Beyond the edges of the swamp, a large field filled his sight, golden grass waving gently in the breeze. Not far in the distance, on the other side of the field, he could see the blue haze of mountains. The air already smelled fresher, and the call of birds was far preferable to the grunts and growls of unknown predators.

"Why couldn't we have ended up here?" Cody bent at the waist as he asked his question, stuffing his feet into his nasty shoes. They were coated in mud and gunk, but better than going barefoot.

"Because Kirit always muddles up the parameters when he triggers the portal spell."

"I do not," Kirit replied irritably. "You can't open a portal into the Dragonlands, and you know it."

"You can into—"

Kirit's angry snarl cut off the budding argument. Nyx snickered some more. Cody was reluctantly impressed by the man's courage. Or maybe it was sheer stupidity. Kirit was looking really annoyed.

Cody wrapped his hand around Kirit's biceps and squeezed. The instant he had Kirit's attention, he smiled. "So, how much farther?"

Kirit smiled back. "Not long." He stepped behind Cody and pulled him back against that broad chest. With a quick nuzzle, he whispered into Cody's ear. "See the base of the mountains? Now go straight up, there's an outcropping. Squint, and you should be able to see the carvings."

Cody did as instructed. It was a long way, but eventually his eyes adjusted and he could make out the well-worn figure, a dragon spread for flight.

"Sweet."

"That is home."

Cody turned and pulled Kirit into a kiss. It just felt right, a celebration of the beginning of his new life. Of course, with Kirit, he quickly lost control, the kiss turning hungry and consuming.

The fierce heat that roared through Cody erased all thoughts, sweeping away the last bit of his earlier irritation and anger. He moaned, tugging until Kirit bent far enough for Cody to drape his arms around his dragon's neck.

Their lips met and parted, each press and retreat fierce and passionate. Cody sucked on Kirit's tongue and pressed closer. He wrapped one leg around Kirit's thigh and used his grip on Kirit's neck to lift his weight. He was happily trying to climb the big, bulky body when an odd sound interrupted his lustful haze.

Curses. Deep, heartfelt curses. Accompanied by a lust-filled groan that was most decidedly not from Kirit.

Cody pulled back, clutching firmly at Kirit's clothing to maintain his precarious position. He looked to one side.

Nyx watched them with hooded, burning eyes. Literally. Flames danced in the dark depths, his narrow pupils almost swallowed by the deepened color. His cock made a noticeable bulge in the front of his tight leather pants. He had one hand on said bulge, rubbing with rough, unsteady motions.

Oh. Okay. Cody had thought they were being attacked or something.

With a mental shrug, he went for Kirit's lips again. He found them just in time to swallow Kirit's rumbling growl.

Cody suddenly found himself back on the ground, still trying to kiss someone who wasn't there anymore. The cursing grew louder, ending in a sharp shout.

By the time he cleared the fuzziness from this head and got past the 'what the fuck happened?' moment, Kirit and Nyx were rolling around on the ground, locked together in some weird wrestling hold.

"Shit. Fuck. Damn." Cody took a hesitant step forwards.

Someone threw a punch. A few grunts and more curses rang through the air. They rolled again, nearly taking out Cody's feet.

"You idiots," Cody bellowed. "Stop it, right now. Kirit, get your ass over here! I mean it!"

They ignored him. Nyx pinned Kirit, straddling his legs, and pulled his fist back.

"Oh, hell, no." Cody leaped into the fray, landing with a solid thump on Nyx's back. "Get off him, you bastard."

He didn't know who started the fight or even what it was about. He didn't care. No one hurt his Kirit.

"Cody!" Kirit yelled in a furious voice.

"Shut up," Cody and Nyx said at the same time.

Cody yanked backwards, gripping Nyx around the neck. Nyx grunted.

Big, egotistical jerk. Cody wasn't sure which one he meant. He planted his feet, shifted his weight, and sent Nyx flying to one side — the other Draak might be big, but he was significantly smaller than Kirit. And Cody had picked up a few tricks over the years.

Nyx rolled to a stop, gaping. He stared at Cody. Then he started laughing.

A moment of shocked silence followed before Kirit joined him. The two idiots were soon sprawled on the ground, deep sounds of amusement filling the air.

"God," Cody mumbled. "This is going to be a really long trip."

Chapter Eleven

The two dragons settled down after their little tiff. In fact, Cody had only seen Kirit that relaxed after sex. Apparently, dragons needed a good fight every so often. Go figure.

They traveled for the rest of the day. Cody couldn't remember the last time he'd walked so much. His feet ached and he just wanted to sleep.

The flat land of the fields gave way to increasingly steep hills as they neared the mountains. The sun was beginning to set when they crested one last rise. A small town lay in front of them, tucked at the base of the mountain.

"Thank God, civilization," Cody said with heartfelt relief. Welcoming smoke curled from rough stone chimneys and lights flickered in some of the windows. He wanted a fire and a bed. And food. His stomach had been rebelling for the last hour.

Kirit grunted something unintelligible. Then he started down a path — around the town. It took Cody a few minutes to realize they were going to skirt the village without going in.

"Wait a minute," he protested. "I'm tired and hungry and why the hell are we going *away* from the people?"

"We live farther up," Nyx said, when it seemed like Kirit was going to remain silent. "Don't worry, it won't take much longer. A few hours, perhaps."

"What, don't you know? And can't we stay back there?" Cody jerked his thumb at the small bastion of civilization that they were in danger of leaving behind. "I mean, nothing says we have to get there tonight, right? It's getting dark." And cold. So much for the whole cold-blooded thing, because that wind was whipping right through Cody's coat. It was like being back in Denver, minus the snow.

While he waited for an answer, he dug his gloves from his pockets and jerked them on. The sun had dipped behind the craggy peaks above, and it was getting colder by the second.

Nyx looked at him searchingly. "Hmm. Perhaps we should stay in Thesauros for the night," he said. "We can stay at Lyrion's hut and continue on tomorrow."

"Yes. Please. Thank you."

Kirit scowled, obviously wanting to argue. Cody took heart, though, since he slowed his steps to a near-halt.

"Please?" he said again.

Ahead of them, the small path narrowed and began to climb, working its way through ever-increasing rock structures. He really didn't want to climb a mountain in the dark.

Kirit sighed, sounding very put-upon. He held out one hand, which Cody took.

"You won't always get your way," Kirit said.

"Wanna bet?" Cody said with a teasing smile.

Kirit made a face, and Nyx started to laugh.

The village of Thesauros was quiet at this time of night. Kirit led the way through the winding streets to a tiny building on the fringes. A sleepy-eyed guard stood in front of the wooden door. Kirit told him to take the night off, slightly amused at the speed with which the young man departed. The Draak were common visitors to the area, and all the local militia knew them on sight, as did the members of the small garrison. Not that Thesauros was a strategically advantageous location, but it *did* contain the only portal in or out of the Dragonlands. Seamus made certain it was well protected.

Lyrion's hut, Draak way station and home to the portal, was just that, a hut. It consisted of one small room built around a central hearth. A chest in one corner was piled high with blankets and furs. No furniture, no central lighting. Just a bunch of torches and a couple of oil lamps. There was a door on each end, one going outside and one that led to the portal.

Kirit had never understood why the wizards liked to hide the portals behind doors, but whenever it came to magic-users, he figured the less he knew, the better.

Kirit took a look at his mate and felt a little guilty. The poor man was tired enough that he didn't even complain about the sparse accommodations.

"Grab some blankets and make up a bed," he told Cody softly. "I'll get a fire started."

Nyx came in, arms loaded with wood. He dumped it into the cold hearth with a loud clatter that made Cody jump.

"Damn." Cody glared at the unrepentant Nyx. He yanked out a wool blanket, then paused. "Food?" he asked hopefully.

Nyx dug through the cupboards. The Draak paid someone in town to make sure the hut was kept provisioned, although they rarely needed it. The hike up the mountain wasn't hard, and they usually continued on, no matter the hour.

Of course, they rarely came though the village at all. Flying was faster.

After a pitiful meal of bread and cheese, Kirit settled into a nice pile of blankets with his mate. He pulled a bearskin over the top—nights grew cold here, very cold.

It only took a few minutes for Nyx to start snoring on his pallet on the other side of the room. Next to Kirit, though, Cody was suddenly restless.

"I thought you were tired," Kirit said.

"I was. I think I'm to that too-tired-to-sleep point." Cody thrashed around a couple of times and smacked Kirit in the nose. Kirit decided to forgo cuddling his mate and turned his back.

Cody lay silent and still for a few minutes, and Kirit began to drift off.

"What was that all about?"

"Huh?" Kirit asked, the question making absolutely no sense to his tired brain. "What was what about?"

"The fight," Cody said, as if it should have been obvious. "From earlier, you and Nyx."

"Oh."

"So? What was it about?"

Kirit rolled back over. "You, of course."

"Me?" Cody asked, sounding offended. "What the hell did I do?"

"Nothing. It was that bastard Nyx," Kirit grumbled. "He was looking at you."

Even the thought made Kirit's blood heat and he drew out a low growl.

"Looking at me? Seriously?" Cody raised one eyebrow in incredulity.

Gods, the man is pretty.

"I'm the only one who gets to look at you."

"That's ridiculous. You'll spend all your time fighting."

Kirit didn't really see anything wrong with that option, and he was stupid enough to voice his opinion. A small fist whacked his shoulder in response. Kirit grinned.

"You are so cute," he told Cody.

He probably shouldn't have said that, either. His cute mate let out an even cuter snarl and launched himself at Kirit. Kirit caught Cody handily and pinned him to the floor.

"Mmm. So cute." He nuzzled behind Cody's ear, flicking out his tongue to taste.

"Stop that," Cody ordered. "I'm mad at you."

He didn't sound mad, though, so Kirit kept licking.

"Stupid dragon."

"That's me," Kirit agreed. "Your stupid dragon."

Cody's pretty green eyes were glazing over with lust and Kirit hummed in contentment.

"This," he whispered into Cody's ear. "Nyx was looking at you like this. This is only for me to see."

"What is?"

"You. Lost in passion. Hot and aroused and...oh, yes. Most definitely. This is mine."

"Yours."

Cody's agreement deserved another kiss. Across the small space, Nyx snorted loudly. Kirit ignored the sound, as he ignored the following protest. A minute later, the door slammed shut, leaving Kirit all alone with his mate. Just the way he liked it. If he had his way, Kirit would lock Cody up with the rest of his jewels, where no one else would dare to take what was his.

Somehow, he didn't think Cody would appreciate that plan.

"Mmmm. Get back here," Cody murmured between kisses.

"I didn't go anywhere."

Cody laughed. Kirit did love that sound, even when he rather thought it was at his expense.

"No," Cody said. "No, you most certainly didn't. And I'm not planning on letting you."

"What?" Somewhere, Kirit had lost the thread of the conversation. The kisses were distracting him.

He ran his hands along Cody's back. When he reached Cody's arse, he just had to squeeze a few times. *Gods, I want in this. Did I remember to pack some – ?*

Kirit realized suddenly that the kisses had stopped. *Well, that won't do at all.*

"Cody?"

A small snore greeted him. Between one kiss and the next, his poor, exhausted mate had fallen asleep.

Damn, he was going to have to be chivalrous. Kirit shifted Cody's weight until he was no longer pressing into Kirit's engorged cock. It didn't help very much — Kirit was still uncomfortable. *Oh, well.*

He wrapped his arms around Cody and resigned himself to a long, sleepless night.

Chapter Twelve

Cody woke with a start. He blinked a few times at the ceiling. It was made of crude timbers. *That's weird. What happened to my plaster – oh.*

About the same time the truth registered, another fact made itself known. He was still on the floor, and no matter how many blankets and furs were piled around him, wood was still damn hard. He rolled over, groaning at the pain that stabbed through his lower back. "Damn."

There had better be an actual bed in Kirit's home, or Cody might revolt. He was really missing his pillow-top mattress.

Cody untangled himself from the bedding and stood, stretching until his back cracked. *Oh, better.* Not great, but better. He was still sore and his legs hurt from all the walking yesterday. He was hungry, too. So where was Kirit? If the big guy was going to leave before Cody could get in a morning blowjob, he could at least be there with food.

He crossed the tiny room in a couple of strides then pushed open the heavy wooden door. Sunlight stabbed at his eyes and he blinked rapidly to clear the spots from his vision. It still took several moments for his sight to adjust. When it did, he took in the vista before him with something approaching incredulity.

Nothing was familiar. Absolutely nothing. There was no concrete, no cars, hell, no *people*. He had the disturbing sensation that someone had dropped him into the middle of a fantasy movie.

The small cabin that had sheltered them stood a little apart from the village and farther up the mountain. A narrow dirt road wound down the hill towards a cluster of wood-framed buildings. A few of the structures were made of brick or stone, but even they weren't very large.

"This is going to take some getting used to."

A shadow caught his attention and Cody shielded his eyes. Nyx was walking up the path in his direction. Cody waited in the doorway for him to approach.

"Good morning," Nyx called cheerfully. "It's about time you woke up. We've been awake for hours."

"Honestly, I'm rather shocked that Kirit didn't pull me out of bed at the crack of dawn," Cody replied.

"He normally would have," Nyx assured Cody. "But a message came in around daybreak. Since we had to change plans anyway, he decided to let you sleep."

"Change plans?" Oh, that didn't sound good. "Do I want to know?"

Nyx shrugged. "I'll let Kirit tell you. Biscuit?"

He held out something round and hard. Cody took it reluctantly. The thing wasn't as bad as it looked, which was good, because he had been a bit afraid he would break a tooth on it. He demolished the biscuit in a few bites, but it didn't do much to satisfy his hunger.

"So, where is the big guy?" Cody asked. "And can I get another biscuit?"

Nyx grinned. "Kirit should be along soon." Nyx swung a pack off his shoulder and dug out two more biscuits. Cody accepted these with much more alacrity.

"He'd better show up soon," he said between bites. "I'm not a patient person."

"I did notice that."

Cody thought he was being teased, but it was hard to tell with these Draak. They did solemn so well.

"There's a stream out back, if you want to clean up and change clothes," Nyx said, changing the subject abruptly.

"God, yes."

Thirty minutes later, Cody was feeling much better. He was clean—albeit cold, because damn but that water had been frigid—and wearing fresh clothing. He absolutely hated wearing clothes two days in a row, particularly underwear. He was spoiled and knew it. It made him a little uncertain about this whole Faerie thing—he was a modern boy used to his modern conveniences.

Cody shoved his dirty clothes into a side pocket of his duffle, turning to look when the door thudded open. Kirit walked in, growling in a low and steady rumble that practically made the walls tremble.

"Problems?" Cody asked his glowering lover.

"We've been summoned," Kirit said, waving a piece of paper as if its very presence explained everything.

"Summoned?"

"Seamus wants to meet you."

Cody was fond of the man, but sometimes... "And who is Seamus?"

"The king." Kirit scowled. "I told him I haven't even taken you home yet, but he won't be put off. I'm tempted to tell him to shove it up his—"

"Holy shit, Kirit, you can't tell a *king* something like that!"

"Of course I can. It's only Seamus."

"The king. The Faerie king."

"That would be the one."

It struck Cody suddenly, how little he really knew Kirit. Who was this man that he could get away with talking to the Faerie king like that?

Another thought struck him, one that wiped away the first. "Well, why the hell does he want to meet *me*?"

"You're my mate."

"Kirit, you do remember I'm human?" Cody resisted the urge to roll his eyes. Sometimes he wondered if Kirit had been dropped on his head when little, because the man could be so incredibly dense.

Kirit sent him one of those *do-I-look-stupid?* glances. At the moment, Cody didn't think Kirit would really want him to answer.

"I need more explanation than the whole mate thing." Cody tried to hide his exasperation.

A shadow darkened the doorway, a low chuckle filling the small room. Nyx ducked through the door, head almost brushing the ceiling when he stood upright.

"We blame it on the battles," he said. "One too many blows to the head makes a nice excuse."

"I am not stupid!" Kirit bellowed.

Cody patted his irritated mate on the chest. "No," he assured Kirit. "Just a little dense sometimes. Don't worry, I'm getting used to it. That's what friends are for." He added the last bit with an expectant look at Nyx. "Explanations."

"Finding a mate is a huge event in our world," Nyx obliged. "I don't know how much about our society the loquacious one here has shared, but the Draak are pretty powerful, both in magic and in standing. It's traditional for any new mate or spouse to be introduced at court. Seamus likes to know his nobles."

Cody got less out of the explanation than he did the fact that both men called the king by his first name. Combined with Kirit's earlier comments...well, he was used to thinking of Kirit as his grumpy, sweet and indulgent lover, not as a powerful man who interacted with kings.

"What about the fact that I'm a man?" Cody asked. "Is that going to be a problem?" That was one thing they had never discussed, surprisingly enough—how homosexuality was viewed in this culture.

"You're my mate."

"Sheesh, it's like talking to a parrot," Cody declared. "He's stuck on repeat again."

Nyx chuckled and shook his head at Kirit. "Nice to see finding your mate hasn't softened you too much, old friend. You're still as stubborn as ever."

Cody turned his glare Nyx. He had to look way up. All the Draak—at least the two he'd met—were so blasted huge. He was growing accustomed to being the short one in the room. At least he didn't let it intimidate him anymore. Much.

Nyx was still laughing when he continued. "No one in Faerie would care if you were a three-headed sloth."

"What's a sloth?" Kirit spoke at the same time as Cody asked,

"Do those actually exist?" *Now, that would be something to see.* Both Nyx and Cody ignored Kirit.

Nyx shrugged. "Haven't a clue. The point is, a mate is a mate. Destiny and the gods control a mating, not us. Man or woman, it makes no difference."

"Unless you're Fayte," Kirit, ever literal, pointed out.

"Wait, what?" Cody blinked in confusion.

"Irrelevant. Focus here, sunshine."

Cody was about ready to tear his hair out. Or slug someone. "I'm trying. Hell, I don't even remember what we were initially talking about!"

"Visiting Seamus," Kirit reminded him.

"Right. The Fae king. Who, apparently, wants to meet me for some weird reason."

"You're my—"

"Shut up, Kirit," Cody and Nyx ordered at the same time.

Kirit scowled. "You asked."

"Not all questions require an answer," Cody said.

"Don't bother," Nyx advised. "We've tried for most of his life to explain the whole rhetorical question thing. He still hasn't gotten it."

"Give me your bag," Kirit said. He looked grumpier than usual, and Cody had the notion his feelings might have gotten hurt. "We'll go to the palace and get the meeting over with. Then, I can take you back to my home and lock the door."

That sounded marvelous to Cody. The last part, that was. Not the whole meeting-the-king part. Cody could do without that.

Cody handed over his bag without a protest. Their fingers brushed when Kirit took the bag, and it suddenly occurred to Cody that he hadn't given his big dragon a proper good morning greeting. No wonder Kirit was so cranky.

Cody pulled Kirit's head down for a good-morning kiss, hot enough to make his toes curl. When he pulled back, they were both panting. Cody adjusted himself in his jeans, his cock making itself known in a most uncomfortable way.

"Seamus can wait," Kirit said. He dropped the bag and yanked Cody close again. He slammed his lips down on Cody's forcefully. Cody could taste the sweetness of his mate and opened his mouth for Kirit's tongue.

A loud throat-clearing broke the haze.

"Damn it, Nyx, don't you have anything better to do?" Cody glared over Kirit's shoulder at Nyx. "I'm saying good morning to my mate."

"And by the time you finish, you'll be able to start saying good night. Look, the sooner we go, the sooner we can leave, huh?"

Logic. Sometimes, Cody hated it. "Fine."

Kirit didn't look like he agreed. Cody snuck another kiss, making sure to keep this one light and affectionate since, apparently, they didn't have the time to get carried away.

"Later, big guy," he promised.

Kirit nodded reluctantly. He picked up Cody's bag again and turned for the front door. As he did, Cody caught the sight of his erection trapped inside his tight leather pants.

Aw, poor Kirit. He looked even more uncomfortable than Cody felt.

"Wait," Cody suddenly called. "I want my boots from my bag. If we're going to be walking all day again, I want to be comfortable, and I think these shoes have about had it."

His sneakers hadn't survived the battle with the swamp very well.

"We won't be walking," Kirit replied, walking out of the door.

"We won't? Then what—" Cody went outside himself and stopped short at the sight in the front yard. "Oh, no. Hell no."

"Don't be difficult."

"I'm not being difficult," Cody insisted. He eyed the horses with utter disgust and tried to avoid thinking about how *big* they were. "It's the twenty-first century. I'm not gonna spend all day on the back of a horse."

Nyx snickered. Kirit glared at him. "You aren't helping," he warned.

"Come on," Cody said. "Can't you guys magic in a car or something?"

"It doesn't work like that," Nyx explained. "Human technology doesn't work on this side of the Veil." He snorted, the sound full of amusement, and turned to Kirit. "Remember the time Desmond bought that cappuccino maker?"

Kirit groaned. "Gods, yes. It took weeks to rebuild the wall in the east wing."

"Focus," Cody snapped. "Horse. Me. Not happening."

"Cody, this is very simple," Kirit said.

Cody did *not* appreciate the patronizing tone. *Just see if he gets sex tonight, after all.* Although, he would be depriving himself, too. Maybe he would just torture the man a little.

Oblivious to the plotting aimed in his direction, Kirit continued, "The capital is one hundred and thirty kilometers from here. We cannot refuse the king, and it would take days to walk. Therefore, you are getting on this horse."

"No, I am not."

Nyx laughed. Kirit snapped his hand out and smacked the other Draak, which only made Nyx laugh harder.

"By Epona's grace, what did I ever do to deserve such friends?" Kirit muttered. "Cody, it's either the ride the horse or fly."

Cody looked at the horse. Looked at Kirit. Growled in irritation. He stopped when he realized he was starting to sound like Kirit.

That, and apparently, the big dragon liked the sound a little too much. Kirit shivered, eyes turning blue, a sure sign of rising passion. They had also shifted, the pupils long and narrow. The heated stare gave Cody a few shivers of his own.

"Don't even think about it," Cody warned.

"Think about what?"

"You can't pull off innocent, so don't bother trying. We don't have time, remember?"

Nyx was still cackling. This time, it was Cody who smacked him.

"Not helping," Cody warned.

"You two are better than Comedy Central," Nyx said.

"Good Lord. No cars, but you know about Comedy Central. What kind of sense does *that* make?" And they were off track again. "I thought we needed to leave," he prodded.

"I'm sure we have time," Kirit said, sounding almost pathetically hopeful.

"Sorry to break up the love fest, but you know Seamus isn't exactly the most patient person around, and we've already wasted several hours."

"Don't remind me."

"Fly," Cody said abruptly, hoping to break up the budding conversational tangent before they wasted even *more* time. He was still stuck on Nyx's earlier statement—the sooner they got there, the sooner they could leave. And the sooner Cody could get sex, preferably in a bed.

"Huh?" Kirit had clearly lost track of the topic. His brow furrowed. "Let's see, there was something about cars...horses...flying! You want to fly?"

"No," Cody said baldly. "But I figure at least it will be faster than the damned horse."

Chapter Thirteen

The trip was just as bad as Cody had feared. Not to mention the fact that Kirit in dragon form was...well, damn scary.

They had trekked behind the cabin, up a little hill, and onto a small rise. The clearing there was big and clearly man-made, with felled trees around the edges. Someone kept it maintained, too. He'd seen parks less manicured.

Once there, Nyx had told him to stand back. Apparently, that hadn't been good enough for Kirit, who had positioned him behind a big fallen tree. Then, there had been this weird rushing sound, a big flash of light, followed by the biggest damn creature Cody had ever seen. From narrow snout to the slender tip of his spiky tail, Kirit stretched across the substantial clearing with barely any room to spare. That big head had swung in his direction. Cody had backed away, but he hadn't been fast enough. Nyx had snagged him before he could escape. Next thing he knew, he'd been about ten feet up, yelping and clutching at air. Nyx had given him instructions on seating and how to hold on and before Cody could work up a protest, there was a lurch, then hell.

Cody was *not* a fan of heights. Man was not meant to go sailing through the sky without anything around him. Besides that, it was damned cold up in the clouds. Cody kept thumping Kirit, trying to get the big jerk to fly lower, but it didn't work. Either Kirit couldn't figure out what Cody was asking, or he just wasn't complying. The dragon was getting a swift kick in the ass when they landed, that was certain. *At least when he changes back, 'cause I don't think I could reach his ass in this form.*

Cody leaned farther down, practically lying atop Kirit's smooth scales. He clung fiercely to the dragon's long neck and tried not to lose his meagre breakfast with each lurch. There was nothing smooth about this flight. Each beat of Kirit's widespread wings sent them bobbing up and down. Not a lot, but enough to make Cody's stomach roil. It was like being on a plane with slight turbulence—only without any safety features. Like a cabin.

Turning his head, Cody used Kirit as a shield as best as he could. They were moving fast enough that the wind whipped into his face. He couldn't keep his eyes open from the force. Not only that, but it was *freezing*. His teeth were chattering. At least, he thought they were, judging by the feel. The only thing he could actually hear was the whistling shriek of air and the deafening flap of leathery wings.

Cody yelped when Kirit banked to one side. He was seated pretty solidly in between Kirit's shoulders, the wing joints holding him in place, but it was still freaking him out. Dragons should come equipped with safety belts.

He squinted, trying to see why they had turned. A flash of red caught his attention. Cody pried his eyes open just in time to see another dragon—*Nyx*, his mind supplied, though he hadn't seen the other man transform—fold his wings in close and plummet almost straight down.

Oh, good God. Kirit better not even think *about it.*

His dragon tilted, front end rising upward. A mighty heave of wings and then—

Oh, fucking hell, I am going to kill him!

Cody knew he probably screamed, but the sound was snatched away. He hung on for dear life as Kirit followed Nyx down. The incline wasn't as steep, the wings not as tightly folded to the side, but it still felt fucking awful.

The loud roar Kirit uttered made his body quake. All around, answering roars echoed in his ears. It sounded like they were suddenly flying through a herd of dragons. *Herd? Flock? What's the proper—?*

Kirit banked sharply to the left, body almost twisting sideways.

Oh, shit. Oh, shit. Cody didn't want to look, didn't want to see the ground rushing at them. He might have bellowed Kirit's name. Hell, he might have yelled for his mummy, for all he knew. He couldn't breathe, couldn't think.

The thundering jolt almost unseated him. Cody yelled, shocked when the sound rang out loudly. No more wind. No more wings.

In a minute, there was going to be no more Kirit. *I really should have picked the horse.*

Cody peered through the gap on the left side between Kirit's wing and jutting shoulder blade. White rock glistened up at him.

"Thank God. Move, arms, move." It took Cody several long minutes to get his arms to obey the command. They seemed to be stuck around Kirit's neck.

Kirit settled back on his haunches with a low huff. Those impressive wings flapped once as Kirit made himself comfortable on the ground.

Cody finally shook off his paralysis. He slid to one side, hitting the dirt with both feet at once and staggering backwards. He heard muffled laughter. *Yeah, that's right, make fun of the human.* God, his face was probably a very unattractive shade of green.

He really was going to kill that damned dragon.

Another bright flash of light pierced the air like before. Cody looked away to protect his eyes—they were damaged enough already from the wind. When he looked back, Kirit stood there, stretching his body toward the sky.

"I am going to kill you," Cody bellowed.

Kirit turned, surprise etched on his face.

With a low growl, Cody launched himself at the smug dragon. His fist slammed into a rock hard ab. Kirit's yelp of surprise mingled with Cody's howl of agony.

"What are you made of, granite?" Cody yelled. "That fucking hurt!"

"You hit me." Kirit's voice was disbelieving, the look on his face confused.

"Well, you deserved it," Cody replied. "What the hell was that whole diving stunt, huh? Were you *trying* to send me plummeting to my death?"

"Of course not." The big guy actually had the gall to look offended.

Cody smacked him again. This time, though, he used the back of his hand and aimed for the stomach. No way in hell was he trying for that steel jaw again.

"Bravo!"

Turning, Cody saw the owner of a nice, smooth tenor voice beaming at him with complete pleasure.

"Kirit should be hit daily. It keeps him humble. And you must be the mate," the man — dragon? — continued in a chipper tone, "I'm Chaos."

Cody brushed at his clothes, feeling grimy and inadequate. He wasn't used to it, and it irritated him. But the men surrounding Cody were enough to make the world's top supermodel feel ugly — male or female. Chaos, in particular, was prettier than most women.

They were all tall. Massively tall. Broad shoulders, slender hips, and tight asses, the muscles of their thighs outlined by skin-hugging leather — again, except for Chaos, who wore a kilt in brightly patterned orange and purple. It clashed horribly with his deep red hair, which hung to mid-back in messy dreadlocks. It was enough to give a guy a headache. Chaos had paired the kilt with a white shirt with puffy sleeves, like something from a pirate movie. It was...interesting.

The other newcomer wasn't wearing a top. Cody couldn't help staring. He'd never seen a chest like that before, not in person, anyway — maybe in a bodybuilding magazine. The guy had to be close to seven and a half feet tall. *I wonder if he has to turn sideways to get through doorways.*

"Mate." Kirit practically rumbled the word, laying one meaty arm across Cody's shoulders. "The Draconis nobles, Raven and Chaos."

Raven was the one without a shirt. He had pitch black hair that spilled around his shoulders in a thick mass, a neatly trimmed patch of hair on his chin, a swirling tribal tattoo by his left eye, and a nasty scar across his forehead. The guy was terrifying, very obviously a warrior, and even more obviously *not* human.

Chaos was the smallest of the quartet of dragons. Built more like Cody, he was lanky but no less impressive, aside from his questionable fashion sense. Even with his skinny torso, Cody figured Chaos could still bench-press a boulder.

Cody also decided he didn't trust the way Chaos was smiling at him. The man screamed 'trouble' with every bright inch.

Then again, the rest of the Draconis, as Kirit had called them, looked like they had sticks shoved up those very fine asses. Maybe he and Chaos would have to get together and chat.

"Come," Raven said. "Seamus is waiting."

"Indeed," Chaos added with irritating cheer. "He gathered all the nobles and everything."

Cody wondered if it was too late to run.

Chapter Fourteen

The palace was something of a surprise to Cody. He wasn't certain what he had imagined—Cinderella's castle, maybe. Instead, it felt almost...Eastern. Oh, the size was typical enough—massive. It sprawled in a one-story, elegant maze, tucked up against a large bluff. The occupants of Faerie did seem to like their hills.

The field Kirit had landed in was just outside the boundaries of the wall encircling the palace. The empty space was apparently set aside particularly for the dragons. And, Nyx had said, weapons training. Cody wasn't surprised. *They have to work out that aggression somehow.*

From the field, they had passed through an opening in one of the walls, then an untamed garden, and finally up to the palace itself.

As they walked, Cody realized it wasn't one building, but rather a set of connected smaller buildings. The hallways were wide and open. The one they currently traversed was open on both sides via a set of arches along the walls. People milled about in a riot of costumes. It was like taking a walk through a history book. He saw the expected plate armor, along with chain mail, silk, lace, some sinfully short tunics and even a few togas. There was also a lot of leather. And more kilts, these thankfully in more eye-pleasing tones than Chaos'.

"Oooh, nice." Cody turned, walking backwards for a few steps, eyes glued to a guy wearing a short piece of pleated plaid and nothing else. The guy winked and grinned.

Kirit growled and yanked Cody down the hall. Chaos laughed.

"Hey, it's not a crime to look," Cody declared. "And y'all have got some very nice eye candy."

"I don't know what that means, but it sounds marvelous," Chaos said.

Kirit growled some more.

"Do you ever wear a kilt?" Cody asked Kirit. The thought made him drool a little bit.

Kirit grunted, a sound Cody interpreted as one of affirmation.

"Oh, God, I think I came in my pants," Cody muttered. The image that popped into his head was enough to send his pulse skyrocketing. He adjusted himself to make room for his cock and tried to spot a dark corner. *Maybe we can make time for a little fun...*

The guys were all staring at him. Cody shrugged. "What?"

Chaos laughed so hard he had to stop walking for a second. "I think we're going to be very good friends," he told Cody when he caught his breath.

"The gods help us all," Nyx said fervently.

I wonder if I should be offended. Then they turned another corner and he was distracted again by the sight of a trio of absolutely stunning stained-glass plates. And the sweaty, half-naked warriors on the other side. *I wonder if there's a war or something that Kirit forgot to mention.* There were weapons everywhere. Hell, even the women were armed, some carrying daggers, and some in full armor with swords.

As they wound deeper into the complex, Cody felt a little like royalty with a cadre of bodyguards. The dragons crowded around him from all sides and everyone they encountered moved aside as they passed. Some of them went so far as to bow to the group.

It was downright weird.

Their destination finally loomed ahead, through a set of open double doors. Cody had to pause and take a closer look. The doors towered to the roof, enormous slabs of dark wood carved with sequential battle scenes from floor to ceiling.

Kirit grabbed Cody's arm again and pulled him away from the fascinating object.

"Hey, I wanted to see how the fight turned out," Cody protested.

"Later."

Once inside, Cody had to stop again and gape some more. He was standing in what had to be the biggest damn room in the entire universe. He was surrounded by glittering marble and soaring ceilings in a space full of elegant people dressed in velvet and jewels. He had never felt more out of place in his life. Their small group hadn't been noticed yet, save for a few people. Those few, however, eyed Cody like gunk scraped off the bottom of a shoe. It didn't bode well.

A silence started at the far end of the grand hall and rushed toward them in an almost visible wave. The crowd parted. Despite the size of the space, Cody could make out a golden platform with matching thrones on the other side.

And I thought the Draak were intimidating. He'd been wrong. They seemed like tame little kittens compared to the man who stood and stalked across the opulent hall. His beauty alone was enough to make anyone feel inferior. Long, gleaming white-blond hair hung in a thick tail down his back to brush his ass. The top sections were braided around the golden stems of a crown. *An actual crown, for Heaven's sake.* Pointed ears emerged from his hair. His face was perfection, long and patrician features, delicate and beautiful but with more than enough masculinity to keep the Fae king from appearing feminine. His leather pants were tucked into knee-length boots. The leather lovingly clung to sleek, muscled thighs. The silk of his thin white shirt did little to hide the chiseled chest muscles of a warrior.

Cody thought he might actually be gaping. And it wasn't just from the king's appearance, although the man was so perfect he didn't actually look real. No, it was the power that rippled off Seamus. The king was not a man to be overlooked. When he entered a room, everyone would notice, and Cody suspected there was never any doubt that Seamus was the most powerful man, physically and by status, in any situation.

Cody tugged at Kirit's sleeve. "Can we sneak away yet?" he whispered.

"I don't think—"

"Kirit!"

Damn, even the man's voice is perfect. Deep and smooth, it resonated easily to every corner of the cavernous room.

Kirit actually smiled at the vision approaching them. The dragon dipped his head in a gesture of respect, the most Cody had yet to see him give anyone.

"Your Majesty," Kirit said when the king stopped a few feet from them.

"Do stop that, you bastard," the king replied mildly. He ran his eyes up and down Cody.

Cody suppressed a shiver. He felt like the king was stripping him bare, although there wasn't anything sexual about the examination. Rather, Cody wouldn't be surprised to find that the king could see right through him and down into his soul. There was so much power in the man's icy eyes. It was a bit creepy.

"So," the king drawled, the slightest hint of an accent in his voice. "This is the new mate."

"Yes, Your Majesty."

"He's human."

"Yes, Your Majesty."

"Kirit, if you don't stop 'yessing' me, I'm going to break your nose."

Kirit smirked. "Yes, Yo—"

Seamus didn't have to smack Kirit. Cody beat him to it. He slammed his balled up fist into Kirit's gut. It was like trying to punch a hole through a brick wall. One of these days, he was going to learn. Cody hissed, shaking his aching hand.

"Will you stop trying to provoke the nice king?" Cody chided.

The king looked at Cody again, this time with amusement and growing interest. "I like you," he said.

"I've been getting that a lot."

Seamus chuckled, the deep sound brimming with mirth. Cody found himself relaxing a little. So far, the king seemed like a decent guy. Intimidating as hell, but decent.

Even Kirit cracked a smile. "Seamus, allow me to present my mate, Cody Markswell of Denver, Colorado, Earth."

To Cody's complete astonishment, the king extended one hand and gave Cody's a firm shake. "I must say, it is a pleasure to meet you, Cody Markswell of Denver, Colorado. It has been far too long since the Draak were blessed with a mate. And such a lovely one, too."

Cody frowned, not quite sure if he should be insulted or not. He really wasn't enamored of that word, 'lovely'.

"He *is* pretty, isn't he?" Kirit said in a proud tone.

Cody thought about slugging the big idiot again, but his hand still throbbed.

"Call me pretty again," he said instead, "and you'll be sleeping alone tonight."

Seamus's laughter rang out, louder this time, causing heads to turn in their direction. Cody winced. Normally, he didn't mind being the center of attention. This attention, however, was far from flattering. He could feel gazes boring into him. Unfriendly gazes.

What did Kirit say about the Fae and humans again?

Come to think of it, he'd never really talked about how the two races got along. Cody had the sinking feeling that humans weren't overly popular around here.

"Come, let me introduce you," Seamus said. Cody ignored the come-hither gesture and eyed up the crowd. "No offense, but I don't really want to be here all day."

There had to be at least a hundred people milling about. Probably more. No, definitely more. The great hall was so big, it dwarfed everything, and made the largest crowd look like the tiniest gathering.

This wasn't a tiny gathering.

"I'll only introduce you to the important people," Seamus promised.

"Make that the interesting people, and you have a deal."

His comment made Seamus laugh, so Cody figured his smart mouth wasn't getting him into too much trouble. At least not yet.

Kirit draped his arm over Cody's shoulders, steering him after the king. Cody didn't balk at the outward show of affection. It wasn't something he was used to, but right now, Cody appreciated the moral support. He had a feeling he would need it.

Chapter Fifteen

Kirit loved this time of day. He could feel the approaching sunrise in the weight of the air and the song of the birds. The barest hints of light were streaming into the hallway, turning the cold marble walls into a warm shade of gold with faint tinges of pink.

He took a deep breath as he walked, relishing the warm, clean scents of the atmosphere. So different from Earth, which tended to smell rather stale. He had missed his home.

Although, he would far prefer his cave to the palace. Unfortunately, despite the casual relationship that existed between him and Seamus, he couldn't ignore a direct order. They may be considered friends, but the Fae was still his king. Kirit was bound to him with ties far stronger and more complicated than mere loyalty or spoken vows.

Kirit turned a corner, rubbing at the stubble on his jaw. He should have shaved before going to meet with Seamus. Kirit figured, though, that if Seamus was going to summon Kirit before dawn, then he could deal with a scruffy appearance.

So Kirit wasn't in the best of moods. After all, Seamus had pulled him from a warm bed and his cuddly mate.

Kirit turned another corner, the path familiar enough he could walk it in his sleep. The well-known surroundings allowed his mind to wander as he walked.

Seamus had taken them around the palace last night, seemingly oblivious when the dragons dropped off one by one — except for Chaos, who pretended to hang on every word expounded by the king as he explained the vast history of the building. Kirit was a bit concerned over Chaos's fascination with Cody. Not that he thought there was cause for jealousy. No, it was more a matter of worry. He could easily picture the two of them becoming good friends.

That's a terrifying thought. The palace would never survive.

Seamus would most likely be amused, though.

Kirit had cut the previous evening short when Cody began yawning. By the time he'd escorted Cody to his suite in the palace, his poor mate had barely been able to keep his eyes open. Once more, Cody had fallen into bed, asleep the instant his head landed on the pillows.

If Kirit weren't so concerned with his mate's health, he might begin to feel deprived. *Two whole days without sex.*

He had planned to greet the day by burying his cock deep inside his mate's ass. Hell, he had even dreamed about it. Then the messenger had knocked on his door with a request from Seamus and all his wonderful plans had crashed into a broken heap.

Hell, with as growly as Kirit was feeling, Seamus was lucky that Kirit was only unshaved. And unarmed.

The hall he was walking ended in a blank wall. Kirit pushed a large door on his right open, stepping into an empty antechamber. Two desks faced the entryway, where normally clerks held court. Like most sane people, they were likely still abed.

"Seamus?" Kirit called.

"Here!"

Dim light spilled from another doorway across the room. With a few quick strides, Kirit entered the welcoming environs of Seamus' personal office.

It was empty.

Damn the Fae and their infernal obsession with subterfuge.

The room wasn't all that large, most of the space taken up by bookcases and an absolutely enormous desk. A small sitting area filled one corner, the sofas facing a large fireplace. The intricately carved stone forming the mantle was a work of art.

Kirit sidestepped an end table and smacked his closed fist against a well-endowed angel, right on top of her breast.

Seamus had a perverted sense of humor.

When nothing happened, Kirit hit the angel again. This time, the back of the fireplace slid up with a soft crunch of stone.

"Don't break my angel," Seamus admonished, the same as he always did.

"I haven't yet," Kirit offered the standard reply.

Kirit ducked and walked through the fireplace. The room on the other side was tiny—and an utter mess.

"Blessed Epona, Seamus, what have you been doing?" Kirit eyed the papers littering the floor. He had to dodge a precarious pile of books on the way to the curved desk wedged into a corner. The desk, too, was threatening to drown beneath maps, documents and open books.

Seamus stood at one of the large bookcases, papers raining down around him as he sorted through the disorganized shelves. He turned at the question, a dark scowl on his refined features. Kirit winced as a large tome slid off the top stack, narrowly missing his leader's head.

"Trying to keep this realm intact while you gallivanted about Earth."

Kirit halted, taken aback by the anger in his king's voice.

Seamus grunted and rubbed at his eyes, perching himself on one corner of his desk. Kirit was impressed that he found room enough to sit, considering the clutter lining the top. "Sorry. It's been a difficult few days."

Without waiting for an invitation, Kirit dropped into one of the large wingback chairs in front of the desk. "What did you need and when can I go home?"

"I'm sorry," Seamus said again. "I know you want to sequester yourself with your mate, but I need you here, at least until the end of the week. I have a delegation from the Evii Islands coming."

"Again?" Kirit snorted in disgust.

"Again. I'm fed up. Perhaps a show of strength would help remind them of their place."

And a show of strength meant the Draak.

"Why do you need all of us?" he asked, tone perilously close to a whine. "Three Draak are impressive enough."

Seamus gave him a pointed look. "And if I let you duck out, then Chaos wouldn't show up. Raven would glower, Nyx would grumble and the Eviatt would laugh."

Seamus' argument was flimsy, but for whatever reason, the king wanted all of them present. Kirit wouldn't be able to dodge this particular duty.

The Evii Islands, a small chain off the Southern coast, had been a thorn in Seamus' side for the last two decades. They were far enough from the center of the Realm that they were left to run themselves for the most part. Unfortunately, that autonomy had given them illusions of independence and grandeur. Equally unfortunately, they outmatched the central government when it came to naval power. It made the situation highly volatile. Both sides needed each other — Seamus needed them for the ships, they needed Seamus for the manpower, not to mention the mutual trade benefits — but the Eviatt were stubborn.

"So," Seamus continued, "When the delegation gets here, I'll have the Draconis stand around and glower while I play hard-ball. That should hopefully knock some sense back into their obstinate heads."

"Hard-ball?" Kirit blinked in confusion. Their king had been picking up what he assumed was Earth slang, although from where was anyone's guess. It was irritating.

Seamus waved away the question, moving from the top of his desk back to the large upholstered armchair behind it. "Not important. Just remember, I want ceremonial armor, full weaponry, all the pageantry." Seamus slid his glasses into place and went back to the letter in front of him.

"You roused me at dawn for *this*?"

Seamus looked at Kirit again, blinking a few times. "Oh. Of course not." He shuffled some papers around, dug out a rolled up piece of parchment, and tossed it at Kirit.

Kirit suppressed a wince. The scroll looked far too old and delicate for such rough treatment. He unrolled it gently, taking in the old-style script and the archaic wording. Then it was his turn to blink.

"The Renewal? Already?"

"Unfortunately."

"But...Cody." The words sounded pathetic, but Kirit *felt* pathetic. The last thing he wanted to do was sequester himself for six months.

"You have some time," Seamus assured him. "We won't need to begin the process until spring."

Kirit let out a breath of relief. "You are very mean," he informed his king.

Seamus just smirked.

"So why bring it up now?" Kirit asked, when the silence began to stretch thin.

"Because you need to be prepared," Seamus said calmly. "And because Desmond is making gloom and doom noises again."

"Desmond is always making...gloom and doom noises." The dour face of Seamus' clerk and assistant was a permanent fixture at the palace.

"True. But I've heard rumors that the Druids have come down out of the mountains. They were seen on the Lallithan coast."

Kirit uttered a particularly vile Latin curse.

"Indeed," Seamus concurred.

The Druids were the ones who had created the Fae plane. They'd controlled the Veil for centuries, and they were the ones to make the decision to close it off during the Gallic Wars. They were also the ones who had decided to open it again shortly after World War Two. Legend held they also opened portals within the

Veil periodically to let in different populations, primarily ones needing shelter from the increasing technological advances of Earth. Beyond that, no one saw them, no one interacted with them. Hell, no one had even *spoken* to them, not since leaving Gaul, as far as Kirit knew. Oh, Seamus almost certainly had contact with them, but then again, with the Druids, one never knew. They were a law unto themselves — they certainly hadn't asked the king before re-opening the Veil. For all Kirit knew, they had just woken up one morning and decided it was the thing to do that day.

If they were re-joining society, it couldn't mean anything positive.

"Have you spoken to them yet?" Kirit asked.

"No. All I have are rumblings right now. I've sent several of scouts out to poke around. When I hear more, you'll be informed. You always are."

Seamus sounded exasperated, but Kirit had no idea why.

"May I go now?" he asked plaintively. "I have a mate waiting in bed, and I want to —"

"Stop right there," Seamus ordered. "Do *not* talk about your sex life with someone who isn't getting any."

"Any what?"

"Think about it for a second," Seamus responded in a dry tone. "I'm sure it will come to you."

Kirit cocked his head, but rustling from the outer office caught his attention. "I believe Desmond has arrived."

"So he has. Get out of here, then, and go have fun with your mate."

Kirit grunted and stood, before heading rapidly for the hidden doorway.

"Kirit?"

He froze, foot in midair, practically twitching with the desire to flee. "Yes?"

"I won't keep you any longer than absolutely necessary. I swear it."

Kirit nodded an acknowledgement and left. He barely spared a glance for the slender blond in the other room. Desmond called a greeting, but Kirit brushed him off. He would apologize later for being rude. Maybe. Desmond really should be used to it by now, anyway. And Kirit had a mate to go seduce. It had been *days*.

He was beginning to suspect a conspiracy.

Chapter Sixteen

It was a conspiracy. It had to be.

Cody rolled over and stared at the stark white ceiling, out-flung hand resting on the cool sheets where Kirit was supposed to be.

"Gonna tie him up in his sleep," Cody said. "This is ridiculous." He had a hot guy as a mate. He wasn't supposed to be sex-deprived.

"Good morning!" The door slammed open, almost drowning out the cheerful greeting.

"No, it's not," Cody said.

Bright hair entered his vision. Cody tilted his head up, looking into the smiling features of Chaos.

"Aww, did somebody miss out on his good-morning kiss?"

"If I wasn't so tired, I'd kick you in the nuts. Go away."

Cody had learned quickly the night before—Chaos required a firm hand.

The dragon plopped onto the bed next to Cody, making the whole thing bounce.

And sometimes even a firm hand wasn't enough.

"Don't you have somewhere to be?" Cody sat up, rubbing his shin where Chaos' pointy knee had stabbed him. "And what time is it, anyway?"

"Around sunrise, I think. And no, Raven gave me the whole day to help you adjust."

"Sunrise?" Cody gaped at Chaos. "You're joking."

He wasn't even going to touch the 'help you adjust' comment. Hopefully, Cody could ditch Chaos somewhere. And hide. Cody had the feeling he was going to become very good at hiding.

Chaos tugged at the blankets. "Come on," he urged. "We have so much to do today. It's going to be fun."

Cody groaned and covered his face with his hands. *I think I'm going to kick* Kirit *in the nuts.*

It would serve the man right for leaving Cody alone with the psycho.

"Fine. If I promise to get up, will you go away?"

"Why would I want to do that?" Chaos asked.

Cody groaned again and wondered if he could outrun a dragon.

"I'm going to take a bath," he announced, tossing off the covers. If he 'accidentally' kicked Chaos, well, it was no more than the obnoxious creature deserved.

"That sounds like a good idea." Chaos stood and stripped off his shirt.

Cody froze. Normally, he could care less, but…

"You do realize Kirit would *not* like that plan."

"Kirit is an old prude."

"Maybe so, but I think if you try to join me in that bath, you're going to find yourself missing some vital body parts."

Chaos raised one eyebrow, leering at Cody. Cody would have taken offense, but it felt more playful than anything else. "It might be worth it."

The door creaked and the air stirred around them. *Damn, the man has impeccable timing.*

"Run," Cody said. "Fast."

Chaos smirked at Cody. Then he turned the expression on an infuriated Kirit, who stood framed nicely in the archway between the bedroom and living area.

"I'm faster than you," Chaos said.

"Don't taunt the enraged dragon," Cody advised.

"He hasn't caught me in decades." With that statement, Chaos whirled on the balls of his feet. Kirit roared and lunged but Chaos was, indeed, quicker. He raced to the balcony and, bypassing the stairs, leaped over the railing. Cody went to look, in time to see the dragon hit the ground in a roll, pop back up, and take off into the shrubbery.

"Huh, he *is* fast." It was as neat an escape as Cody had seen. Chaos had even managed to remember to take his shirt with him. He wondered vaguely what Chaos would have done if the balcony was farther off the ground, instead of barely a story high.

Cody became aware of a low, steady rumbling about the same time steel bands wrapped around his waist and yanked him back into the room. Cody rubbed at Kirit's tense forearms in an automatic soothing gesture, but the muscles remained taut. Then it struck Cody what he was doing.

Why the hell am I trying to calm him down? Hadn't he been wishing earlier for a round of hot, sweaty sex? And nothing was better than possessive sex. Cody would let Kirit reaffirm his claim in the best possible way. Enjoyment would most definitely be had by all.

Cody wiggled, loosening Kirit's hold just enough to turn around. He couldn't quite reach his dragon's mouth, but by standing on his tiptoes, he managed to land a kiss on Kirit's chin.

Kirit gave him a bemused look. Cody grinned.

"Come on, big guy, take me to bed."

Kirit smiled, the expression growing wider by the second. "I have a better idea."

"Oh?"

With a low sound of pleasure, Kirit swept Cody up in his arms. Cody yelped, then smacked at his dragon's broad shoulders.

"Put me down, you idiot! I am absolutely not the heroine from a Victorian romance novel."

"Of course not," Kirit replied seriously, with the cutest little frown. "You're not a girl."

"Glad you noticed. Stop carrying me around."

"I like holding you."

Cody was pretty sure he wasn't going to win this argument. And pretty sure he didn't want to, either. Not that he would be telling Kirit. The big dragon was smug enough already.

"So, what's your better idea?"

Kirit grinned. He carried Cody across the room and through an archway adjacent to the balcony. This one led to the smallest room Cody had seen in the palace so far, although that didn't mean much. The Fae built large.

It was a bathing room, and Cody instantly fell in love. It was dim, the only light coming from narrow windows set high in the walls. The air was warm and humid, steam rising off the patterned tile floor. A large body of water took up the entire center of the room. It was somewhere between a giant hot tub and a small pool. Steam rose off the water, too, and Cody couldn't wait to test it out.

"Put me down," he demanded, somewhat surprised when Kirit obliged without protest. Cod immediately went to the side of the pool and dipped his fingers in the water. *Oh, yeah, that's nice.*

He sent a taunting grin Kirit's way and began stripping. Since he was only wearing a pair of sweats and one of his oldest T-shirts, that didn't take long.

"Gonna join me?"

Kirit didn't reply, too busy staring at Cody.

"You've got a little drool," Cody teased, then burst out laughing when Kirit actually checked. "Come on, big guy, time to get wet and slippery."

Kirit watched Cody slide into the water and had to take a couple of deep breaths. Oh, his mate was special—all that creamy skin, the sultry laugh. If Kirit moved, he was going to lose control. It could go one of two ways—either he would pounce on his mate, or he'd come right there, without a touch. He'd never gotten so hard, so fast. Or at least, not since the last time Cody had smiled at him.

He really did need to do something about that. Later. Much, much later.

Cody ducked under the surface of the pool and came back up, water streaming off him. He shook his head, spraying drops everywhere. He smiled at Kirit, the expression open and happy.

Kirit growled and jumped in, grabbing his mate around the waist and swooping in for a rough kiss. Cody clutched at Kirit's shoulders for a minute, then pushed him away, laughing even while Kirit tried to continue kissing.

He had never tried that before, kissing someone who was laughing. It was difficult.

"Hang on, hang on," Cody said, still chuckling. "This would work better if you got naked, big guy."

Oh, damnation.

Warmth spread across Kirit's cheeks. He hadn't blushed in...well, a very long time.

"I won't tell," Cody whispered in his ear. Meanwhile, he tried to yank off Kirit's tunic. The damp fabric was clingy and didn't want to let go.

"A moment," Kirit said. He reluctantly set Cody aside and managed to work his shirt over his head. He tossed it away, where it landed on the tile with a loud plop. Then he went to work on the rest of his clothes. It took longer than it would have if he had bothered to take his clothes off *before* he jumped in the water, but eventually he managed to strip down to skin.

Naked, the air hit his upper body with a slight chill. Goose bumps prickled his arms and his nipples drew up tightly. He bent his knees, ducking further into the water.

Cody hummed, the sound full of pleasure. He ran his hands along Kirit's chest, pausing briefly to press against his erect nipples, before moving outward to his shoulders. Kirit closed his eyes and savored the caress. Cody massaged the tense muscles near his neck and in his upper arms.

"Feels nice," Kirit mumbled.

"Good. It's supposed to." Cody kept working the muscles, even as he leaned closer and brushed soft kisses along the side of Kirit's jaw. The water helped, keeping Cody afloat and providing easier access to Kirit's top half. Having a short mate wasn't always easy, although Kirit personally liked how they fit together.

Then a door slammed and Nyx's voice yelled his name.

Kirit roared, the sound rattling the walls. "Go away!" He bellowed.

"Ouch," Cody said. "Warn a guy next time, would you?"

"Sorry, Kirit." Nyx appeared in the entryway and Kirit simply had to roar again. He shoved Cody under the water.

"No looking," he ordered Nyx.

Cody came back up, sputtering and gasping. "Damn it, Kirit!"

Nyx, the bastard, was laughing. The look of anger on Cody's face didn't bode well for Kirit's plans.

"Go away, Nyx. Now."

"I brought food."

"Now!"

Nyx left, but he had ruined the mood quite nicely.

Or at least, Kirit thought he had. But that was before Cody swam closer and enclosed Kirit's still-hard cock in one fist.

"Forget about Nyx," Cody said.

It was an order Kirit was glad to obey. "Touch me." His voice came out in a low grumble. The surface of the water glittered with a slight tinge of color—his scales were emerging. They always did when Cody touched him.

"Gladly."

Cody pressed their bodies together. He wrapped his thighs around Kirit's, rubbing their erections together. The warm water created the most marvelous friction. Kirit closed his eyes in pure pleasure.

The water, Cody's touch, even the humid air all combined to ensure that Kirit was likely not going to make it to full intercourse this time. He couldn't bring himself to mind. It was, in his opinion, the best part of having a mate. There was always a next time.

Kirit moved backwards until his knees hit the bench that ran the length of one side of the pool. He sat, running his hands along Cody's back, feeling the flex and play of lean muscle under damp skin. Cody knelt, one leg on either side of Kirit's hips, and rose up. They kissed again, which was rapidly becoming one of Kirit's favorite pastimes.

"Mmm. S'good. But you're not worked up enough."

"What?" Kirit gasped. He licked along the bottom row of Cody's teeth, tasting mint and spice. *When did Cody find the time to clean his teeth?*

"Come on, big guy. Give me all of it."

"All of...all of what?" Kirit tilted his head and let Cody ravage his mouth more deeply. Cody kept moving, too, pressing and retreating, each brush maddeningly light, enough to tease but not enough to push either of them over the edge.

"All of you."

"I'm...gods, I can't think when you touch me."

"That's the idea, big guy. But we're not there yet. Your tongue isn't forked."

"Like that, do you?"

Cody's little moan was answer enough and Kirit chuckled. It was hard, concentrating on anything other than Cody's fingers, his cock, the heat, but he managed long enough to partially shift. His back tingled. Damn, almost too far. He didn't need to sprout wings in the bath.

"Oh, yeah." Cody groaned, sucking on Kirit's tongue, teasing at the slit that now ran down the middle. More tingles rippled up his spine, ones of pure arousal. "That's the stuff."

Kirit grunted and pressed one hand against Cody's lower back. His palm spanned from one hip almost to the other. He used the grip to force Cody up against him. While their lips parted and met, the sounds loud in the empty room, he kept up a constant rhythm of press and retreat.

"Wait, wait." Cody tried to pull away. Kirit snarled and wouldn't let him. *No getting away, mate.*

"I want more."

Far be it for Kirit to deny his mate, especially when Cody was leaning to one side and rummaging through the bottles neatly aligned on a nearby shelf. He snagged one—a lightly fragranced bath oil.

"This should do," Cody declared. He tipped backwards in order to free both hands. Kirit held him steady, kneading the tops of his thighs and palming the tight curves of his ass. Damn, but he loved his mate's ass.

Cody opened the bottle with a loud pop, the cork flying across the room. Kirit smirked.

"Eager, little one?"

"Not little," Cody said, but the protest was more out of habit than anything else. He was far too busy working two fingers into his ass. Kirit reached down, ostensibly helping. Mostly, he wanted to feel Cody's fingers moving in and out. There was something intensely erotic about the action.

"I wish to see," Kirit said, caressing the edges of Cody's hole with light fingers.

"Later." Cody shoved Kirit's hand away and rose up on his knees. He held the base of Kirit's cock, and the grip had Kirit moaning in need. Then, in one swift motion, Cody slid down, enveloping Kirit in heaven. It was smooth and effortless, then Cody's ass was resting against Kirit's groin.

"Oh, mate. So good. Move. Please." Kirit wasn't too proud to beg, not with Cody holding him so close that he could feel his mate's heartbeat. Cody held the intimate embrace, tightening his muscles in a delicious taunt.

Kirit growled, at the end of his tether. Cody laughed. Using Kirit's shoulders for balance, he rose, almost pulling off Kirit's cock before sinking back down. He began a swift, pounding tempo. Kirit could do little but hold on and let his mate control the sex.

"Right there," Cody muttered. "Can feel you, so deep. Need you, Kirit. So much."

Kirit braced his feet against the bottom of the pool. Each motion Cody made had water splashing up around them, the spray chilly against his heated skin. His scales rippled along his arms and chest, reflecting the rising of his desire. It spiraled higher, pulling him towards his climax.

Not yet. He didn't want to come yet. He wanted more, wanted to keep feeling Cody moving on him and in him. Could, in fact, stay this way all day and be entirely happy. The arousal was a delicious pain tightening his muscles and making his heart pound.

"Come on, big guy. Gimme."

Cody leaned forward, but instead of taking a kiss, he offered his neck in a beautifully submissive move. It was so unusual for his proud mate that Kirit couldn't resist the offer. With a sound that was a cross between a snarl and a growl, he buried his fangs in the sweet spot between neck and shoulder.

Cody shouted, back bowing as he shot. Cum splattered Kirit's chest, hot and thick, mixing with the water to run down his abdomen. Kirit growled again, his own climax ripping through him without warning. His balls drew up painfully tight as he came, flooding his perfect mate's channel to overflowing. The sensations seemed to draw on forever as he cradled his mate close, suckling at the skin still caught between his teeth.

Slowly, so slowly, the pleasure faded, leaving behind a tingling buzz in every inch of his body. He hummed in happiness, taking one last swipe with his still-forked tongue before withdrawing his fangs. Cody collapsed against him, breathing hard.

"Damn, big guy, that just keeps getting better."

Kirit hummed again, this time in wordless agreement. He couldn't stop touching, running his hands along his mate's sides and keeping Cody pinned to his chest. He didn't want to let go.

Eventually, though, he had to. If for no other reason than the cum was beginning to dry on his chest where the water didn't reach.

"Come, mate, let me tend you."

Cody didn't offer any protest when Kirit retrieved a cloth and another bottle. He took great pleasure in scrubbing every inch of pale skin within reach. Then he made Cody stand and paid particular attention to Cody's smooth balls and now-limp cock. He kept his grip light, knowing how sensitive the skin would be. When he finished his inspection, he turned Cody around and, just as gently, cleaned out the red and swollen hole that still bore his seed. He regretted having to wipe it away, but his mate's comfort came first. He could console himself with the thought that his scent would linger.

Cody's eyes were half-closed in sleepy bliss by the time Kirit had finished.

"I am afraid we do not have time for a nap," Kirit said. "We will be missed before long."

"That's not fair." Cody didn't look happy at the thought. "Can't we hide here for the day?"

"Not for the day." Kirit's voice reflected his regret. "But perhaps for a while."

He lifted Cody in his arms and took the narrow set of steps out of the tub. Instead of going back into the bedroom, he crossed to the far side of the room. There was a little alcove there, hidden behind a heavy tapestry. He pushed the depiction of a stocky unicorn aside and stepped into his favorite place in the palace. It was small, barely large enough for his other form, and every inch of the floor—and a good portion of the walls—was covered in gold and jewels. This was his makeshift hoard, a fraction of the size of the one in the mountains, but enough to keep his dragon happy when in the palace. He could have used the Royal Treasury, but this was private and just his.

"Wow." Cody looked around in awe. Kirit set him down on a pile of gold and Cody reached out, trailing his fingers along a necklace glittering with rubies. "This is...holy shit, Kirit."

"My jewels," Kirit said with pride. "You fit so nicely."

The half-smile on Cody's face abruptly soured. "I'm not an object for you to collect."

"No," Kirit agreed. "You are a jewel, the most precious of all treasure. Far more important than any mere object."

"I'm not sure that's any better."

"Hmmm." Kirit brushed damp brown hair off Cody's forehead. "Rest for a moment while I finish grooming. Then we can hide for a bit. Not long, but there is no need to venture out until we are forced."

He left Cody with his hoard and dunked back into the pool, scrubbing his scales almost ruthlessly in his haste. He wanted to spend as much time as possible with his treasures before duty called.

Chapter Seventeen

Cody was going to scream. The frustration just kept building, and the worst part? He couldn't even say what the main source was. Some of it, no doubt, had to do with Chaos following him like an eager puppy. The rest could be placed firmly at the feet of his beloved mate. *Cue the sarcasm.*

After their romp in the water the previous day, Cody had been feeling quite good about his decision to move to Faerie. They had spent the day together, dodging Chaos and making themselves seen often enough to keep the king and Raven happy.

Then, he'd woken up this morning. And Kirit was, once again, missing. *I really am going to tie him to the bed, just see if I don't.*

Cody turned another corner, nodding politely at a passing soldier. The man nodded back. The soldier was the only other person in sight but even after he'd passed by, Cody still felt like someone was watching him.

Cody looked over his shoulder, scanning the immediate vicinity. There was being watched, and there was being *watched*. Cody expected a certain amount of staring—he was odd, unique and mated to an intimidating Draconis noble. Looks came with the territory.

But these looks made his skin crawl.

"Goddamn it," Cody said. He so did not need this.

After the fourth corner in a row, he began to get irritated. Cody halted mid-stride. He felt like he was running away, and that just wouldn't do. He planted his feet, crossed his arms over his chest, and waited.

A tall, muscular man turned the corner and almost ran right into Cody. The look of surprise on the stranger's broad face was oddly satisfying.

"Looking for someone?" Cody goaded.

The man snarled—actually snarled, with teeth and everything.

"Dude, that works better if you have fangs," Cody pointed out. *Really, does this guy think he's intimidating?* "I live with a dragon. You're gonna have to do better than that."

The man spat something in a language Cody had no hope of understanding. Then he pushed by Cody, bumping their shoulders as he left.

"Good grief, did I go back to high school and not know it?" Cody said, turning to watch the man walk away. *Sheesh*. That was just weird. And irritating.

Cody scowled, wondering what the hell that whole business was about. And what, exactly, the man had said. Because it was probably a really good insult.

"Who are you talking to?"

Cody yelled, tripping over his own feet. "Damn it, Chaos!"

"And a good day to you." Chaos fell into step next to Cody and began to chatter. Cody didn't pay much attention to the words, focusing instead on trying not to get hopelessly lost.

They wandered the halls together as Cody looked for Kirit. He wouldn't even begin to guess what Chaos was looking for.

His sanity, maybe.

"Do you ever stop talking?" he asked, interrupting yet another string of endless, meaningless patter.

"Sometimes," Chaos replied in seriously.

"God, you're irritating." Cody turned another corner, squinting in the bright sunlight that spilled through the window up ahead. He'd given up on losing Chaos almost an hour ago. In truth, the man was beginning to grow on him, but Cody wasn't going to admit to that, not even under threat of torture. Chaos was impossible enough as it was.

They passed yet another cluster of men.

"Aren't there any women in Faerie?"

"Of course. Just not in this part of the palace."

"This, or any other part." Cody hadn't seen any, not since the night of his arrival.

"You'll see some eventually. Why, do you have a thing for girls, too? Does Kirit know?" Chaos gave a look that was likely supposed to be a leer. He looked ridiculous.

"I really don't like you at the moment."

"Don't worry, I'll grow on you."

"Like a fungus," Cody muttered.

"Not nice." Chaos sounded way too cheerful for a man who had just been insulted.

"Don't you have anything else to do?"

"Nope. By the way, we've been down this hallway before," Chaos pointed out.

"I know." Cody stopped, scowled then turned. "This damn place is like a maze."

"Would you like a map?" Chaos asked with amusement.

"Why, do you have one?"

"No, but I'm sure I could come up with something."

"Would it get you to go away?" Cody sighed. "Never mind, I think I know the answer. And why the hell am I leading, anyway?"

"Because I don't know where you're going," Chaos said.

"I'm trying to find that blasted dragon of mine, so I can hit him for abandoning me."

"Oooh, I want to see that. Will you kiss and make up afterwards?"

Cody didn't dignify that with an answer. He rounded another corner and ran into yet another group of men. He walked backwards for a minute, studying them with curiosity, only facing forward again turned around when he smacked into a wall.

"Nice one," Chaos said.

Cody grunted, rubbing the back of his head. "That hurt."

"Stone usually does."

Cody tried to trip Chaos. Chaos, the rat, dodged.

"What was so interesting, anyway?" Chaos looked over his shoulder and shook his head. "It's just a bunch of average, everyday soldiers, no different than the last three groups. Hardly celebrities."

"Huh?" Cody stopped mid-rub. It wasn't helping the throbbing, anyway. "Oh, them. Just wondering. They weren't speaking English. Does Faerie have its own language?"

"Sort of."

Chaos took a few rapid steps. Cody realized the warrior had no intention of continuing the explanation.

"Hey, jerk-off!" he yelled, his patience stretching past the breaking point.

Chaos stopped again. "I don't know what that means."

"It wasn't nice. And you're annoying."

"So they tell me."

Cody growled. Chaos nodded approvingly.

"You're coming along quite nicely," he said. "We'll turn you into a proper Draak yet."

Would anyone notice if Cody shoved him off a balcony? *Nah, wouldn't work. The guy can fly. Maybe a nice rockslide...*

"Oooh, you're planning my demise, aren't you?"

Cody blinked a few times.

"I know that look," Chaos confided. "It's one of Raven's favorites."

Cody uttered a few choice curse words and decided he might as well give up on finding Kirit. Maybe, if he stayed in one place, Kirit would find him. It was a thought, anyway, and it appealed more than continuing to wander the halls and have people stare at him. *You would think they'd never seen a human.*

Cody reached a familiar hallway and headed for Kirit's suite, a place he was quickly coming to think of as his sanctuary. It was quiet and secluded. And no one looked at him oddly. He threw his entire body into shoving the door open far enough to sneak through. He definitely needed to remember to talk to someone about that. Maybe Kirit could open the door with no problems, but to Cody, the thing weighed a ton.

On the other side of the two-foot thick, solid wood double doors was the room Kirit used when he stayed at the capital. Well, Kirit called it a room. Cody called it a frickin' palatial suite—three enormous rooms, including that absolutely fabulous bathroom. The main room combined a living area and bedroom, walls lined with open arches leading to the giant balcony. *Hmm, what would it take to get Chaos to jump off it again? Maybe this time, I can help out...* The third room was a study of sorts. It was the first room through the doors, kind of public before the more private sections, sporting couches, chairs and a large desk. The open archway leading to the bedroom was at the far end. Cody had to admit, he liked it here. Well, inside the rooms, anyway.

Cody went to close the door, but a loud protest stopped him. Cody didn't apologize, just left Chaos jammed in the half-open doorway.

"That wasn't very nice," Chaos said, squirming free and letting the door bang closed. Cody noted with envy that *he* didn't have any problems with its weight.

"Sue me."

"I don't know what that means."

Cody groaned. He walked into the bedroom, bypassed the still-rumpled bed and instead flopped face-first onto the massive pile of pillows in one corner. He grabbed one overstuffed velvet pillow, inexplicably shaped like a heart, and screamed into it. Then he rolled over and stared at the ceiling. The nest was comfy, at least.

Chaos dropped down beside him. Cody's determination to ignore the Draak only lasted a few moments. Chaos was pretty much un-ignorable. *Dis-ignorable? Whatever.*

"So..."

Cody could actually *feel* Chaos staring at him. He looked sideways without moving the rest of his body. The slender dragon lay on his side, head propped on one hand, studying Cody like a scientist with a fascinating specimen.

"Sheesh, don't you have someone else you can bother?"

"No."

"Well, find someone."

"Don't want to."

Cody covered his face with the stuffed heart and yelled again.

"Why are you doing that?"

Cody flung the pillow at Chaos' head. He chuckled with satisfaction when it smacked the guy right in his smirk.

"How are you still alive?" Cody asked. "I mean, really. I would have thought someone would have killed you by now out of sheer irritation. Raven, maybe."

"Raven is good at avoiding me. But don't worry, I'll figure out his hiding place sooner or later."

Cody burst out laughing.

"See, you *do* like me."

Cody just laughed harder. All right, so maybe Chaos *was* growing on him. It was like having a giant, talkative puppy following him around.

When Cody's laughter finally trailed off, they lay side by side. Chaos readily joined Cody in his ceiling contemplation, silent for once.

"Tell me about them," Cody said.

"About who?"

"The dragons. They just...don't seem to fit, you know? With the rest of the Fae." The Fae that he had met in his admittedly short stay were all stuck-up, overdressed jerks. Being around them, even for this brief amount of time, made him feel like someone had dropped him into a period movie, complete with phony smiles and court intrigue.

The Draak rarely smiled and wouldn't know intrigue if it smacked them in the face. They preferred the 'when it doubt, hit it' philosophy. At least, Kirit did, and Cody had trouble imagining any of the other Draak behaving differently. Except Chaos, but Chaos didn't behave like *anyone.*

"They—we—don't, not really. For one thing, we're older. We've been in Faerie longer, too."

"That's...odd."

Dragons had been in Faerie longer than the Fae. Something was screwy with that picture.

Chaos shrugged, an interesting feat when he was still lying down. "They only started calling it Faerie around the eighteen hundreds, when stories about it were a fad. The Druids created the plane, I don't even know how long ago. With the rest of the earth, maybe. They're ancient. Hell, I think MacInerny has been around even longer than the earth. He certainly looks it."

"So what did the Druids call it?"

Cody wasn't going to touch the statement on MacInerny, whoever the hell that was. It made his head hurt.

"Nothing, as far as I know. It was kind of a shelter at first. Then the Draak crossed over permanently and the Druids sealed off access to the portals."

"When was that?"

"A while ago."

"Define a while."

Chaos shifted in the nest, brow furrowing slightly in thought. "It was...let's see, I'm not so good with human dates. A couple centuries, I think. Raven and

Seamus left when that little upstart general moved in. Caesar?"

Cody choked. He had to sit up and cough a few times before he could breathe again.

"Caesar?" he asked incredulously. "As in Julius? Raven knew Julius Caesar?"

"I don't know if Raven ever actually *met* the man."

"Good grief, how old are you guys?"

"Hmmm." Chaos pursed his lips in thought. "Raven is the oldest. I think most of his clutch was killed off during the Gallic Wars. We—Nyx, Kirit and I—were the next clutch born, and that was…well, I'm not certain, to be honest. Time runs differently in Faerie, remember?"

Okay. Cody had to take some more calming breaths. "Harper mentioned that, but he didn't go into details. If I go home, I'm not going to find flying cars, am I?"

"I don't—"

"Know what that means, yes. Chaos, Julius Caesar died like over two thousand years ago."

"Wow, Raven is old."

"No shit."

They lay in silence for several moments.

"Why did they cross over? Raven and Seamus, I mean."

"Hmmm? Oh. Things were changing, I guess. The Romans were conquering everything, damn their hides, and the magic was vanishing. It's not something Raven and Seamus really talk about."

"Oh." Cody chewed on his lip. "Well, damn. This is turning depressing."

"Little bit, yeah?"

"So, pick a better topic."

"Eh, who needs conversation? Want to go watch the men training? They usually strip down. It's quite a lovely sight."

"I don't think Kirit would approve of me going and drooling over half-naked men."

"That's what makes it so fun, isn't it?"

Cody chortled. "Hell, yes, I'm in."

He'd worry about Caesar, his wayward mate, and ancient men later. Much, much later.

Chapter Eighteen

Time passed slowly in the palace. Each day dragged on until he wanted to scream. Every so often Chaos would appear to liven things up, and Kirit would pop in for sex. Then it was back to the slow trickle of time.

All right, so it had only been three days since they'd arrived at the palace. Still, Cody wasn't used to all the inactivity.

Bored. Bored. Bored.

Cody stabbed at the meat on his plate. He wasn't quite certain what it was. Some kind of venison, he thought. It was kind of limp and chewy. He wasn't a fan. Cody poked his food some more. The clink of his silverware against the plate echoed loudly in the room. Unable to handle any more stares without Kirit to act as a shield, Cody had opted for the noon meal in his room.

Kirit was an important man. Cody got that, he really did. It didn't however, make him any happier to be left on his own in a strange place, surrounded by strange people—both the ones he didn't know, and the ones who were just plain weird.

Speaking of weird...

As if conjured by his thoughts, Chaos burst into the room. The concept of knocking, Cody had discovered, was quite beyond the dragon.

"How are you this bright and cheery morning?" Chaos asked with irritating perkiness.

"It's afternoon," Cody retorted. "And my meat tastes funny."

"Oooh, someone is testy today. You must be spending too much time with Kirit."

"Try not enough," Cody grumbled. Kirit was developing a habit of going who-knows-where before Cody even got up in the morning, staying away all day, and only reappearing in the evening.

"I have the cure," Chaos said, pulling Cody's attention away from his morose thoughts. "There's going to be an exhibition match this afternoon. I thought you might want to watch."

Cody glared at Chaos. "No. Thank you. I'm going to stay here with my chewy meat and my pile of pillows. I'm having a sulk, if you don't mind."

"That doesn't sound like much fun."

"It's marvelous, actually. So, go away now."

Chaos sat down at the low table next to Cody. Not that Cody really expected anything else. Chaos did exactly what he wanted, and didn't listen to anyone. Ever. Cody was beginning to wonder if the man needed hearing aids. He'd made the mistake of asking that very question, in his best sarcastic tone. The subsequent conversation was convoluted and made Cody's head hurt simply remembering it. Apparently, they didn't have hearing aids in Faerie.

"You're very annoying," he told Chaos.

"So they say." Chaos snuck a piece of meat off Cody's plate. Cody would have complained, but he wasn't going to eat it, anyway.

"Stop pouting," Chaos said. "You'll get wrinkles."

"Sorry," Cody said, and meant it. "I just don't like the palace all that much."

"Neither does Kirit. If it's any consolation, I think Seamus is starting to feel guilty for keeping the two of you here. He thought the Eviatt ambassadors would be here by now."

"I still don't understand why we have to wait for them."

"Neither do I," Chaos admitted. "But it's Seamus. He always has a reason for everything, even if it's beyond the understanding of the rest of us mere mortals."

Cody sighed, then began to grow irritated with himself for the sound. This wasn't like him. Sure, he was in a strange environment, surrounded by strange people and a culture that confused him in a myriad of ways. That didn't mean he had to be such a brat about it.

"You said something about an exhibition match?"

"Oh, yeah." Chaos grinned, his expression wide and happy. "Raven and Kirit are giving a demonstration to some new recruits. You should come watch."

That sounded infinitely more appealing than staying inside with his chewy meat.

"Lead on," he said firmly.

"Excellent. I always like watching those two impress the hell out of the baby soldiers."

Cody slipped on a pair of boots and checked his appearance in the full-length mirror. He still wasn't used to the clothing, although it was admittedly comfortable. The loose cotton trousers and long tunic looked more like lounging clothes than every day wear, though. He kind of missed his jeans and T-shirts. But he was trying to fit in to Kirit's world, and that meant looking the part.

Cody followed Chaos from the room. They took a now-familiar path out of the palace and down a small rise. He was getting better at navigating the maze, although he only had a few places he could get to with any sort of confidence—the throne room, the dining room, a small library in the same wing as the suite, and the training grounds. The rest of the place confused him horribly.

Less than a half hour later, Cody perched on the low stone wall, letting the sun beat down on his shoulders as he watched the people walk by. The palace loomed at his back, ominous and lurking.

Okay, so he was maybe being dramatic. He couldn't seem to help it lately.

Chaos poked him in the side. "There they are."

Cody sat up straighter. The little wall they were using as a bench encircled an arena of sorts. Really, that was giving it too much credit. Mostly, it was a big, empty patch of dirt. The soldiers—of which there were an amazing amount, considering the peaceful state of the country—used the space for training Today, a small crowd had gathered to watch. Most of them were, as Chaos had put it, 'baby soldiers'—new recruits to the army, the majority of them appearing to be between their late teens and early twenties. An air of excitement hung around them as they waited eagerly for the senior warriors.

"If we're really lucky," Chaos said with malicious glee, "they'll pick one of the new recruits to demonstrate on. It's fun to watch them impress the babies, but it's even more fun to watch Kirit and Raven scare them."

"You're evil."

"This is not news."

While they waited, Cody scanned the audience. Most of the people watching were men, and obviously soldiers. There was a lot of shiny metal—chain mail was the most common, but he saw one or two in plate armor. He wasn't certain why they felt the need to load up their bodies with God only knows how much metal just to watch other people fight, but whatever made them happy.

There were also a lot of pointy, sharp objects— swords, knives, spears, axes, arrows. And those were only the visible ones. These people liked their weapons.

Even the ones who weren't warriors.

Cody eyed an approaching group warily. He recognized a couple of them—not because they had been introduced, but because they tended to sneer when he was around.

"I think I want to find another place to sit," he said.

"Why?" Chaos turned, craning his head to see. "Oh. Can't say I blame you. If I thought Seamus wouldn't notice, I would have done something about that lot by now. Unfortunately, he counts them every day."

Cody snorted in delight. "He *counts* them?"

Chaos shrugged, a smile flirting on his lips. "That way he doesn't actually have to get close to them."

"Don't listen to Chaos. Seamus doesn't count his nobles." Cody turned to see Nyx standing behind them, his own smile firmly in place. "He has Desmond do it."

Chaos applauded in approval. Nyx gave a little bow. "Thank you, thank you. You know, the party is over there."

He gestured to the other side of the field. Cody looked at the group. When a loud round of laughter erupted, he decided that was most definitely the place to be.

"Let's go," he said, hopping down off the wall.

"Kirit is going to complain that I'm corrupting you again."

Chaos got down too, though, and quickly took up the lead. At Cody's questioning expression, Chaos grinned mischievously. "They have alcohol."

"That they do," Nyx said with amusement. "A *lot* of alcohol. Just don't drink the stuff out of the black barrel."

"Wow, this is turning into a regular carnival," Cody observed.

"Raven and Kirit don't spar in public very often. Most of the palace usually turns out to watch. I'm sure even Seamus is here somewhere," Nyx said.

"Oh, there he is now," Chaos said. "What do you know? We should go say hello."

Chaos changed course mid-stride and Cody followed, ignoring the well-dressed man who tried to gain his attention. The Fae likely just wanted to aim more poorly disguised insults Cody's way.

Seamus saw them coming. A look of long-suffering tolerance settled on his face, but he stayed where he was. Cody figured he knew better than to run. Chaos was an amazing tracker.

"Is your name really Chaos?" Cody asked. "Because that just seems a little too fitting." It had been nagging at him for a while.

"No," Chaos said. "It's just one of those nicknames that stuck."

"So what's your real name?"

Chaos came to a halt, a strange expression crossing his features. It was mostly consternation, but there was also a hint of…confusion, loss, maybe?

Then he shrugged, the emotions sliding away. "Darned if I remember. It's been too long since anyone used it. I've been Chaos since before I could fly."

Cody assumed that meant a kid, but wasn't certain. He didn't want Chaos to go off on a tangent, though, so he let it be.

"Damn, now you've got me curious," Chaos declared. "Say, Raven, what's my name?" He hailed as the man passed by, half-naked and looking stern.

Raven gave one of those patented Draak grunts in acknowledgement. "What the hell kind of question is that?" he groused before moving on.

"I take it he doesn't remember, either," Cody said dryly.

"Maybe Seamus knows."

Cody watched in amusement as Chaos made a beeline for the king. A minute later, a loud, "Good Lord, you're joking," echoed through the air. Heads turned.

"So?" Cody asked a disgruntled Chaos when he returned.

"I'm sticking with Chaos."

Now Cody *had* to know. He'd go straight to the source.

"I made Seamus swear not to tell you," Chaos said.

Cody laughed. "We'll see about that."

"No, we won't."

Sometime during their little talk, Seamus had vanished. Cody would just have to find him later, because he really, really wanted to know.

He let it go for the moment, and allowed Chaos to drag him back onto their original course.

Soon, Cody found himself in the middle of a group of men—and, surprisingly, women. It also didn't escape his notice that no one here was wearing armor. He did see a lot of kilts, plain fabric and some extremely short tunics. Weapons were in evidence, of course, but they were well-worn and sharply honed, not flashy and adorned.

Someone shoved a crude wooden mug into Cody's hand and he took a tentative sip. The bitter taste of fermented wheat hit his tongue and he smiled.

"Oh, that's fantastic."

"Go slow," Nyx warned. "It's strong."

Looking at the crowd, which was growing larger by the minute, Cody wouldn't doubt it. These people looked like they lived hard, fought hard and drank hard. In short, they were his kind of people.

Someone let out a raucous cheer, which was quickly taken up by others. Cody looked up to see Kirit and Raven stride onto the field. He swallowed his beer a little too fast and almost choked, but damn. They were quite the pair.

The two dragons towered over everyone, their bulk making every other warrior look puny. They were stripped to the waist, displaying each muscle of their upper bodies to perfection. Alone they were impressive, but together, bristling with adrenaline? Holy hell. They were both primed for a fight, and it showed. Cody could kind of see why Seamus wanted to use them to intimidate those ambassadors. Take those two, throw in Nyx and Chaos, and that would be all the deterrent ever needed. The mere sight would be enough to stop a war before it started. Who would want to fight *that*?

Raven lifted one hand in the air, eliciting more cheers.

"They're like the rock stars of Faerie, aren't they?" Cody observed.

"I don't know what that means," Chaos said.

Nyx groaned. "Shut up, Chaos."

"What?"

"Have another beer," Cody advised.

Chaos quite eagerly took the suggestion to heart, pushing through people toward the kegs.

"And get me one while you're at it," Cody shouted after him. His was almost gone, too fast really, but it was the best damn thing he'd tasted since he'd arrived in Faerie.

A big, burly man he'd never seen before clapped Cody on the shoulder.

"Come," he bellowed. "There is a better vantage point over there."

Cody ducked the thick arm that waved vaguely to the left. It was the size of a tree trunk. The guy wasn't tall, but he was definitely beefy. Cody could tell, because he wasn't wearing much. His entire ensemble consisted of a kilt that was a little too short and a pair of battered boots.

Cody followed, praying that the guy didn't try to bend over. It would provide a view that Cody really didn't want to see. *What is it with these people and the slutty clothes?*

The man seemed friendly, if overly inebriated, and he was right about the vantage point. Cody trailed in his wake as the man pushed his way to the edge of the arena. Cody winced sympathetically as he bowled a few people over. Cody called swift apologies as he passed through the aftermath. Most of the victims looked resigned and greeted the man, Domius, by name.

Cody settled into a position between Domius and a pretty woman with dark hair. She smiled at him and he nodded in turn. He'd barely stopped moving when someone grabbed his shoulder.

"Don't do that," Nyx said with a deep scowl. "Kirit would kill me if I lost you."

"Oh, relax. I was with my new friend here," Cody said, pointing a finger at Domius.

"Domius." Nyx sounded resigned, too. "How have you been?"

"Wonderful, old boy. Say, I found this one wandering. Who does he belong to?"

Cody tried to surreptitiously lean to one side. The man was *loud.*

"He's Kirit's," Nyx said.

"Good for Kirit! 'Bout time the boy found someone."

"He'll be glad to hear you approve."

Domius beamed happily and didn't appear to notice the sarcasm in the reply.

"I found the beer!" Chaos shoved Domius aside and presented Cody with a mug about twice the size of the last one.

"Tha—"

A loud cheer from the crowd cut Cody off. He turned to see Kirit launch himself at Raven. Raven sidestepped, swiping out with sharp…claws?

Chaos whistled. "They're going full out today."

Nyx snorted in derision. "Why? They're supposed to be demonstrating fighting techniques for the new recruits. I highly doubt any of those boys will be growing wings any time soon."

Chaos grinned. "Can't you guess? They're showing off for our newest resident."

Cody smiled in return. "Aww, how cute."

Nyx looked at Cody in disbelief. "Only you would think that was cute." He gestured at the combatants going at each other with determined viciousness.

They moved swiftly, completely absorbed in the fight. Both men's fangs were on display, claws flashing in the sunlight. They spun and separated, circling around the arena. As Raven passed, Cody got a good glimpse of his face. His skin looked...odd. It took him a second to realize the man had sprouted scales. Blue-tinted scales. Kirit was sporting his own coating of white-tinged scales. They glittered with an iridescent glow that almost exactly matched his eyes. Kirit shook his shoulders, settling himself, and the scales spread until they covered his chest and back.

With a low roar, Kirit launched himself into the air. Literally. Between one instant and the next, wings burst from his back.

"Shit, I didn't know he could do that," Cody said, startled.

"They don't go halves very often," Domius said. "Quite the sight, eh?"

Silence fell over the audience as the pair twirled and spun in a deadly dance. They didn't use any weapons besides those provided by nature—claws and fangs, wings and tails. Kirit tossed Raven over his shoulder. Raven flipped in mid-air, touched down and spun, already striking out. Cody winced when his blow drew blood. Kirit shook it off and landed a nasty uppercut to Raven's jaw. Raven staggered backwards, using his wings to keep himself upright.

The battle seemed to last for hours. The men were obviously pulling their strikes, but only enough to avoid inflicting any permanent damage. They were both soon bleeding, bruised and scratched.

They were also grinning manically and clearly having the time of their lives. The new recruits, on the other hand, were looking a bit pale.

Chaos chuckled, the sound wicked. "They're scaring the babies. Isn't it great?"

"Oh, do shut up, Chaos," Cody said. He couldn't pull his eyes from the arena. His adrenaline was pumping, heart pounding, as if he was the one fighting. There was something utterly magnificent about the two creatures locked in combat. It would have been a riveting sight, even if it wasn't his Kirit. Knowing all those gleaming, straining muscles were his to stroke and lick? *Damn. Just…damn.*

"You're thinking about sex again," Chaos made the familiar complaint.

"You bet. Wouldn't you be?"

Nyx chuckled and Chaos grimaced.

"That's nasty. They're like my brothers, yeah?"

"The Lynalin—"

"Don't even go there," Chaos interrupted Nyx. Apparently, Kirit wasn't the only one who was a bit too literal. "Ooooh, swords."

Cody scowled. Kirit and Raven had snagged weapons from a couple of waiting squires. The proficiency they displayed was impressive, but he really didn't like seeing Kirit facing the weapon.

"If Raven hurts my Kirit, he'll regret it," Cody said.

"Exhibition, remember?" Nyx reassured him. "No dismemberment or death allowed."

"That still leaves a lot of wiggle room."

"I don't—"

"Know what that means," everyone around Chaos finished in unison.

"I need more beer."

Nyx heaved a sigh as Chaos disappeared into the crowd. Again. "Maybe I can get Raven to send him to Earth for a while."

Cody bit his tongue, but he really hoped Raven wouldn't. At least not until he and Kirit could leave. Right now, Chaos was the only friend Cody had in Faerie.

Without Chaos to distract them, Nyx and Cody were able to turn their complete attention back to the arena. Cody kind of wished Chaos would come back. It was impressive, but the longer the fight went on, the more tense he grew. Both men were dripping with sweat and more blood than he was comfortable with. He hadn't minded the claws, but for some reason, the swords made him nervous, even if both men wielded them as if they were an extension of their bodies.

"Come on," he whispered. "Someone end this."

"Soon," Nyx replied.

As if in response to his words, Raven ducked and brought their weapons together. With a painful wrench, he sent Kirit's blade soaring to one side. He followed that with a sweep of his feet, and Kirit went down in a heap. Cody's lungs burned and he realized he had stopped breathing. Raven's blade dipped to rest against Kirit's throat and Cody almost launched himself into the arena. Only Nyx's sudden fierce grip stopped him.

Then a cheer went up from the crowd and Raven stepped back. He reached out a hand and helped Kirit up.

"Well, that's done," Domius declared. "Who's ready for some fun?"

Someone tossed Kirit a cloth as he exited the arena. He caught it and wiped the sweat from his face, still breathing heavily. His shoulder and back stung from a couple of deep cuts, but he ignored the minor ache, knowing it would vanish quickly. A human would be incapacitated, but scales provided better armor than any metal. Only a few of Raven's swipes had gotten through the protection.

"Excellent match," Raven murmured, swiping at some of the blood and perspiration on his torso. "You've gotten faster."

"Since when, yesterday?"

Raven grunted. Kirit tossed his damp towel at the commander's head. Raven dodged.

By mutual unspoken agreement, they stopped in front of the cluster of wide-eyed new recruits.

"And that's how it's done," Raven announced, flashing a grin full of sharp, pointy teeth.

One of the kids hit the ground. Kirit shook his head. "You're as bad as Chaos."

Both of them took an unreasonable delight in frightening the young ones.

"Oi, Kirit!"

Kirit turned at the hail. Everand, one of the senior officers, jogged towards them.

"Everand." Kirit clasped forearms with the man

"Good to see you, my lord. Fantastic exhibition. It's only a shame the Eviatt contingent weren't here to watch. They would have made peace faster than you could take a breath."

"They were *supposed* to be here," Kirit complained. "I swear, a turtle moves faster than that group."

"Speaking of groups, the Bagaudasii *are* here."

Behind him, Raven groaned. "Don't tell me they brought their own alcohol again."

Everand nodded, a wide grin splitting his craggy features. "Five big barrels of *courmi*. Seamus is furious."

"Because they brought the beer, or because he can't drink it while the Fae are watching?"

"The latter, of course. It's a good batch. Your mate is certainly enjoying it."

That had Kirit's head turning quickly. "Cody is with the Bagaudasii?"

"Indeed. He seems to be fitting in quite nicely."

Kirit cursed and headed back across the field in a near jog.

"Hold up, Kirit," Raven called. "Where are you going?"

"To rescue my mate from the Bagaudasii," he replied.

"I do believe it should be the other way around."

At the smooth voice, Kirit came to an abrupt halt. He scowled at the man blocking his path.

"Lord Magisteri."

"Lord Morkenslayne."

Pleasantries dispensed, Kirit wondered how much trouble he would be in if he bit the irritating man. Raven gripped his shoulder and leaned in close.

"You can't eat him," he whispered into Kirit's ear.

He just wanted a little nibble. It would make the bastard go away.

Kirit resigned himself to making conversation before he could find his mate. "What did you need, my lord?"

Magisteri smiled, the expression cold on his distinguished features. "You put on quite the performance today. Most impressive. Of course, I am uncertain how much your mate witnessed. He has been availing himself of the refreshments."

You can't hit him, you can't hit him.

Kirit bared his teeth in something resembling a smile. "I am glad to hear he has been enjoying himself. Cody has found palace life to be rather dull on occasion."

"Hmm. I am unsurprised. It would be difficult at best for a human to find a place among us."

Kirit scowled, searching for another veiled comment to respond with. He could practically hear Raven willing him to walk away. Subterfuge was a Fae talent, not a draconic one.

"I could use a drink," Raven said in a loud voice. "Couldn't you use a drink? Excuse us please, Lord Magisteri."

Raven grabbed Kirit by the shoulder and steered him past the smirking noble.

"Wait, I wasn't finished," Kirit protested.

"No." Raven waited until they passed out of earshot of Magisteri before he continued. "I know you, Kirit. Magisteri would poke, you would lose your temper and attack, and then Seamus would have to deal with the whole mess. Then Seamus would drag me into the middle, wondering why I cannot control my own. So, we are going to find your mate and maybe a couple of mugs of ale along the way. You can't penetrate Magisteri's arrogance, you should know that by now. And you most certainly cannot do it with words."

"Was that a comment on my intelligence?" Kirit asked mildly. He wasn't eloquent and he could admit it.

"Do be quiet."

Several times people stopped them, wanting to discuss the bout, but Kirit kept the conversations short, wanting to get to Cody. He could hear the

Bagaudasii before he could see them. The alcohol had clearly been flowing freely for some time.

The hour was growing later, the sun beginning to sink low in the sky. Torches were being lit, accompanied by the occasional bluish glow of witch-light. The majority of the light, though, came from a huge bonfire. The Bagaudasii had set up camp in a far corner of the lower bailey, the fire crackling merrily in the niche created by the intersection of two of the outer walls. It was growing bigger by the minute as people added fuel, spilling a bright circle onto the hard-packed dirt and trampled grass. Someone had found a fiddle, someone else a set of pipes, and already the circle was filling up with whirling dancers, some more sober than others.

Cody was in the middle of it all. Kirit watched for a minute, knowing he was wearing a slightly sappy smile. He couldn't help it. Cody was laughing, looking happier than Kirit could remember seeing him since they had arrived in Faerie. He would do just about anything to keep that expression on his Treasure's face.

"You should dance with him," Raven urged.

"He's happy."

"He would be happier with you there."

Kirit shook his head. He loved seeing Cody dancing with such abandon. At the same time, he could admit that it hurt a bit. *He* wanted to be the one to put that look on Cody's face.

Then Cody looked over, saw Kirit, and Kirit forgot to be hurt. The smile grew, becoming incandescent, as Cody beckoned for Kirit to come closer.

"What did I tell you?" Raven said.

Kirit hit Raven with the back of his hand and went to join his mate.

"Hey, big guy." Cody grinned widely, wrapping his arms—and the rest of himself—around Kirit. Kirit grinned back.

"You are drunk," he observed.

Holding up one hand, Cody spread his thumb and forefinger about an inch apart. "Just a little."

Kirit thought it was more than a little. Cody pulled him into the middle of the group of dancers and the music picked up in tempo.

"I don't dance," he said, even as his feet moved back and forth.

"We're not dancing," Cody argued. "We're just wiggling."

Kirit couldn't really argue with that statement. He didn't think Cody was capable of anything more intricate than 'wiggling', anyway, not with the amount of alcohol in his body.

"Did you enjoy the demonstration?" Kirit asked.

"You were hot."

"That was not quite what I meant," Kirit said with a smile.

"Gonna show me those wings again? Later? In private?"

"If you wish."

It gave Kirit a little thrill. He knew it was very alien, his dragon half. He preferred the dragon form to the human, though, and always had. He wanted Cody to feel comfortable with both sides of him.

"When are we going home?"

The question caught Kirit by surprise and he blinked for a minute before he could puzzle it out. "And where is home, my little treasure?" he asked as softly as he could and still be heard over the music.

"I don't know," Cody admitted. Kirit immediately regretted the question as the happiness slid away from Cody's face.

The impromptu musical group finished the reel and moved into a ballad. Kirit slowed his movements and pulled Cody in tight to his body. He ran his hand up and down Cody's back, finally settling his fingers in the soft hair at the nape of Cody's neck.

"I know this has been difficult," Kirit said. "We will leave soon. The Eviatt ambassadors will arrive, Seamus will dismiss me, and we can return to the mountains. You will like it there. It is beautiful and peaceful and private. And if you are still unhappy..." Kirit paused, but his Treasure meant everything. "If you are still unhappy, I will take you back to Earth."

"I don't really want to go back," Cody said. "It's not home anymore. But home sure as hell isn't this palace. I mean, it's beautiful, but it feels so cold, you know? I guess I'm just feeling a little disconnected. So much has changed."

"You have me, and you will always have me." Frustration edged at Kirit's mind. He knew he wasn't saying the right things, but damned if he knew what words would make Cody feel better. Words were most definitely not his area of expertise. Nyx was the charmer—and, surprisingly enough, Chaos, when he exerted himself.

"Yep." Cody smiled and hugged Kirit tightly. "My big, grumpy dragon."

Kirit growled, just to make Cody laugh.

"Am I really going to be enough for you?"

"Damn, you're a maudlin drunk."

Cody pulled away far enough to poke Kirit in the side. "Come on. You're *ancient*. You've seen and done things I can't even imagine. What can you possibly see in a rent boy from the city? I didn't finish high school and I don't have any significant talents. Unless you count the ability to deep-throat an above-average-sized cock."

Kirit thought that was a pretty significant accomplishment, himself, especially as he'd been the recipient several times. But he was distracted by the rest of the statement. He scowled and clapped one hand over Cody's mouth to stop the flow of self-derogatory words. "Stop it," he ordered. "You're perfect."

Cody tugged the fingers aside, rolling his eyes in exasperation. Kirit let go.

"I'm far from perfect," he retorted.

Kirit opened his mouth to protest again, but Cody cut him off.

"Fine, agree to disagree. I just mean, you're important and gifted and you deserve a whole hell of a lot better than me."

"No, I don't." Kirit hoped the certainty he felt came through in his words. Cody was everything he'd ever wanted.

Cody sighed. "Ignore me. You're right, I'm a maudlin drunk. Maybe more alcohol would help."

Kirit groped Cody's perfect ass, already dreaming of what he wanted to do to it. "Maybe food would be a better plan."

"Or more dancing. Dancing makes things better."

"I am not certain of that."

"That's because dragons don't know how to have fun."

As if on cue, the ballad ended and something much livelier began. Kirit grunted, but let Cody move him with the music. He wasn't actually dancing, per se. It was more of following Cody's lead as his mate stomped around with abandon. Kirit had to admit, it was enjoyable. He caught Nyx and Chaos at the edge of the crowd, watching him and laughing. Chaos gave Kirit a thumbs-up. Kirit wondered where he had picked up the gesture. He returned it with an older, ruder gesture.

Chaos, as expected, threw back his head and cackled loudly. Then he leered at a girl in a skimpy, filmy dress and followed her out of sight. Kirit shook his head.

"Hey, big guy, over here." Cody grabbed his chin and tugged Kirit's head back around. Kirit smiled and leaned down for a kiss. He only meant to take a taste, but then he couldn't make himself let go. He delved deeper, tongue tangling with Cody's. Cody groaned and pushed closer, until Kirit could feel the ridges of his stomach and the hard bulge of his cock.

"I think I'm done dancing," Cody said.

"Me, too."

Kirit pulled back, grabbed Cody's hand, and dragged him away from the crowd. A few lewd comments followed them, but Kirit ignored them.

Occasionally, even Chaos could have good ideas. Kirit couldn't take Cody away from here, not just yet, but maybe he could distract Cody for a time.

Chapter Nineteen

He was being watched again.

Cody slowed his steps, keeping an eye on his surroundings. He was supposed to be at dinner right now. Seamus had ordered the Draak to be more sociable, amid much protesting. Cody wasn't too happy about it, either. He preferred dining in his room with his big dragon. It was about the only time together they had. Otherwise, Kirit was off training soldiers, sparring, or doing other warrior-type duties. Seamus knew his Draak well and worked hard to keep them busy. If they were busy, they couldn't cause problems.

"Would work better if he just let us leave," Cody mumbled. He didn't know what Kirit's home was like, but it had to be better than here.

Recently, he had been getting that tickling sensation in the back of his neck which signaled someone with unfriendly intentions was hovering just out of sight. He used to get the same feeling when Johnnie, the obnoxious wannabe pimp, would have his goons keep an eye on Cody. Every so often he would catch a flash of movement, and he was pretty sure it was always the same guy. Cody didn't know his name, but remembered running into him during one of his first days at the palace. The man — Fae — had been distinctly unfriendly.

Cody briefly considered telling Kirit. He discarded the notion just as quickly. He had nothing solid to give the big guy. Plus, he didn't relish being stuck in their suite by himself. He knew Kirit well — the dragon would lock Cody up for his own protection. And that simply wouldn't do. It was hard enough finding things to occupy his time when he could wander and explore.

Maybe he should tell Chaos. Despite his initial snarky attitude towards the hyperactive idiot, Cody really didn't know what he would do without Chaos. The man was, at the moment, keeping him sane. Weird, considering Chaos' mental state, but true. Between the boredom, Kirit's constant disappearing acts, and the 'parties', Cody was at his wits end. Throw in the hostility from the Fae and he was starting to long for his old life.

If only going back to Earth didn't mean giving up Kirit. According to Chaos, the big dragon would follow him, but the Draak simply couldn't survive on the other side of the Veil, not indefinitely. Something about the magical matrix.

Yet one more thing about this damned mess I don't understand.

Cody was growing sick of feeling like an idiot.

It took Cody ten minutes to make his way to the dining hall. *This place is just too frickin' huge.* Cody needed one of those little scooter things to get around. Hmm, maybe he should suggest it to Desmond,

Seamus' secretary. *Surely one of the court wizard guys can come up with something…*

The dining hall was stuffed full of people, with one notable exception—no Kirit. Cody cursed. He wove through the crowd until he reached the table on the far side of the room, where he plopped down in between Nyx and Chaos.

"Where's Kirit?"

Nyx shrugged. Chaos simply shook his head—Cody figured it was a little hard to talk with that much food stuffed in his mouth.

Their small group ate in relatively undisturbed silence. The dining hall was almost as large as the throne room, lined wall-to-wall with long carved wooden tables sitting parallel to each other. Another table at the front of the room sat perpendicular to the others, which was where Seamus sat, when he managed to make it to dinner. Technically, as some of the highest ranking nobles at court, the Draak were supposed to be up there with the king. That, however, was a little too much social activity to expect of the dragons. Instead, they staked out the most isolated table, and people generally knew to leave them alone. The dragons took everything far too seriously, in Cody's opinion, but they *really* took eating seriously.

A lot of fuel was required to keep those big bodies going.

Cody ate absent-mindedly studying the crowd as he did. With his back to the wall the way it was, he had an excellent view of the flashy group. By and large, the nobles were a rather silly, foppish, and useless bunch. He was always surprised that the dragons—Kirit in particular—hadn't lost their patience and disemboweled someone yet.

"Who's that?" Cody poked Chaos in the side, nodding to the small cluster of nobles a few feet away. He had to blink as the light glinted off one woman's jewel-encrusted dress and nearly blinded him.

How the hell can she even walk, weighed down with all that junk?

"Which one?" Chaos asked.

"The big one with the permanent scowl. Looks kind of like a bulldog, but crankier." Cody was pretty certain it was the guy who'd been watching him. It was always a good idea to identify your enemies.

"I don't—"

"—know what that means, yes. Third from the right. Dark hair. Crooked nose."

"Ah, Ellar."

"Ellar? Nice." Cody snickered, although really, that wasn't the strangest name he'd heard lately.

"Ellar is the king's nephew. He's also an absolute numbskull. How did you put it...cranky? Yes, that fits nicely."

"I ran into him a while back. Or should I say, he ran into me. I don't think he likes me very much."

"Ellar doesn't like anyone." Nyx joined the conversation.

"I can see it," Cody said, watching the man surreptitiously. Ellar seemed to have a limited range of facial expressions—scowl, deep scowl and deeper scowl. *Yep, cranky.* "He looks like he needs to get laid."

"No one would have him," Chaos said.

Cody tried to hold back a laugh and ended up snorting his wine. "Now, that's just mean."

Chaos shrugged, as usual completely unrepentant. "Perhaps, but it's the truth."

"I would think his position alone would be attractive, even if he isn't." Cody had realized quickly that the Fae mingling throughout the royal court were very attached to rank. Personally, he didn't get it, but whatever.

"It might," Nyx said, "If Seamus actually *liked* his nephew. As it is, he spends an amazing amount of time trying to find ways to send Ellar away from the palace."

"Wow, I'm just feeling the love all over the place."

Chaos shrugged again. "Ellar creates his own problems. If he would remove the stick from his arse on occasion, he might find people kinder."

This time, Cody couldn't stop his laughter, even if it did make people stare. On the far side of Nyx, Raven grunted in irritation. Cody noticed, however, that he didn't dispute Chaos' description.

Cody shoved his plate aside. He leaned his head on Chaos' shoulder and contemplated taking a nap. It seemed like he took a lot of naps lately.

"Better not let Kirit see you," Nyx cautioned.

Cody waved aside his concern. Chaos made a nice pillow. Besides, the guy might dress like a total queen, but he could definitely take care of himself.

"Maybe next time, Kirit will show up when he's supposed to," Cody retorted. "Then I could use *him* as a pillow."

As if on cue, a low growl ripped through the buzz of conversation. Chaos immediately sat up and shoved Cody aside.

"Damn it, Chaos, I was comfortable," Cody groused.

"Sorry, my friend, but I like my head on my shoulders and my balls between my legs. Kirit has absolutely no sense of humor these days."

True.

Kirit walked up behind Cody and hauled him to his feet. Then, the big dragon sat back down, plopping

Cody onto his lap. He folded muscular arms around Cody's waist and snarled warningly at the table in general.

"Yes, yes," Cody said, patting Kirit's forearms. "They all know I belong to you. Where the hell have you been, anyway?"

Kirit grunted. Cody rolled his eyes. Really, the longer they were here, the less Kirit spoke. If they didn't leave soon, Cody was going to have to learn sign language or something.

"Words," he said. "Words are really useful, big guy. You might try them."

Nyx slapped Kirit on the shoulder. "I was waiting for you to show up," he told Kirit. "I've got good news. Seamus told me the Eviatt ambassadors will be here within the next two days. Two more days after that, at the most, and we can all leave."

"It's about time," Kirit said. He gave Cody a little squeeze. "Hear that, mate? We will go home soon."

Seeing Ellar's unfriendly eyes turn his way, Cody knew it couldn't be too soon for his taste.

Kirit pulled Cody's plate back in front of them. He urged Cody to eat more, but didn't eat much himself. Cody had noticed that, along with the diminishing speech, Kirit's appetite was lessening. Raven and Chaos seemed to handle the palace with aplomb, but Kirit and Nyx grew more uncomfortable with each passing day, although Kirit more than Nyx. Seamus did a good job of keeping them busy, but it seemed each day they spent a little longer training. And by training, Cody meant battering at each other with sharp, shiny objects. After the exhibition a few days ago, Cody had made a point of providing them with an audience. It was the highlight of his day, watching the dragons spar. Skin shiny with sweat, muscles working, it was a sight to behold.

"He's thinking of sex again," Chaos complained.

"When is he not thinking of sex?" Nyx retorted.

Raven grunted. Kirit smirked.

The Fae stared. Seamus glared.

Cody sighed. He hoped those ambassadors hurried.

"Kirit, Seamus would like to speak with you."

Cody looked up to see Desmond hovering in front of their table. The man was short, slight and fidgety. He also ran the palace with an iron fist. Cody had yet to figure out the man's position—Seamus called him a secretary, but he did so with amusement in his voice.

"Can it not wait?" Kirit sounded put out. Cody wasn't sure if it was because of having his meal interrupted, or having his cuddle time interrupted. For a big, burly warrior, Kirit was extremely fond of cuddling.

"No."

Cody glared at Desmond. Desmond seemed unfazed.

"Very well," Kirit said. "Tell him I will be there shortly."

Desmond didn't move.

"I think you're supposed to go with him," Cody pointed out in a faux whisper.

Desmond nodded. "If I leave without you, I will only have to track you down again."

"He does know you well," Nyx said.

Kirit very gently set Cody to one side. "Lead on."

Cody watched him go, regretting the loss of his cuddle, but enjoying the view of Kirit's ass. "I wonder what Seamus wants now," he mused.

"Who knows? Seamus has been acting odd of late," Nyx said. "His actions are making even less sense than usual."

"Maybe *he* needs to get laid," Cody said.

Chaos snickered. "I dare you to say that to his face."

"No, thanks."

"Here," Chaos said. "Have a piece of broccoli."

He dropped the vegetable on Cody's plate. Cody stared at it, then at the very strange dragon next to him. "Thanks," he said sarcastically.

"Don't say I never give you anything," Chaos said.

On Chaos' other side, Nyx was eyeing him warily and inching farther away.

"I think he's cracked," Cody told Nyx.

"He popped out of his egg...cracked."

Cody couldn't help it. He laughed, long and hard, until he could barely breathe. Now Nyx was looking at *him* warily.

"Egg...cracked..." Cody gasped out between laughs.

"You're a very strange human," Chaos said. "Eat your broccoli."

God, but he was getting attached to these guys. Looking at Chaos' self-satisfied grin, Cody figured the other man did it on purpose. He also figured that most people underestimated Chaos. Chaos would prefer it that way.

"Yes, mother, I'll eat my vegetables," Cody said when he could speak again.

Chaos nodded once in approval. Cody flicked a piece of bread at him. Chaos caught it handily and ate it. Chaos ate *everything*.

"I wonder if there's any more dessert," Nyx said, looking mournfully at his empty plate.

"You had three," Cody said.

"Yes, but it's *chocolate*."

"Here." Cody passed over his bowl of some kind of pudding concoction. Nyx took it without argument. The guy really did love his chocolate. He even ate it for breakfast.

"I have no idea how you stay so ripped," Cody said, taking a brief moment to admire Nyx's rippling physique.

"Ripped?"

"You. The muscles."

"Ah." Nyx grinned, showcasing some very pointy teeth. Even in his human form, Nyx looked more like a reptile than the others, with his sharp teeth and his eyes with the slit pupils. It had creeped Cody out at first, but he was getting used to it.

Raven grunted again and pushed away from the table. He walked away without a word. Cody stared, trying to think if he'd said anything to offend Raven.

Chaos patted Cody's shoulder. "Raven is even crankier than Kirit," he said. "Don't take it personally. I never do. Eat your broccoli."

Cody glared but complied, if for no other reason than to shut the man up. As he chewed, he wondered what he was going to do with himself the rest of the evening. He'd spent all day reading, and he was so damn *bored*.

A shadow fell over his plate and Cody looked up. Kirit stood there, a small grin tilting the corners of his mouth.

"Seamus says he has no need of me for the next twenty-four hours, and that I should find something to occupy myself with before I injure one of his men."

Ignoring the pouting Chaos, Cody wiggled his way out from under the table. Benches might seat more people than chairs, but they were murder to get off of. He used Chaos to balance as he pulled his legs free.

He might have kicked the man in the shin, too. Then he was free and grabbing Kirit's hand.

"Come on, big guy. Let's go have some fun."

It looked like Cody suddenly had a full schedule, and it made him very, very happy. Judging by the smile on Kirit's face, it made him happy, too.

And really, that was Cody's major goal in life right now—making his dragon smile.

It wasn't like he had any other goals. Maybe he should work on that.

Tomorrow.

Or the day after.

Chapter Twenty

Cody hesitated outside the gilt door. He took a deep, bracing breath and tried to muster his courage. Then he wanted to bang his head against a wall.

What am I doing? God, I'm turning into a big baby.

He'd never been shy a day in his life. He'd certainly never suffered from a near-debilitating attack of nerves at the thought of a room full of people. Hell, usually a room full of people was his element. Maybe Kirit's anti-social attitude was rubbing off on him.

"Are you going in or coming out?"

Cody jumped. "Shit, Desmond, would you make some noise next time?"

"Pardon, young sir."

"Quit calling me that." Cody scowled at the prissy little man with his perfect hair and perfect skin. "You're not old enough."

Desmond arched one perfect eyebrow. Cody scowled.

Can't the man have just one flaw?

"Would you care to wager on that?" Desmond said.

"Stupid Fae and their ageless perfection," Cody said under his breath.

"Which is it, my lord? In or out?" Desmond politely ignored the insult to his species. Desmond was always polite. Cody often wanted to poke him, just to make sure he was flesh and blood and not some kind of robot. *No, wait, what do they call it in fantasy literature? Golem, that's it. I swear to God, Desmond has to be a golem.*

"In, I suppose," Cody said, shoving aside the random thoughts that insisted on spinning around in his head.

Desmond opened the door and motioned Cody inside with a small half-bow. Cody manfully resisted the urge to mess up Desmond's carefully styled hair. He understood why one of Chaos' favorite pastimes was tormenting the castle steward. That much perfection was unnatural. *Golem, has to be.*

The minute he entered the room, Cody forgot about Desmond and his plastic perfection. Every eye turned his way. He tried not to squirm, but a weird feeling tingled along his spine. His fight-or-flight instinct was kicking in and, for once, he wanted to pick flight.

Cody shoved it, too, aside. Raven had been making more noises about sending Chaos away on some errand, and it had made Cody panic. What on earth would he do without Chaos to keep him occupied? The thought had made him realize how ridiculous he was being. This was his home now. It was past time to make an effort to fit in.

He had been told by a servant that Seamus had tea every afternoon in one of the salons, and many of the upper nobility—of which Cody was, apparently, now a member—joined him. Cody had thought, *"Perfect, an intimate gathering."* Seeing all the stares, and the cold, haughty faces of the Fae, made him reconsider his plan.

Then a woman with the most amazing braids patted the couch next to her. She was rounder than most of the Fae he'd met, carrying more than a few extra pounds. Like many Fae, she wore silks and satins, with an impressive amount of lace added for good measure. The bright green dress was a little gaudy, but it suited her blonde hair and pretty features.

"Dragon-mate," she said with a smile. "How lovely that you could join us."

"Umm, thanks. Call me Cody, please." He sat gingerly — the piece of furniture was delicate, and the cushion harder than wood. It was one of those pretty parlor pieces that were made for looks, and absolutely not comfort. Cody figured it was deliberate.

"Cody." The woman smiled again, and Cody smiled back. It was hard not to, when confronted with such a radiant face and those rounded, dimpled cheeks. "I'm Lisette. Well, Lady Mountebank, but that's far too formal. I've been dying to talk to you ever since I heard Lord Kirit mated a human. I've never been to Earth, and I want to hear all about it."

"Wow, that…might take a while. It's a big place."

"Good. New stories."

Cody half expected Lisette to clap her hands in delight. "If I have to listen to the tale about Lord Ashton and the goat again, I swear, I'll be forced to take drastic action."

Oh, yeah, I'm going to like her.

"I've gotta ask. How long does it take to do your hair like that?" Cody knew it was probably rude, but he was absolutely fascinated by her hair. It was piled atop her head in what seemed like millions of tiny braids. He really wanted to touch, but that would definitely be rude. And likely get him slapped, too.

"Days," she confided solemnly. "I only did it for my wedding last month."

"Congratulations."

"You two certainly look cozy over here. Lisette, don't tell me you're stepping out on Henri already?"

Lisette scowled, the expression turning the corners of her full lips down, causing deep wrinkles to form on either side of her mouth. She still looked like a cherub, but now she was a very annoyed cherub.

"Do go away, Ellar," she said in a tart voice. "I can speak with whomever I choose. No one is interested in your sordid opinions."

Ah, so this is Ellar. Cody had never seen the king's cousin up close before. Ellar was usually lurking in the shadows.

Cody wasn't impressed. Ellar was of average height and rather plain. Cody tried, but he couldn't see the slightest resemblance to Seamus. *Maybe the eyes...nah.* They were the same color as Seamus', but beady. Really, Ellar just looked like the quintessential schoolyard bully, albeit all grown up.

"And I see the human decided to grace us with his presence today," Ellar continued, blithely ignoring Lisette.

"I don't think we've been introduced." Cody put on his best professional smile and held out his hand. "Cody Markswell. And you are?"

Ellar eyed Cody's hand as if it were covered in poison ivy. "You know quite well who I am."

"I can't see how." Cody gritted his teeth. *Just pretend he's that damn banker that used to come around at precisely ten oh-two every Thursday afternoon. Damn anal, cheap bastard.*

Ellar waved his hand. The gesture was ridiculous, more suited to the foppish than the stocky. "Everyone knows who I am."

"I don't listen to gossip. You should try it some time." Cody knew he shouldn't poke at the man, but he couldn't seem to help himself. Beside him, Lisette coughed in what might have been aborted laughter.

Ellar drew himself up tall. Cody barely refrained from rolling his eyes. *Really, is it necessary to fulfill every stereotype?*

"I happen to be the king's cousin."

"Good for you."

Those around them whispered while Ellar looked outraged. Cody didn't think it was his imagination that thought the whispers sounded amused. Someone like Ellar wouldn't have made himself a lot of friends.

"Come, Ellar, stop pestering the poor human. I'm certain he only understands half of what you say, anyway. I've heard they're all mentally deficient." The lady who had spoken snapped open her fan and waved it. She was tall and thin, her mean-spirited attitude affecting what would have otherwise been a beautiful face.

Or maybe it was Cody they were laughing at.

"Do be quiet," Lisette ordered. "Ignorance is never attractive."

"Better ignorant than fat," the woman retorted.

"That was uncalled for," another man said, rising to his feet.

Oh, good Lord. Cody had visions of a brawl in Seamus' sitting room, the tea service flying against the wall and silk and ribbons floating through the air while the Fae slapped and pinched each other. He really couldn't see this crowd fighting dirty. They were too refined.

A throat cleared in the doorway and interrupted the escalating tension.

"Good afternoon."

Cody was relieved at Seamus' entrance. "I think I could really use a cup of tea," he told Lisette.

Something stronger would be even better, but Cody didn't think he'd find it here.

"Indeed." Seamus smiled, the expression tight and thin-lipped. Someone clearly wasn't happy. "Ellar, a word?"

Ellar scowled down at Cody.

Cody smiled and winked. "Better go, Ellar. I don't think Seamus is feeling very patient."

There was no response, but the gleam in Ellar's eyes made Cody feel very uneasy. He shifted, suddenly wanting to run again.

"I suppose I shouldn't expect any better," Ellar murmured, as if to himself. "You are, after all, only a human."

"And what's wrong with being a human?"

Again, Cody was ignored. Ellar seemed to be in his own little world as he mused, "It isn't as if Kirit would be able to do any better. Not many would have an imbecilic oaf such as him."

"Now wait a minute!" Cody stood fast, almost knocking Ellar to the floor. "Say what you want about me, but leave Kirit out of it."

"Ellar!"

Out of the corner of his eye, Cody could see Seamus approaching, but all his attention was focused on Ellar's ugly face.

"Everyone knows it's the truth." Ellar sneered. "Kirit is all muscle and very little brain. All of the dragons, actually. Brute strength and no finesse."

"I'd like to see you say that to one of them directly."

"That would be beneath me."

"Beneath you?" Cody sputtered. "What the hell is that supposed to mean?" Cody could feel his ears heating, which only happened when he got really, really angry. Ellar was pushing all his buttons. Cody thought it was deliberate. There was a calculating gleam in Ellar's eyes. But Cody couldn't stop taking the bait. If it were just Cody, sure, but Ellar had to go and bring the dragons into it.

"I am royalty. I have no need to consort with riffraff."

"Riffraff?" Cody's voice rose a couple of notes and he stepped forward, crowding into Ellar's personal space.

"Ell—"

"I suppose that's better than an ugly, flat-faced, backwards son of a donkey!" Cody yelled.

Pain exploded in Cody's face. He flew backwards and slammed into the wall, vision going fuzzy.

I probably should have expected that.

* * * *

Kirit rolled lazily to one side, letting the heat of the sun soak into his scales. He purred with happiness. There was nothing as splendid as basking during midday. He felt like he could take a deep breath for the first time in ages. He knew he looked like an undignified idiot, lying half on his back in the middle of the field, wings outstretched, but he didn't care. Now he just needed his little mate and a short nap.

Since he didn't know where Cody had gone to, he decided to settle for the nap.

Someone cleared their throat nearby. Kirit ignored them in favor of studying a cloud formation that looked like a fat duck.

"Lord Kirit?"

Kirit's stomach rumbled ominously, fire churning in his gut. Stress. That was what the humans called it. It was a nasty bugger. Maybe if he pretended the person was a teeny, tiny bug and Kirit couldn't see him...

"Lord Kirit!"

"You're a little too big to hide," Raven said.

Damn it, there goes my nap.

Kirit gave a mental snarl and refused to look at anything but the clouds. *"I'm basking, you bastard. Go away, and take the annoyance with you."*

"I'm afraid I can't comply," Raven said, a note of amusement in his voice.

"What did he say?" The annoyance asked.

Dragons weren't capable of speech. Which was fine to Kirit, as he would rather not speak to anyone, in general. It did not, unfortunately, work with his clutch-mates. All the dragons—and Seamus—were able to communicate mentally. It came in handy during battle. Any other time, Kirit would rather do without that particular 'gift'.

"I don't believe you wish to know," Raven told the man. "Now stop pouting, Kirit, and listen to the man."

"Unless he is going to tell me I can take my mate and go home to my treasures, I'm not interested."

"Kirit."

Kirit heaved a sigh powerful enough to make the grass sway. He rolled again and slowly lumbered to his feet. On the ground, he wasn't the most graceful of creatures. He plopped down on his ass and curled his tail around his front legs. One more stretch of his wings, and he tucked them along his back. Then he blinked at the pair standing a few feet away and tilted his head.

"If you insist."

"Kirit." Raven was rapidly growing irritated. His eyes brightened, a small haze of yellow surrounding his pupils.

Kirit's gut churned again, but if he lit the field on fire, he would never hear the end of it.

His nap was most definitely a dream of the past.

He closed his eyes in resignation and reached for his human form. The world contracted with an almost inaudible pop. The instant his scales were gone, he wanted them back. His skin felt tight and itchy, the air too close. It took him a moment to remind himself how to use his lungs, and he was cold. Again. He always hated the transformation from dragon to human. It left him floundering, feeling powerless and tiny. Insignificant.

"Give me the message," Kirit ordered, his voice coming out around a low, heavy grumble as his vocal cords readjusted to human speech.

Then the messenger opened his mouth, and Kirit wished he had given in to the stress and set the grass aflame. It might have alleviated some of the tension trying to pull his shoulders up around his ears.

The ambassadors were, once more, delayed.

Kirit clenched his hand and released, over and over. The urge to start a fire resurged, stronger than ever, and it took sheer stubborn will to squash it. The poor messenger ducked his head and scurried away.

"Easy," Raven murmured softly, cutting through Kirit's mounting fury.

Kirit shook his shoulders, but it didn't help. Gods above, he shouldn't be this anxious, not over something that wasn't really all that unexpected. For whatever reason, though, emotions were riding him hard today. Before his aborted basking session, he'd spent half the morning in the sky, trying to ease the irritation, and he still felt ready to rip apart the first person to look at him crosswise. Spending some much-needed time with his mate would undoubtedly help, but Kirit was reluctant to inflict his mood on Cody. He knew he was neglecting his most precious jewel, but he still found himself spending more and more time away as the days went on. Not because he didn't want to be around his mate, but because he wanted it *too* much.

"Where is Seamus?" Kirit asked abruptly.

"In his office, I would imagine. Why?"

"Because my patience is gone. I need to leave, before I splatter Seamus' shiny floors with blood and guts."

"That bad?"

"Worse."

Kirit turned and stalked away, knowing every line of his body was screaming 'stay away'. He stepped from the warm sun and into the cool hallways, navigating the twisting maze of corridors with the ease of familiarity. He reached the doors of Seamus' private study in minutes and pushed his way inside without bothering to knock.

"We're going home," he announced.

Damn. That announcement would have had more impact if he hadn't made it to an empty room.

Kirit scratched his chin, trying to think of where else the king could be at this hour. He wanted to leave today. He'd reached his quota of court days ago. Right after he arrived, truth be told. Last night, he had dreamed about the mountains. And making love to his mate. Without interruption. Their last two 'make-out sessions', as Cody called them, had been halted by annoying people wanting things they didn't need. Even his promised twenty-four hours hadn't been free from annoyances.

"I assume you're looking for Seamus?"

Desmond's familiar voice broke through his thoughts. Kirit turned and mustered his best smile. Desmond took a step back.

Oh, yes, definitely time to go home. Desmond was generally unflappable.

"Yes, have you seen him?"

"He's in the east receiving room having tea, I believe."

Kirit grunted his acknowledgement and headed back into the halls. He would just take off with his mate, but that would make Seamus extremely irritable, and no one wanted that. The Fae king had a nasty temper, and it was a rule of his that the Draak needed permission to leave the palace. Kirit remembered when the king instituted that particular command—it had little to do with control and everything to do with frustration. Seamus had grown tired of searching for his Draak, only to find they had disappeared sometime during the night. He had no issues with them leaving. He simply wanted to know when they did so.

Kirit was close to the east wing when he heard the shouting. He planned to ignore it. He was on a very important mission. No distractions.

Except...

One voice rang above the others and Kirit bolted. Cody. That was Cody yelling.

His heart stuttered, then pounded with a mad rhythm. He tasted fear, sour in the back of his mouth.

It vaguely registered that the yelling came from the very room he'd been heading for, but Kirit shoved the thought aside as unimportant. He pushed through the small crowd that had gathered in the hall.

The roar that ripped from his throat vibrated through the walls and Kirit felt his control of his human form slipping.

"Cody!" he bellowed his mate's name, a red haze crossing his vision. A bulky figure had Cody pinned to the wall, bodies far too close. The man—Ellar, the king's cousin, he recognized in some distant part of his brain—had his hand around Cody's throat. They were pressed together from chest to thigh, but there was nothing lustful about the position.

Grabbing Ellar around the neck, Kirit ripped him away from Cody.

He snarled—the sound full of fury and death. He tightened his grip and extended his claws drawing blood.

"Kirit!"

He paid no attention to Seamus' shout.

"Kirit!"

He grinned, knowing it was a very unpleasant expression. The terror on Ellar's face was extremely satisfying.

"I'm going to kill you," Kirit said evenly. "And I am going to enjoy it. Very much."

"Kirit!"

The new voice penetrated his haze and he turned his head. Cody stood there, looking haggard around the edges and more beautiful than anything Kirit had ever seen. Even with the redness around one eye that would likely turn into a beautiful array of colors tomorrow.

"Kirit, put the idiot down," Cody said calmly. He placed one hand on Kirit's arm, stroking gently. "That's it, come on, big guy. I need a hug, huh?"

He growled and squeezed some more.

"Please, Kirit?"

With another snarl, Kirit opened his hand and let his prey drop. He snagged Cody and pulled him close, burying his nose in Cody's hair and inhaling the beloved scent of his Treasure.

"He hurt you," he said.

"No, I'm fine, promise."

From behind, Kirit heard a series of painful-sounding coughs. They made him happy. He turned, still clutching Cody close. He bared his fangs at the prone figure at his feet.

"How dare you?" Ellar demanded. His voice croaked a bit on the words. "You attacked a member of the royal family. I'll have you—"

"Do shut up," Seamus interrupted in an icy voice.

"Seamus—"

"I said, shut up." Seamus looked furious. In fact, Kirit couldn't remember the last time he had seen the king so angry. A chill snaked along his spine.

Enim merda. He could only hope the fury was directed at Ellar and not at Kirit. Or worse, at Cody. That thought was enough to renew Kirit's growling.

Cody couldn't stop shaking. *What the fuck?* It wasn't like he had been injured badly. Hell, the king's jerk of a cousin had only managed to land one punch before Kirit had gone all snarly on his arse. No big deal, right? Not something that hadn't happened dozens of times in the past. His usual response was anger and indignation. Instead, he was being all weird and freaked out.

It only took a minute for him to realize he wasn't scared for himself. No, the so-called attack wasn't all that big of an issue. It was Kirit he was worried about.

The big guy had actually tried to kill a member of the royal family. That wasn't good.

Cody clutched tighter to his mate, watching Seamus warily. He couldn't read the expression on the king's face. It was blank and impassive as he leaned over and offered a hand to his cousin. Seamus hauled Ellar to his feet—then, in the next motion, grabbed him in a move quite similar to Kirit's.

"Know this," Seamus snarled, doing an impressive imitation of a Draak. He slammed his nephew into the wall, digging his fingers into the younger man's neck. Ellar gasped for air in a grim parody of the way Cody had minutes before. "The only reason you're still breathing is because, as much as I might dislike the reality, you are kin. But touch the Draak's mate again—touch *anyone's* mate again—and I won't interfere. I'll allow Kirit to rip out your insides and the only thing I'll concern myself with will be who is stuck cleaning up the mess."

He yanked his hand away, watching dispassionately as Ellar fell to the ground, choking and coughing for a second time as he tried to get air into his tortured lungs. With a last disdainful look, Seamus turned and walked out of the room. His grand exit wasn't hampered in the slightest by the audience that had gathered outside.

"Damn," Cody said. "Remind me not to piss him off."

Kirit was, by this point, almost squeezing the air out of *Cody's* lungs. The only reason Cody didn't protest was because he could feel the tension still running through the dragon's big frame.

"He had best listen," Kirit said. The growl wasn't quite gone from his voice and his fangs were still extended, giving him a slight lisp when he spoke.

Instead of making him sound weak, it added an additional element of menace to his tone. "Next time, I'll do just what Seamus said and damn the consequences. My jewel. Mine!"

Cody patted the arms circling him reassuringly. He seemed to be doing that a lot lately. "We know," he said. "Now why don't you take me back to our rooms and fuck me into the mattress?"

It was the best way Cody knew to soothe the beast Ellar had raised in his lover.

Kirit gave one last vicious snarl before dragging Cody from the room. Behind them, a litany of shouts erupted. Cody tried to get a look over his shoulder to find out what was going on, but Kirit was moving too fast.

When Cody tripped for the third time, he dug in his heels.

"Slow down, big guy," he ordered.

Kirit slowed, but only long enough to grab Cody around the waist. Cody's yell echoed throughout the marble halls as Kirit tossed him into the air. All the breath whooshed from his lungs as he landed on Kirit's shoulder.

Sheesh. Here we go again.

It seemed like he spent far too much of his time draped over Kirit's shoulder.

The dragon started moving again, practically running down the hall. Then they were free of the palace, the sun bearing down on them with searing heat, and Kirit *was* running.

If Kirit tried to take flight, they were going to have words. Not-nice words.

"Kirit…where…would you sto…ugh."

Cody gave up trying to speak. The jouncing made it a painful, rather fruitless, endeavor.

"Kirit!"

The bellow sounded like Raven. A pissed-off Raven.

Kirit still didn't stop. It was entirely possible he didn't even hear the other man. He seemed focused on making his escape and dragging Cody along for the ride.

They left the palace grounds through the east gate. The soldiers guarding the entrance moved out of their way. They passed through shadow as they went through the massive curtain wall, then they were back in sunlight and plunging down the hill, gaining momentum at a frightening speed. They hit the bottom and Kirit kept going straight into the trees.

Ooh, goody, outdoor sex. Cody was a fan.

The thick tree cover was a welcome change from the unrelenting sun. The air was cool and damp, smelling strongly of must and leaves. They didn't go far before Kirit slowed. One tree looked pretty much the same as another to Cody, but Kirit found one that apparently passed inspection. He dropped Cody at the base, then followed suit. Cody grunted as the familiar weight of his dragon landed on top.

"Easy, big guy. I'm right here, huh?"

Kirit growled, capturing Cody's mouth in a bruising kiss. Cody lay back and let the dragon have his way. Cody heard the tell-tale sound of ripping as Kirit went to work on his clothes.

"Hey, none of that." Cody tried to push Kirit away. "I'm not walking back to the palace butt-naked. Give me a second."

Kirit didn't seem to even notice that Cody was talking. He worked with clumsy, frantic motions at the fastenings on Cody's clothing. Cody decided to help before he was left wearing scraps. The shirt was a loss, but the tights — which he was never, ever wearing again—were stretchy. They slid off more or less in one piece until they hit his boots.

"Kirit."

Kirit was busy nibbling on Cody's neck. The caress was slightly scratchy and Kirit's tongue was longer than usual.

"Oh, damn," Cody whispered. Then he yanked on Kirit's hair until he could connect their mouths again. He loved kissing his mate when Kirit was losing control of his human form. Something about that forked dragon tongue...

Trailing his mouth back up, Kirit pressed light kisses around Cody's sore eye. The tenderness in the gesture was at odds with the harsh, grasping touch of Kirit's hands. The dichotomy was extremely arousing, and Cody was hard and leaking pre-cum, which seemed to please Kirit a great deal.

It was over almost before it began. Cody would swear Kirit used magic to undress—one second he was fully clothed, and in the next came the delightful press of naked skin. Kirit latched onto Cody's shoulder with sharp teeth, growling low as he rubbed against Cody.

The heat of Kirit's penis was scorching against Cody's belly. Cody tried to slow Kirit down, but the big dragon was single-minded in his purpose. Cody could only hang on and let Kirit soothe his possessive streak.

They humped and bucked, writhing on the ground in a tangle of limbs. Gasps melded with the rush of the wind through the branches. The noises Kirit made became less and less human as the passion built. In the dappled sunlight, Cody could see the flex and play of muscle, highlighted by the flow and retreat of glittering scales. He rubbed the nearest patch, loving the feel. Surprisingly pliable, the scales were warm and scratchy beneath his fingers. He found one patch in particular, right behind Kirit's ear, which made the dragon rumble in bliss. He kept up a steady pressure, earning another frantic melding of lips and tongue.

Cody's climax crashed over him with unstoppable force. He shouted, sending several birds into flight, and grabbed onto Kirit, clinging tightly. Kirit stiffened, too, and for one endless moment, Cody couldn't breathe. Kirit's weight pressed him into the ground, debris digging into his back. Cody barely noticed, preoccupied with riding out the waves of his orgasm. Kirit rubbed a few more times then collapsed. Cody grunted and pushed until Kirit rolled to one side.

Holy shit. It was fast and brutal and Cody loved every single second. He lay on his back in the leaves, panting and sweating. Cody stroked Kirit's chest as he tried to catch his breath. The heated skin under his fingertips was slick with sweat, Kirit also breathed heavily from exertion.

"Wow," he said to the tree branches overhead.

"Hmmm." Kirit's hum sounded quite satisfied. Cody just knew his lover was smirking.

"Feel better now?" Cody teased.

Kirit rumbled happily, the sound not the slightest bit human.

"You did good," Cody said. "Wanna go again?"

Kirit turned his head, eyes widening in disbelief. "You can become aroused again? After that?"

"Give me a few minutes." More like a few hours, but teasing Kirit was just so much fun.

"We don't have time," Kirit said. "Someone will come looking soon. Besides, you need to pack."

"Pack? What for?"

"We are returning to the mountains. Tonight."

Reality intruded on Cody's post-sex euphoria. "The ambassadors still haven't arrived."

"I no longer care." Kirit turned on his side, staring at Cody with fierce possessiveness. "You were harmed." He brushed the backs of his fingers across Cody's cheek, again caressing the area where Cody could feel a bruise forming. "I am taking you where you will be safe."

"You can't protect me from everything," Cody said. "Not without locking me into the equivalent of Rapunzel's tower."

"I do not know this Rapunzel, but a tower sounds like an excellent idea."

"Try it and you'll be sorry."

Kirit flopped down next to Cody. He stared up at the trees, running his fingers along Cody's side.

"Promise me," he ordered.

"Promise you what?"

"That you will go nowhere unescorted. I know not why Ellar risked the king's wrath to attack you, but I have never trusted him. He will try again."

"I can take care of myself."

"Promise me."

Cody changed the subject, hoping Kirit wouldn't notice that he'd never actually responded to the demand—he had no intention of dragging a babysitter along everywhere he went. "You know, we're technically still at the capital."

"Hmmm, that's a wonderful idea, mate. We will simply stay here. I am sure I could bribe Chaos to bring us food."

"I bet he would work for voyeur privileges."

"No one looks at you." Kirit didn't sound too snarly, and his features were soft with happiness.

"We've really gotta work on your possessive streak."

"My possessive streak functions quite nicely."

"That's the point," Cody replied.

Cody cuddled into his mate's side. *Yeah, we should just stay here.* This was nice. No one watching, no one wanting something. Just him, his mate and nature. Which was kind of weird in itself, since Cody had never been a big fan of nature before. He'd always been a city boy, but maybe it had more to do with not knowing anything else.

Then a low rumble—one not from his dragon—caught Cody's attention, and he changed his mind about becoming nature-boy.

"Come on, big guy," Cody said, sitting up. "Find my pants. I don't really want to get wet."

Kirit groaned. "Stupid weather. Two weeks of perfect, sunny days, and the one time I want to hide outdoors with my mate, it decides to rain."

"Sorry. Take it up with Seamus. He's the all-powerful king of everything."

"I don't believe even Seamus can do anything about the weather."

"Then what good is he?" Cody muttered. "Can't control the weather, can't control his relatives, hell, can't even deal with diplomats on his own." He really didn't want to go back. But he was shivering a bit. The air was chilling rapidly from the approaching storm. Dark gray encroached on the horizon and lightning broke the solid mass of clouds in the distance.

Kirit huffed. He stood and stretched. He gave Cody a slow kiss and smiled. *Damn, I love how that looks on his face.*

Stepping away, Kirit left the shelter of the trees for the more open spaces between the forest and the palace. A dull flash of light burned Cody's eyes and he closed them.

"Warn a guy, will you."

A low chuff was his only answer. Cody opened his eyes and made his own low noise, this one of pure irritation.

"What the hell, Kirit?"

Reptilian eyes blinked at him, the long, narrow head tilting to one side.

"Don't give me that look," Cody grumbled, fishing his tights out of a nearby bush. It took him a few tugs to free the fabric, along with a few new rips and tears. "Goddamn stuff is worse than pantyhose." And he should know — he'd done his share of drag back in the day. Heels made his legs look *awesome*.

Thunder rumbled again, much closer this time. Kirit shook his wings out and stared at Cody.

"Hell, no," Cody said. "I'd rather get wet." He was never flying without an airplane again.

Kirit grumbled, the sound amusingly human, strange coming out of that sharp-teethed muzzle. Really, Kirit's dragon was a rather amusing creature. His legs were too short, body too long, his face a near perfect triangle. With the oversized eyes and his habit of sitting oh-so-properly, front feet together, he looked a bit like a scaly cat. With wings. It was a weird combination. A lizard-cat.

With no warning, the clouds suddenly burst, depositing their heavy load like an upturned bucket. A bottomless bucket. Cody was instantly soaked.

Kirit herded him to the edge of the trees. Cody watched, jealous, as the water slid off Kirit's iridescent scales. The foliage cleared some, and Kirit stretched his wings out again, providing a make-shift umbrella for Cody. They went a little bit farther, Kirit waddling and off-balance. Cody couldn't help the fit of giggles, even though it made Kirit blow smoke out his nose. Dragons really weren't meant to be land-bound.

Instead of heading for the palace, Kirit found a spot that seemed to pass his inspection—not that it looked any different from anywhere else. Cody wasn't going to argue, though. He hadn't spent a lot of time with Kirit in his dragon form—except for that day he'd found Kirit in the bathing room—a dragon in a bathtub was quite the sight—but he knew it was no fun to argue with something that couldn't argue back.

Kirit plopped down on the soggy ground and assumed that cat pose of his, front feet together, tail wrapped around his lower body. Cody shook his head in amusement, but took up the offer of shelter. He shoved at Kirit's feet, avoiding the nasty hooked claws, until he could snuggle up between Kirit's front legs. Kirit ducked his head and wrapped his wings around them both.

"Damn, this is awesome." Water ran down Kirit's wings, visible through the pale, translucent membranes as long streams of a darker color. It was like being in a really fantastic tent, dry and almost hot with all the heat Kirit's body produced in this form.

Kirit rumbled, a very happy sound, and rubbed his muzzle along the top of Cody's head.

"Watch the teeth."

Kirit rumbled again, what Cody figured was a dragon's version of laughter. Despite the storm raging outside, Kirit seemed more content than he had in quite a while. Cody settled in for a good cuddle and listened to the wind blow, safe and protected with his dragon.

He could definitely grow to like this side of his mate. Of course, eventually the storm would pass and they would have to go back to the palace. But that was a worry for later. For now, Cody would snuggle and try to dream up ways to duck the escort he just knew Kirit would put to watching him.

Chapter Twenty-One

This is utterly ridiculous.

Cody poked his head into the hallway, looking left, then right. Once assured that the coast was clear, he made his escape.

This time, he almost made it out of the wing before he could feel someone watching him.

Cody stopped, his boots squeaking on the slick floor. He heaved a dramatic sigh, making sure the sound carried through the empty corridor.

It worked. Nyx appeared in front of him, seemingly from nowhere. Cody didn't bother to ask. The Draak reveled in being enigmatic and Cody wouldn't be able to get a straight answer. He knew this. He'd tried.

"You can stop following me already," he told Nyx.

"No, I can't," Nyx retorted. "Kirit insists. Sorry, but he's scarier than you are."

Cody glared. "Are you sure about that?"

"Kirit is going to smother you. Accept it."

Cody wasn't sure who he wanted to smack more, Nyx or Kirit. "I can take care of myself."

"Experience says otherwise."

Cody would argue, but that would be hard considering he still sported the damning evidence. He had developed a nice shiner from where Ellar had slugged him. It was embarrassing, damn it. Cody was usually faster than that.

"He took me by surprise," Cody said with a scowl. "I wasn't expecting to be accosted ten feet from the king. I'm ready for the bastard now, though."

"Of course you are."

Nyx clearly didn't believe him. Cody couldn't blame him all that much. Like Nyx had so nicely pointed out, his track record so far wasn't fantastic.

Cody uttered a few choice curses under his breath when he heard footsteps coming their way. Nyx had that look on his face, the 'I'm going to lecture you now' look. All the Draak did it well. Except for Chaos, who was usually on the same end of those looks as Cody.

The gardens were visible through an opening to his left, so Cody headed that way, knowing Nyx would follow. They *always* followed.

"I haven't seen you around in a while," Cody said over his shoulder. He was the curious sort, but he also wouldn't mind diverting the coming conversation.

"Seamus sent me to track down the wayward Eviatt contingent."

"I don't think they really exist," Cody speculated. "I mean, Seamus has been talking about them since I've arrived, but have you seen any sign of foreign ambassadors? Because I sure as hell haven't."

Nyx snorted. "You may be right. I certainly couldn't find them."

"I wish they'd hurry up so we could leave."

"Huh."

Cody turned his head to take in the surprise on Nyx's face. He looked forward again when he tripped over a loose stone in the path, only to get whacked in the face with a thick patch of greenery. *Damn.* He was swiftly coming to the conclusion that nature wasn't his thing. Even the carefully cultivated, civilized gardens hated him.

But then he thought of the forest yesterday, and he grinned. Maybe not *all* nature was bad.

"What's up with the surprised face?" Cody rounded a corner as he asked the question and saw a bench up ahead. He claimed it quickly. It was easier to concentrate on a conversation when he didn't have to battle the garden at the same time.

"I don't know. I suppose I assumed you would prefer the luxuries available at the palace. Kirit does live in a cave, after all. A very nice cave, true, but it *is* still a cave."

"I wouldn't know," Cody complained. "Since I have yet to see it. Either way, if it comes down to a choice between a cave and the lovely group of staring, inquisitive idiots inside, I'll take the cave, thank you very much." Which wasn't entirely fair. Some of them had been quite nice yesterday, at least before Ellar had started that fight.

"I can't say I blame you for that." Nyx paused, pursing his lips.

Here it comes.

"Kirit only wants to keep you safe."

Yep, just as he thought. The dragons were nearly impossible to distract when they had an idea in their heads.

Well, nearly *impossible. I know a few tried and true methods to distract one particular Draak...*

"You're a mate," Nyx continued.

"Here we go again." Cody shook his head, more in amusement than irritation. "I think I've had this conversation before. Several times."

"You're special."

Cody gave up. "It's like talking to one of those blasted dolls," he told a big, pink flowery bush. "They just repeat the same thing over and over. Irritating, dense dragons."

"Indeed."

Cody yelped, catching himself before he tumbled off the bench. "God, would you people stop *doing* that?"

It wasn't proper to glare at a king, but Cody couldn't bring himself to care. After all, Seamus certainly didn't. *And if he did, then he would stop* sneaking up on people!

Seamus chuckled. Uninvited, he took a seat on the stone bench next to Cody. "The dragons are a bit single-minded, as I'm sure you've noticed. I've found it to be a useful, albeit annoying, personality trait."

"I resent that," Nyx said.

The king waved a hand. "Resentment duly noted. Now, go away. I wish to speak with Cody in private for a moment."

Nyx opened his mouth, most likely to protest, but the king cut him off with a stern glare. Cody didn't think he was imagining the humor lurking in Seamus' eyes.

"I promise to escort him safely back to the palace."

Yep, there was amusement in his voice. Cody felt his mood lighten abruptly as the ridiculousness of the whole thing hit him.

"I suppose so." Nyx said the words slowly, reluctance obvious.

"Oh, go away, already," Cody ordered. "Or I'll demonstrate why you don't need to worry about my safety."

Seamus laughed, the sound booming and unrestrained. Nyx finally obeyed, but only after one last warning glare in Cody's direction.

"They are certainly protective."

"Like jail wardens," Cody muttered. "I can't turn around without tripping over one."

"I don't believe they quite know what to make of you. It's been a very long time since one of the Draak mated, and then it was to a woman. While Elena was a strong woman in her own way, she was perfectly content with her role in life."

"And what was that?" Cody almost didn't want to ask, but he knew it would bug him if he didn't.

"A…helpmeet, for lack of a better term. I believe it would be called a housewife on Earth. She ensured Raven's home was in order and would have never thought to argue with him, let alone disobey. He was the head of the household, and in truth, I believe she preferred it that way."

"*Raven?*" Cody asked, astonished. "Raven was *mated?* To a *girl?*"

"Ummm. Many years ago."

"What happened to her?"

"She died," Seamus said shortly. The expression on his face discouraged further questions.

Cody was reckless, but he wasn't stupid, so he didn't push.

"I believe that's partially why they are all so protective. Elena's death devastated the entire clutch. They don't handle change well, and they handle loss even worse."

"I understand, but I'm not Elena."

"No, you most certainly are not."

Cody couldn't figure out if he was being insulted or complimented.

"This is not why I sought you out," Seamus said abruptly. "I wanted to extend my apologies for the...incident yesterday. Ellar's behavior was inexcusable. I cannot imagine what possessed him to attack you, in full sight of my court and I, no less. Ellar is far from the most intelligent Fae in the palace, but I wouldn't have said he was quite that stupid, either."

"Hatred doesn't leave much room for intelligence," Cody said. "And I might have provoked him. Just a bit."

Okay, so it was maybe more than a bit. No one would be happy being called a flat-faced, back-ass-wards son of a donkey. Or something along those lines, anyway—Cody honestly couldn't remember what he'd said. He had been irritated at the time and not really giving his words due consideration. Ellar had been snide, Cody had snapped, and then there had been some blood.

"Be that as it may, he should have known better. Or at the very least, controlled himself. He may technically be superior in standing, but he should know by now that I like you more than I do him."

"Wouldn't your court be thrilled with that pronouncement?"

"My court can kiss my ass."

Cody choked and stared in shock. "Good lord, who are you and what have you done with the king?"

Seamus chuckled, his smile just this side of wicked. "My nobles are a necessary evil. I stroke their egos on occasion, then do precisely what I wish. They remain happy in their oblivion and I can return to ignoring them for a time."

The word 'stroke' had Cody's mind dropping into the gutter. He had to blink rapidly a few times to rid himself of the mental image that popped up.

"I really don't want to know what you and that bunch get up to in your spare time."

"And I am not even going to pretend to understand that statement. Kirit came to see me this morning."

Cody blinked at the rapid subject change. "Huh?"

"Kirit came to see me." Seamus smiled. "He was quite prepared to wrap you up and spirit you away. I believe he had visions of you, him, and an isolated mountain. I also believe he had no intention of returning, possibly for centuries."

"Overprotective, possessive idiot." Cody said the words fondly, though.

"He's a dragon. They can't help themselves. I convinced him, however, to remain for a few more days. There is an event tonight that requires your presence."

"Because heaven forbid I look like I'm running."

Seamus' expression of surprise was not at all flattering.

"What?" Cody rolled his eyes. "Frankly, they remind me of the crowd I used to hang around with back on earth. All the posturing and bullshit. It's all about appearances, I get that."

"Indeed." Seamus looked pleased. "I will depend on you, then, to keep Kirit in line, shall I?"

"I'll try, but no promises." Hell, if anyone started anything, it just might be Kirit keeping Cody in line.

"This will be a more formal affair than those prior, so I suggest you consult Desmond as to clothing. Nyx or Raven would also serve. Whatever you do, please do not ask Chaos."

Cody winced. "God, no. That man has absolutely no sense of taste."

"I resent that!"

"How does he *do* that?" Cody asked.

Seamus stood. Cody stood, also. "I will bid you good-day, dragon-mate."

"See ya around."

The king turned to go.

"Oh, wait!" Cody called. "Before I forget..."

"Oh, no you don't!" Chaos quite literally popped out of a bush. "My real name is a deep, dark secret and Seamus is not sharing it."

Seamus just laughed and walked away. Before he vanished, though, he turned and winked in Cody's direction.

"I'll find out eventually," Cody promised Chaos. "So, this event. What should I know about it?"

Chaos' grin was a little frightening. He took Cody's arm and steered him back into one of the palace's connecting hallways.

"Seamus holds them periodically. I believe he gains some perverse amusement in putting all his opposition in one place so he can watch them jostle for position. There's drinking, dancing and hours of polite conversation between people who would really rather stick each other with sharp objects."

"So, a party," Cody clarified dryly. "Oh, joy. Any chance I can get in and out without being seen?" He sighed in frustration as a bunch of ornately dressed men parted to let him through. It didn't escape his notice that they worked very hard to avoid brushing against him. It seems the gossip mongers were working overtime, considering the wary way people looked at him.

"Likely not. I would help you hide and avoid the torture entirely, but I don't believe it's optional," Chaos said. "Seamus yelled a lot the last time I tried to skip attending one of his gatherings. It was kind of scary."

"That's what I thought." A yelling Seamus. Cody shuddered at the thought. "Where are we going?"

"Clothes," Chaos said cheerfully.

"You really don't listen to a word anyone says, do you?"

"Not at all. Life is more fun that way."

Chapter Twenty-Two

Kirit was literally vibrating with tension. He had never experienced such a thing before, and it was annoying. He never imagined having a mate would be so stressful. He had already picked a fight with Nyx once today, and let Chaos pick a fight with him. It hadn't helped. And now he was trapped in this crowded room, with Seamus' 'court', and all he wanted was to snatch his mate from their clutches and hide.

"Tone it down."

Kirit hadn't heard Raven arrive, but the warning in his voice was clear.

"I'm fine."

"You're growling."

Oh, so he was. Kirit swallowed several times, trying to stop the incessant rumbling. *There, better.*

For a few minutes, at least.

"Are you certain he's worth it?" Raven asked.

The growling began again, louder than ever, as Kirit turned to glare at his former friend. "He's perfect!"

"Then why are you so touchy?"

Kirit looked away, still growling.

"He's human. I know you want to fit him into your life, but it might not—"

"He's mine. I'm not giving him up."

Raven rubbed at the back of his neck. "I'm not asking you to. I'm only wondering if the Fae court is the best place for the two of you. Cody is uncomfortable, and you're seeing threats around every corner."

"Seamus won't let me leave," Kirit said. "Three days, he promised."

"You can last that long, surely? Then you can take your mate to your hideaway. Or...well, there's always Tamalla."

"I am *not* living in Tamalla." Kirit wrinkled his nose in disgust.

A rapidly growing city some distance from the capital, Tamalla embraced all things Earth. He'd been there once, and that was enough. If Kirit had wanted to live like that, he would have stayed on the other side of the Veil. At least there, everything was real, and not just an illusion or a pale imitation. Besides, Kirit loved Faerie and their ancient traditions. He had no desire to embrace the so-called 'modern world'.

"Kirit, he's not happy," Raven continued. Kirit wondered how much trouble he would be in if he tackled his commander. What point, exactly, was Raven trying to make? Kirit *couldn't* leave.

"So long as he's unhappy," Raven continued, oblivious to Kirit's rising annoyance, "You'll be unhappy. The last thing this court needs is an unhappy Draak."

"I'm completely happy," Kirit insisted stubbornly, just to be contrary.

Raven grunted. "If this is happy, then I'm a flying monkey."

What? Kirit looked at Raven in confusion. "I don't—"

"Know what that means," Raven finished. "You've been spending too much time with Chaos."

Kirit rumbled happily. "It's quality time. I think I broke his nose this afternoon."

"You two are going to drive me insane."

"Too late, old man," Chaos called cheerfully. He trotted up to them and smacked Raven on the shoulder. The bigger man stumbled forward a step from the force of the blow. "You left sanity behind long, long ago."

"Why couldn't you have broken his jaw instead of his nose?" Raven asked Kirit.

"He's a quick little bastard," Kirit retorted.

"Hey, K, you should go rescue Cody. Last I saw, he was hiding out in a corner. Go ask him to dance or something."

"I don't dance," Kirit replied. And damn, but that sounded a lot more pompous out loud than it had in his head.

"You were dancing quite nicely a few days ago."

Kirit didn't bother to dignify the comment with a reply.

"Go on."

Chaos gave him a push. Kirit was tempted to dig in his heels, but...well, it *had* been a while since he had sought out his mate. He wouldn't mind a quick cuddle. Maybe a kiss. And if they ended up leaving the gathering early, that would be all right, too.

With a short nod, Kirit left his clutch-mates without another word. Chaos called out something about rudeness. Since it was coming from Chaos, Kirit ignored the words.

He wove through the small crowd with ease, mostly because people stepped aside when they saw him coming. There were definite advantages to being a Draak, particularly one with his reputation. Not only was he considered an extremely dangerous warrior, but he was also known to be cranky and snarly. And that was on a good day. It kept people at a nice distance. Kirit was quite happy with the system. If he had to be stuck at the palace, the least people could do was leave him alone.

Kirit found Cody in a corner, just as Chaos had said. His mate was leaning against the wall, sipping a glass of clear liquid. He didn't notice Kirit immediately, so Kirit took the opportunity to study his beautiful lover. It wasn't often that Kirit had the chance to simply look.

Cody wore the clothes of Kirit's world well, the snug black leather pants showcasing his long legs. The pants were tucked into shiny knee-high boots, which did an equally nice job showcasing his calves. A red and black tunic stretched tightly across his shoulders. Belted at the waist, the fabric was pulled taut over his chest and was just short enough that sometimes, when he moved, Kirit could see hints of his package, cupped lovingly by the pants.

The red of his tunic only accentuated his mate's beauty, in Kirit's unbiased opinion. His dark hair had been carefully spiked, the color of his clothing bringing out the hints of red in his brown locks. He had gained a bit more color to his skin as well, most likely from the time spent outside watching the soldiers. Each day, he came and observed the training for longer periods. Chaos said he watched them with longing, but Kirit dismissed that as ridiculous. His mate was most definitely *not* a fighter.

The lovely golden tan brushing Cody's skin made his eyes seem even greener. Kirit loved those eyes which seemed to see everything, and sparkled brighter than any jewel with life and happiness.

Normally, anyway. Kirit noted with a scowl that, at this particular moment, Cody looked sad and rather lonely. That look had been on his mate's face more and more of late.

Kirit moved to his mate's side and pulled Cody close. It made him purr happily when Cody automatically sunk into the embrace.

"Greetings, my own," Kirit said, nuzzling behind Cody's ear.

"Mmm. Where have you been?"

"Talking to Raven."

Another noncommittal sound. Cody didn't move out of Kirit's arms, but he did keep sipping his drink and watching the crowd. Kirit searched his mind for something, anything, to cheer up his most precious jewel.

"Would you dance with me?" The words popped out before Kirit could stop them. He winced inwardly.

Cody patted Kirit's arm with his free hand. "That's okay, lover-boy. I'm fine right here."

Kirit's furrowed his brow as he struggled with his words. Damn, but he was horrible at this. Clearly, his mate needed soothing. Too bad Kirit didn't know how to soothe. Maybe he could find something to kill...he could bring back some weapons as a trophy. Would his mate like that?

"You're growling again," Cody said. "I'm fine, Kirit, honest. Just tired, I guess."

"Then we must return to our chambers," Kirit declared immediately. "You should rest."

"Rest." Amusement radiated from Cody. "Is that what we're calling it now?"

"Oh, hush," Kirit scolded gently. And his cheeks were most emphatically *not* hot.

A low buzz started across the room. Kirit caught a flash of green and knew Seamus had arrived. He looked from Seamus back to his mate.

That damned sadness was still in those pretty eyes.

Enough.

"Wait here for a moment," he said quietly. "I will return shortly."

Cody made another of those noncommittal sounds. They were starting to drive Kirit nuts.

With swift, determined strides, he ploughed his way across the room.

"Seamus, we are leaving," he announced before he even stopped in front of his king.

"Oh, is Cody not feeling well?"

"No, not the party," Kirit corrected. "We're going home."

Seamus looked equal parts tired and irritated. "Kirit, I still need—"

"You said a week. I waited two. Then you said four days, and it has been six. I have no more patience. We are leaving."

They were drawing a crowd now, the Fae watching with morbid fascination. His skin crawled, the dragon rising to the surface. He wanted to shift and eat them all. He pictured the throne room engulfed in flames, the thought oh-so-tempting.

Something of his thoughts must have shown on his face, because Seamus suddenly looked alarmed. With a quick motion, he gestured Kirit into the hall. Once out of earshot, he glared at Kirit.

"Calm down," he ordered, steel in his tone.

"Cody is unhappy," Kirit replied, his own voice equally hard.

"Kirit—"

"No. Your insistence on my presence never made any sense, but I was willing to comply. I thought perhaps spending time here would help Cody adjust. But he is bored and miserable and my patience is gone. We will be leaving in the morning. End of discussion."

Seamus' eyes flashed, something dangerous rising in their depths.

Let it. Kirit would welcome the confrontation.

"Remember to whom you are speaking."

Kirit growled and flashed his fangs. His skin prickled again and he knew scales were shimmering into existence along his face and arms.

"Don't test me, dragon."

"I will do what I wish, fairy."

Seamus snarled, the cultured mask falling away to reveal the dangerous creature underneath. Kirit cracked his knuckles and grinned, shifting his weight in preparation.

Loud shouts erupted from the room behind Seamus.

Both men whirled, confrontation forgotten. Desmond appeared in the entranceway, out of breath and looking alarmed.

"Your Highness, the dragon mate—"

Seamus and Kirit pushed past him and headed back into the throne room at a run.

Cody watched Kirit follow Seamus out of the room. He gulped down the last of his wine, then stared into the empty cup morosely.

"How long are you going to keep this up?"

Cody turned to see Nyx surveying him with dissatisfaction.

"Keep what up?" Cody pretended ignorance.

"This whole façade," Nyx said, gesturing at Cody. "What happened to the vibrant man who laid me on the ground when you thought I was attacking Kirit? The one who tramped through a bog while taking to task one of the most powerful creatures in Faerie? The bold and brave Cody who left behind his entire world for a man he barely knew, one who wasn't even human?"

"I think he left his balls in that damned swamp," Cody said, still staring at the bottom of his cup. Nyx growled and snatched the glassware from his hand.

"Oh, do grow up," he ordered. "Self-pity truly does not suit you."

"Is that what this is? I've never experienced it before."

He didn't like it. Nyx had a point. What the hell was he trying to prove? And who was he trying to prove it to?

Well, that last question was easy enough to answer. Kirit. And really, the first one wasn't hard, either. He didn't want Kirit thinking he'd made a mistake. Cody didn't have a whole lot going for him, aside from looks. He knew that. So, he had been trying to make himself into the ideal mate. Someone Kirit wouldn't be ashamed of.

"You know, Kirit fell in love with *you*, not whatever image you are trying to present."

"Kirit didn't fall in love with me at all," Cody retorted, not realizing it was bothering him until the words spilled out. "He fell in love with the idea of a mate. Any mate. I just happened to be the one he found."

Nyx gave Cody a strange look. His mouth twisted, brow wrinkling. "I thought you were smarter than this."

"Oh, go jump in the moat."

"We don't have a moat."

Cody growled.

"There!" Nyx beamed triumphantly. "There you are!"

Cody wondered how much trouble he would get in if he started a fight in the middle of the royal ballroom. It would certainly enliven the dull atmosphere.

Then someone tackled him, and the fight began anyway. Cody slid across the slick marble floor, fetching up against a woman's legs. He knew it was a woman, because he was instantly swallowed in fabric. Cody fought his way free of the massive pile of silk, spitting out pieces of fabric around some creative cursing. Screams and shouts rang out, and Cody distantly thought, *Why the hell does this man keep attacking me in public venues? What kind of an idiot is he?*

"Cody!"

Cody ignored Nyx's shout, finally managing to battle free of the clinging skirts. The woman who owned those skirts was batting at his head with something. A fan, he realized, when he looked up and got whacked in the nose.

"Would you quit it?" he demanded.

"When you get out from under my dress," she screeched in indignation.

"I'm trying, lady."

He stood, but not before receiving a few more hits from the fan.

Nyx skidded to a halt next to him. "What the hell was that about?" he asked, brushing dust off Cody.

"Damned if I know. Who hit me?"

"Him." Nyx gestured over one shoulder with his thumb. Cody really wasn't surprised to see Ellar glaring at him from a few feet away.

"I've had enough," Cody declared. He pushed up the sleeves of his tunic and shrugged his shoulders, then moved his head from side to side until his neck cracked. "Tell Seamus I didn't start it, but I'm damn well going to finish it."

"I feel like I should stop you," Nyx said.

Cody turned and raised one eyebrow questioningly.

Nyx grinned. "Break his nose for me, will you?"

"With pleasure."

Cody stalked across the floor, sight set firmly on Ellar. Some of the smug superiority left Ellar's face, replaced by the first hints of nervousness.

Good. The bastard should be nervous.

"Ten *guldarii* on Cody!" Someone shouted from across the room. Cody thought it was Chaos. He waved one hand in acknowledgement. Then he balled up his fist and slugged Ellar in the jaw.

"I am fed up, you goddamned, arrogant Fae," he said as Ellar landed on his arse. "What the hell are you doing?" He propped his hands on his hips and glared down at the prone nobleman. "Attacking a dragon's mate in the middle of a royal gathering? I mean, really, how dumb *are* you?"

Ellar didn't say anything, but he did make a vague noise of fury before launching himself at Cody. Cody sidestepped, swiping out with one foot. Ellar tripped and took out that same poor lady. She screeched some more. Then she began smacking Ellar with her fan. Cody was amused. In retrospect, laughing probably wasn't the best idea, but he couldn't hold it in.

The lady was muttering in a distinctly unladylike way as she regained her feet. She kicked Ellar in the hip for good measure. Cody was beginning to like her—she was feisty. He grinned, ignoring the indignant glare he received in return. He bowed in her direction.

"Well done, my lady."

She huffed, gathered her skirts in one hand, and shoved through the crowd toward the door. Everyone moved out of her way with alacrity.

Nobody bothered to help Ellar to his feet. That, right there, was pretty telling, to Cody's mind.

"Are we done?" he asked Ellar. "Because this is getting ridiculous."

"Humans have no place in Faerie," Ellar said, standing on unsteady feet. He'd lost a shoe somewhere. "Go back to Earth and leave us in peace."

Cody pinched the bridge of his nose. "Swear to God, Faeries make no sense."

"Cease using that term!"

"Then stop calling me 'human' like it's something nasty."

"It is!"

"Oh, that's it." Cody dropped his hand and moved towards Ellar with purpose. He had been willing to let this go, but now? It was time to show the Fae that humans weren't scum and that Cody, at least, could more than hold his own. He had hoped that time would be enough to gain him acceptance, but he had no problem forcing the issue. If they couldn't accept him then, by God, they could respect him. And if he couldn't get respect, he'd take fear. It worked for Kirit.

Cody let Ellar take the first swing. The blow landed solidly on his chin. Cody shook off the stars, grinned, and hit back. Ellar staggered. Cody followed it up quickly with a kick to the back of his knees. Then he got in a nice groin shot.

What could he say? He'd grown up on the streets. He fought dirty.

Ellar howled in pain. Cody ignored it and kicked him in the stomach. He was rearing back for another blow when strong arms grabbed him around the waist.

"Enough, he is through."

Raven pulled him away from the semi-conscious man.

"Oh, come on. A few more, just for good measure," Cody cajoled.

"I think not."

Cody stilled at Seamus' voice. He watched gleefully as a couple of guys in uniform came and dragged the king's cousin away. Ellar couldn't stand fully upright. It made Cody happy.

It was also rather anticlimactic.

Raven let Cody go as soon as Ellar was out of sight. Cody turned, looking for Kirit. He could hear his dragon growling somewhere nearby. Instead, he saw a group of plainly dressed men staring at him with horror.

"Impeccable timing, gentlemen," Seamus said dryly. Cody squinted at the badges on their tunics. There were several small lumps within the design. He thought they were supposed to be islands, and he sighed, not sure if it was in relief or exasperation.

"What do you know," Chaos declared gleefully. "They really do exist."

Seamus' closed his eyes briefly. Then he pasted on an overly bright smile. "Welcome, men of Eviatt. Shall we begin discussions this evening, or would you prefer to wait for morning?"

Cody took that as his cue. Attention momentarily diverted, he ducked into the crowd.

To his utter shock, he made it out of the room without being stopped by anyone, including Kirit. *Where is my mate?* Cody paused in the hallway, chewing on his lip as he scanned his surroundings. No sign of Kirit. It was quite the change from the last time Cody and Ellar had clashed.

"He went that way."

Cody looked at the man who had spoken, someone he had never met before. The man was Fae, but he had a look of sympathy on his face, rather than one of disdain.

After giving his thanks, Cody jogged in the indicated direction. He followed the hallway to the end and went out of the door into the courtyard, just in time to see a flash of white against the dark sky. He froze and looked up.

Kirit dipped his wings once, then soared out of sight.

"Well, hell," Cody muttered. "What is that all about?"

He reluctantly went back inside. Bed. It was definitely time for bed. And hopefully his wayward mate would show up sooner rather than later.

Chapter Twenty-Three

"What are you doing?"

Cody didn't look up from his book. "What does it look like, idiot?"

Chaos snatched the book from Cody's hands and used it to smack him on the shoulder. "Pouting, that's what. The ambassadors are here, you completely beat the hell out of Ellar, so why are we not happy?"

"I don't know why *you're* not happy," Cody retorted. "But me? *I'm* not happy because I have a crabby dragon in my suite."

Chaos plopped down on top of a nearby table. The delicate, carved wooden legs groaned in protest and Cody watched carefully. He really wanted to see Chaos get dumped on his ass.

"So, what's wrong with Kirit now?"

Cody shook his head. "It's stupid."

"This is Kirit, of course it's stupid. Let me guess. He's all fussy because he didn't get to play the hero."

"You do know him well."

It was infuriating. The last time Cody was attacked, they'd had hot and wild sex afterwards. This time,

Kirit just grunted a lot. He had come back after his flight, taken a quick bath then vanished again. Cody had only seen him in passing since then. He assumed the arrival of the Eviatt ambassadors meant they could go home soon, but he wasn't certain, since apparently Kirit wasn't speaking to him at the moment.

"Kirit insists on seeing me as the helpless damsel," Cody complained. "I'm not, but he wants me to be, and it's driving me crazy. Nyx even lectured me on it last night. Says I shouldn't try to be somebody I'm not just to please Kirit. But when I'm myself, Kirit gets crabby. I can't win."

"Sure you can. We just need a plan."

"Why don't I like the sound of that?"

"Because *you* know *me* well."

"Too well."

"Come on, it will be fun."

"Fun. Right."

"Let's go for a walk."

Chaos didn't wait for an answer. He grabbed Cody's elbow and pulled him from the chair, then out of the door.

"I've been reading all these stories from Earth. About dragons and humans and knights."

"Oh, good Lord." Cody didn't like where this was going.

"Just listen," Chaos insisted, still hauling Cody down the hallway. Cody thought about trying to dig in his heels, but he knew from experience that Chaos was a lot stronger than he looked. "So in all those stories, they leave a sacrifice for the dragon. It's stupid, obviously, because what in the name of the realms would I do with a virgin? I like my partners a little bit more...worldly than that, if you get my meaning."

"Too much information, Chaos."

"My point here is the damsel-in-distress trope. We can use that."

"In case you haven't noticed, I'm not a damsel," Cody pointed out wryly. "And no, I will *not* put on a dress."

"You would look pretty damn good in a dress. You have the delicate—"

"Finish that sentence and I'm pushing you off the first balcony I see."

"Stay on topic. If we set you up as a sacrifice, then Kirit can rescue you. A little backwards, true, but I think it could work. Kirit would get to be the hero and then he would cease pouting."

"I thought the goal here was to be myself." Cody wasn't sure about the wisdom of this plan. In fact, he rather thought it was a bad idea. After all, it was *Chaos'* idea.

"Yes, but dragons don't deal well with change, and Kirit is worse than most. You need to ease him into accepting your independence. If we can placate him for the time being, then get the two of you out of this blasted palace, you should have all the time you need to work on his attitude."

"I don't know. The whole thing seems rather counter-intuitive."

"And that is why it will work."

"I'm not sure I follow your logic."

The idea was growing on Cody, though. Kirit needed to be, well, needed. He'd been deprived of the opportunity to rescue Cody from Ellar, and he hadn't taken it well that Cody could look out for himself. *If we do this right, it could certainly smooth out some of Kirit's ruffled feathers...er, scales.*

"I know I'm going to regret this, but okay."

"Excellent!"

Cody immediately wanted to take back his agreement. Anytime Chaos looked that excited, something usually went horribly awry. He didn't recant the words, though, and less than a quarter of an hour later, he found himself following Chaos out beyond the boundaries of the palace's walls and into the hills, after a brief detour for some rope. The rope made Cody nervous.

They hiked up a steep incline to a hill that looked…damaged. Like someone had sheared the top off it at one point. Jagged rocks pointed to the sky, a stark contrast to the rest of the pastoral landscape.

"Here we go," Chaos announced. "This will do nicely."

Cody sighed. "Okay, let's get this over with."

"It will work, I promise."

They hadn't counted on the ogre.

* * * *

The creature heading Cody's direction was extremely ugly and extremely large. The hunched shoulders rested just under the large ears that protruded from the side of its misshapen head. Two large tusks curled up out of black lips and a wide hooked nose completed the picture. It looked dangerous. And irritated. Or was irritated as an ogre could look, with those inflexible features.

At least, he thought it was an ogre. Cody couldn't be certain, since he'd never seen an ogre before. They weren't exactly a common sight in Denver.

"Shit. Fuck. Damn." Cody ran through ever curse he knew—and a few he made up on the spot—as he struggled against the ropes. They held him firmly against the huge rock, and all he managed to do was scrape his elbows raw. Damn that Chaos, anyway. The idiot was entirely too good at tying knots.

The fact that Cody had agreed to this entire scheme was beside the point.

The ogre came to a stumbling halt, blinking tiny eyes at Cody. Cody froze and hoped that ogres were kind of like the T-Rex in Jurassic Park—if he didn't move, maybe it wouldn't see him.

The ogre roared, an ear-jarring sound.

"Damn it," Cody said again. "I guess ogres aren't anything like dinosaurs. Just my luck."

He wriggled again, trying to dig his nails into the edges of the knot holding his wrists together. Muscles screamed in protest as he contorted himself in unnatural ways, scrabbling ineffectually to pull the ropes apart.

He felt something give just as the ogre broke into a shambling run.

A bellow echoed over the hills. Kirit ignored it, too focused on pounding information out of his irritating clutch-mate.

Chaos, on the other hand, froze and cocked his head, apparently oblivious to the fist ready to slam into his nose. "Was that an ogre?"

Grunting in annoyance, Kirit lowered his arm. "Really? You have to ask?"

"Oh, shite, it *was* an ogre."

Chaos broke free of Kirit's hold and ran in the direction of the sound.

"Most sane people run *away* from ogres, not toward them," Kirit yelled after him.

"Cody!"

That one word sent panic racing through Kirit, especially as he had been trying without success to pry Cody's location out of Chaos for the last fifteen minutes. He took off after Chaos and quickly outpaced him as another bellow split the silence.

The pair crested the nearest rise, gaining a clear view into the valley below. Kirit let out a roar of his own, heart almost stopping at the sight.

Cody sprinted in their direction, coming down the hill on the other side of the small depression. A massive ogre followed right on his heels, each step making the ground tremble. Goddamn it, Kirit had told Seamus they should clear out the ogre nest near the city. But no, Seamus insisted they were creatures of nature and had just as much right to live there as anyone else.

In Kirit's opinion, they were stupid, smelly and dangerous pests. He rather thought the current situation demonstrated his point nicely. He would have been more pleased it if wasn't Cody being pursued by one of said pests.

Cody spotted them and altered course. It was an odd sort of race, the tiny human and the oversized ogre. The ogre, unfortunately, was winning. After all, it could cover as much distance in one step as Cody could in twenty. This ogre was big enough to have some giant blood in it, not that giants would interbreed with ogres.

Shaking off the inconsequential thoughts, Kirit stopped running.

"Kirit?" Chaos yelled. "What are you doing?"

Kirit just growled in response, then let go of his human form. The world snapped into focus, everything sharper and clearer than before. He shook out his wings and took to the sky, quickly drawing near to Cody's pursuer.

Even for an ogre, the thing was ugly. Green-tinted skin wrinkled along an oversized skull. A set of lopsided tusks were prominently displayed. The way they bulged should have been comical, but instead increased the menace factor. The huge mouth gaped as the thing roared.

Kirit roared back. He was louder.

The ogre stumbled in its awkward run and furrowed its prominent brow. Kirit roared again, adding a little heat this time. Then he dove, swooping around the creature and raking his claws along its hunched shoulders. The ogre turned in circles, confused.

Meanwhile, Cody had taken shelter in a ditch. He began to pelt the ogre with rocks. One smacked Kirit between the eyes and he huffed irritably.

You are not *helping, mate,* he thought.

Another stone whacked his wing. The distance was impressive. The way it threw him off balance was not. Wonderful, he was being felled by his own side.

"Chaos, would you please *take away my mate's arsenal?"* He bellowed mentally at his clutch-mate. Chaos' amusement came through the link loud and clear, even without words.

"What's the matter, Kirit? Scared of a few rocks?"

"Chaos!"

Below, Chaos cupped his hands over his mouth and yelled, "Cody! Get over here!"

"This is your fault, Chaos!" Cody yelled back. He threw another chunk of rock. Kirit managed to dodge this one, and it hit its intended target. The ogre growled in annoyance.

"How is this my fault?" Chaos yelled.

"It was your fucking idea!"

"Would you please stop arguing and get my mate out of here?" Kirit didn't know which one was more

irritating, his clutch-mate or his Treasure. Both of them were getting locked up for the next six months. In separate rooms, because clearly putting the two of them together was not a good plan.

"I'm doing the best I can."

"No, you're not. You're yelling at him across the field while I avoid projectiles and an angry ogre."

Kirit felt sorry for the poor ogre. It was grumbling and turning in circles, thoroughly befuddled. It kept swiping futilely at the air. Then Cody shouted, and that instant of distraction was all it took. The ogre slammed one massive fist into Kirit's back. Kirit roared in pain, spiraling out of control. He vaguely heard Cody screaming his name, but he was too focused on trying not to slam headfirst into the ground. Agony radiated up and down his spine, making it almost impossible to coordinate his wings. He floundered, gained a little ground—and went down. Hard.

Dirt sprayed up around Kirit as he skidded along the grass, digging up a nice, deep furrow. He finally ploughed to a halt with a loud crash. He lay there, gasping for breath, and trying to decide which part of his body hurt the worst. His conclusion was everything.

Stupid ogre. Stupid Chaos. Stupid me.

Kirit made an abortive effort to rise, but only ended flopping around on the ground like a beached whale. *I am never going to hear the end of this tale. Laid low by a thrice-cursed ogre, of all things.*

And his mate. Kirit couldn't forget his beloved mate, or his mate's rocks.

"Kirit!" Cody dropped to the ground next to him and placed one small hand on Kirit's still-heaving side. "Are you hurt? Oh, God, I think you're bleeding!"

"Cody, get back." Chaos appeared and dragged Cody away. "Hurt dragons aren't exactly rational."

"It's Kirit, you dumbass." Cody broke free and came right back. "Besides, you have an ogre to worry about."

Chaos spat a nice, dirty word in Latin. Kirit agreed. He renewed his struggle to regain his feet. No matter how badly he hurt, his mate needed protection. It was an ogre, how bad could the damage truly be?

Another shaft of pain ripped through Kirit and he stopped moving. So, perhaps he was wrong. That type of ache was most definitely not minor.

"Stop moving, you idiot," Cody said. "Would it help if you changed back?"

It would. But there was still the ogre. He could feel the approaching vibrations in the ground. The ogre might have been confused and bewildered, but it was still intent on its prey.

"Chaos, change," Cody ordered. "I'll get more rocks."

"Don't be stupid," Chaos said. "I can handle this. You need to get Kirit back to a manageable size, then both of you need to get out of here."

Fuck that. Cody said it out loud, too, for emphasis. "I am not running off and leaving you behind. Besides, look at Kirit. Does it look like he can move, let alone run?"

Chaos cursed again. Cody felt like doing the same. *Damn it, this is all my fault.* Kirit was in agony, there was a rampaging ogre headed their way, and for what? No good reason that Cody could come up with. What the hell had he been trying to prove, anyway?

That he needed Kirit? Hell, he didn't need a life-threatening situation for that.

He should have just sucked up his pride and told Kirit those terrifying words—which suddenly didn't seem quite so terrifying, after all.

"I am never listening to you again," Cody told Chaos.

A wave of heat washed over Cody. He blinked. A half-naked Kirit blinked back at him from within a crater of dirt. What remained of his clothes were tattered and filthy. Cody couldn't even begin to explain that one.

"I could have told you that," Kirit said around a gasp. "Never listen to Chaos. Ever."

"What happened to your clothes?" Cody asked rather stupidly.

"Focus, Cody!"

Cody ground his teeth together. He wasn't going to slug Chaos. He wasn't. They needed the idiot at the moment. He could break Chaos' nose later, once the danger was past.

"I'll hold him still," Kirit said. "And you can hit him."

"Sounds like a most excellent plan. Can you move yet?"

Kirit made it to his hands and knees, swaying slightly from the effort. The ground heaved and knocked him back down.

"Shit, here comes the ogre."

Cody grabbed Kirit under the arms and tried to get him at least semi-upright. He wasn't having much luck until Chaos joined the effort. Kirit couldn't stand straight, though, and was leaning heavily on Cody.

"I think he broke something in his back," Chaos said.

"What?" Cody couldn't help the slight screech in his voice because...well, broken back. *That's, like, the worst injury possible, isn't it?*

"Stop worrying, mate, I heal quickly."

"It's really not a major injury for one of us," Chaos assured Cody. "But he can't heal here. So, get moving."

Cody slung Kirit's arm over his shoulder and followed the command. Or at least, did so as best as he could. Kirit weighed a lot, even in human form. The man was so blasted big.

Kirit stumbled along, clearly trying to hold his own and not place too much of a burden on Cody. They were moving, but it was slowly. Too slowly.

Behind Cody, a loud, rumbling roar came, answered by a sharper, clearer one. He didn't turn to look, just kept putting one foot in front of another. A wave of heat hit his back. He hoped that meant Chaos had finally taken dragon form. They needed a distraction.

Another wave of heat washed over them, and this time Cody did look.

"Oh, shit. Down!" He yanked on Kirit, taking them both to the ground. Chaos whipped over their heads, far too close.

"What is he doing?" Kirit asked.

"I don't know, but this is really not a good place to be right now."

Unfortunately, now that they were down, Cody didn't think he could get them back up.

"I need to change again," Kirit said. "It will speed the healing process, hopefully enough that I can get back in the air."

"Then do— Oh, shit." Cody stared in horror at the wall of fire coming their way. *If we live through this, I am going to kill Chaos.* He didn't think anyone would stop him, either.

Kirit looked to see what had Cody so transfixed. Then it was his turn to tackle them both to the ground. He covered Cody from head to foot, trying to shelter Cody from the coming firestorm.

It would figure that Chaos' plan for getting rid of an ogre would be to set the entire countryside on fire.

The temperature soared. Cody gasped for breath, sweat pouring off him. Flames at Kirit's arms, which were wrapped tightly around Cody. Then the flames moved closer until they brushed against Cody's skin.

To his utter shock, there was no pain. He pulled free and held his arm out, caught between terror and fascination. The fire danced along his arm, a brilliant array of shades from burnt orange and deep red, into a pale blue and purple. Not ordinary fire, clearly, but even that didn't explain why he wasn't being burned.

It was strange, watching himself catch on fire. He was breathing hard, close to hyperventilating, waiting for agony that never came.

"Dragon-mate," Kirit whispered into Cody's ear, barely audible over the crackling and snapping of the conflagration surrounding them. "My Treasure."

"I'm still going to kill Chaos," Cody said.

"I can find many who will aid you."

"Including you?"

"Including me."

Kirit pushed up onto his hands and knees. Cody looked up into the familiar sharp features, watching as a smile widened Kirit's narrow lips.

"I love you," he blurted out. *Okay, maybe not the most appropriate time.* He wouldn't take back the words, though, not after seeing the pure, unadulterated joy that spread across Kirit's face. His eyes lightened to white, a color Cody had only seen on the dragon.

"My Treasure," Kirit said again.

Cody laughed, finally getting it. "Yes. Yes, I am."

Still smiling, Kirit looked towards the sky. A familiar ripple and a flash of light, then Cody was underneath a crouching dragon. With one mighty heave, Kirit took to the sky again. Cody got up in time to see Kirit and Chaos diving on the ogre in perfect tandem.

The ogre, for all that it lacked mental acuity, knew when it was beat. It turned and fled in that weird, lumbering gait.

Chaos landed and, faster than Cody could blink, turned back to human. He held up his hands, doing something magical to get the flames under control.

Something grabbed onto Cody's shoulders and he was suddenly dangling in mid-air. He had time to catch a glimpse of Chaos down below, face expressing stupefaction. It made Cody happy.

Then they were going higher and all thoughts vanished.

He really hated flying.

Chapter Twenty-Four

Cody swallowed hard, fighting down nausea from their short flight. He wanted to berate Kirit, but was afraid if he opened his mouth, he might puke. He let Kirit herd him through the halls without protest and into the first empty room they came across. The instant they were inside, Kirit pinned Cody against the wall.

"My Treasure," Kirit purred, rubbing the sides of their faces together.

"I'm sorry," Cody gasped, wiggling against Kirit's hard body, wanting to get as close as possible. "I am so sorry."

"You should be," Kirit said, albeit without any anger. "Do not put yourself in danger like that again."

"Not about that," Cody clarified. "Well, I am sorry about the whole ogre thing, but I meant for not understanding."

Kirit stopped nuzzling and began licking. He moved his way across Cody's cheek until he reached Cody's lips, taking a hard, passionate kiss. Cody tried to pull away to keep talking, but he didn't want to let go any more than Kirit did.

"Sorry. About...about...a...hang on, big guy." Cody put both hands on Kirit's chest and shoved. As much as he wanted to make out with his dragon, he needed to get these words out. "Just listen for a minute."

"Anything for you, my mate."

The look of bliss on Kirit's face made Cody laugh. The guy looked like he'd gotten into a really good batch of drugs.

"We can go back to the other in a minute. I need to say this." Cody ran his fingers through Kirit's hair, making certain he had the dragon's full attention. "I didn't understand, before. I thought any mate would do. I didn't realize that it was me you wanted."

"Of course it was you." Kirit's look of bliss transformed into an affronted scowl. "You're my Treasure."

"I am. But, big guy, you never said what a Treasure *was*."

"My beloved." Kirit started nuzzling again. "My heart and soul. The center of my world."

"Your love."

"Yes. My love."

"I get that, now. When we were out there, it hit me. You're not the only one who can be a little dense sometimes."

"You're perfect."

"Focus, Kirit," Cody said with another laugh.

"But you taste so good."

"Taste later, listen now. I love you. And you love me, don't you? Just like I am. I don't have to prove anything to anyone, and I certainly don't have to prove anything to you."

245

"No. No proving...to...anyone." Kirit's brow furrowed and he moved back, staring at nothing in particular. "Proving...the gods take it, I'm going to kill him!"

"Huh?" Cody blinked, unsure what happened to their conversation. "Chaos? 'Cause I know we already—"

"No, Seamus!"

"How the hell did Seamus get into this?"

"Proving. Think, mate. It was never about the ambassadors. He was being an interfering bastard, and I'm going to—"

"Oh, damn." The light finally clicked on, and Cody realized he was scowling, too. "That...that...oooh."

"How dare he?" Kirit stepped back, raking his hands through his hair.

"Okay, calm down." Cody bit his lip and tried to think through the maze of revelations popping through his head. "Okay. Enough of this bullshit. We're done here. At the palace. Forget the ambassadors, forget Raven, forget Seamus, forget everyone. You go pack. I'm going to find the king. Then we're heading to the mountains. Today. Right now."

"No, I will go and find the king."

"Nuh-uh. You'll take a bite out of him and then we'll never get out of this place. So you get our things and I'll meet you in the front courtyard."

Kirit looked like he wanted to argue, but instead he just stole another kiss before striding down the hall. Chaos watched him go—all right, he watched that gorgeous ass. Who could blame him? Kirit was a mess and barely clothed. There was, in fact, a nice hole in his pants situated right over one tight butt cheek. Cody wanted to stick his fingers into the space and caress the smooth skin, but he had other things to do first.

Cody watched Kirit disappear from sight, then went in the opposite direction. It was time to confront Seamus.

He did make a little detour first. It wasn't hard to find one of the men from Eviatt. The entire group was in what Seamus called the central receiving room. Basically, it was where he stuck people when he didn't want to deal with them, but couldn't risk offending them, either.

"Which one of you is in charge?" Cody asked. "Anybody?"

After a long moment, one thin man stood and raised his hand. There was reluctance in his movements and fright on his face.

Damn, they recognize me.

Cody put on his best reassuring smile. "I have a couple of quick questions, then I'll leave you alone. Promise."

The thin man stepped forward and nodded. "Ask your questions, sir. I cannot promise to answer."

Diplomats. "I just wanted to know what took you so long to get here. It's been, like, weeks."

A portly man shot to his feet, face turning red. "It was a disaster," he proclaimed in a voice that would be perfect for the stage. Cody could totally picture him doing Shakespeare.

"Such a horrid experience," the man continued.

"Sorry, what was your name?"

"Lewin. Lewin mac Ardwin."

Cody swallowed a snicker. "Lewin. Great. Nice to meet you. So, tell me the whole story."

Lewin clasped his hands in front of his chest. The other ambassadors groaned.

"We had been traveling for less than a day when royal guards met us on the road. We were so flattered. A royal escort! How propitious a sign. Surely our negations would proceed favorably."

"The action, Lewin, the action," Cody urged.

Lewin kept right on talking. "They bore a letter from the king, placing all necessary funds and equipment at our service. Of course, we immediately hired a carriage. We are men of the sea! Walking does not sit naturally on our constitutions."

Cody highly doubted that Lewin had spent a day at sea in his life.

"We were only thirty miles from our home when the first disaster struck."

First?

"Our carriage lost its wheels! Not just one, no, all four! They went rolling with merry glee down a hill, leaving us trapped in a toppled cage of death! It was such a traumatic experience. We immediately set up camp to nurse our wounds."

Cody didn't see any wounds. *Oh, wait, I think the guy has a tiny bruise on his cheek.*

"Of course, the guards were ever so solicitous. They insisted we tarry for two days to recover. Then, to recoup the time lost to our mishap, the guide provided by the royal escort suggested a shortcut. But the terrain had changed!"

I doubt that. Cody was seeing a suspicious pattern here, although Lewin clearly remained oblivious.

"It was dreadful, never have I been subjected to such a place. A swamp, full of pitfalls and demonic creatures. We wandered through the muck for four days, miserable, wet and continuously plagued by horrible bugs. Finally, our apologetic guide led us to civilization. I daresay without him, we would still be lost in that quagmire!"

No, because without him, you would never have been in that quagmire.

Cody had a hard time not laughing, although really, it wasn't funny.

"I have never been so happy as when we arrived at an inn. We stayed there for two more days, again to recoup. I still have a horrible bite on my leg from those bugs. All red and swollen, you should see."

"No, no, that's okay!" Cody held up his hand to stop Lewin, who looked more than happy to drop his pants and show Cody his bite. "What happened next?"

"This time when we left, Markus insisted we stick to the roads." Lewin waved at the third ambassador, who sat in the corner, presumably trying to hide. "He has a map, you see, and the crossroads are all well marked. And yet, we still managed to become lost! We were nearly to Breckens before we realized our mistake."

Cody looked appropriately appalled, even though he hadn't the slightest idea where Breckens was.

"We lost several more days retracing our steps. Then there was a festival in Bernhardt, and all the roads leading north were closed, so we were delayed for several more days. Oh, but the feasting, and the revelry! I must admit, I did not truly mind that delay. There was—"

"Yes, I'm sure it was a lovely party." Cody wanted to wrap this up, because he had the feeling that Lewin could go on for hours. "Thanks, gentlemen, you've been very helpful."

"But I didn't tell you yet about the Minotaur!"

Cody winced and decided it was time for a hasty retreat. Although, he was rather curious. *A Minotaur? No, better run while I can.*

Suspicions confirmed, Cody went hunting. Several sources and multiple rooms later, he finally tracked Seamus down in his office. He didn't bother to knock, just shoved the door open. Then he paused. He might have gaped a little, too.

The king was in the fireplace.

Cody paused halfway across the office and watched the king. Seamus stood, open book in hand, inside the gaping opening of the massive fireplace taking up one entire wall.

Huh. Maybe I hit my head out there.

Seamus looked up from his reading. "Oh, good day, Cody. What can I do for you?"

"You do realize you're standing in the fireplace?"

"Yes, so I am."

"Guess I'm not seeing things, then."

Seamus chuckled and closed his book, clutching it in one hand. He stepped out onto the carpet, turned and fondled a carving of an angel. Cody blinked some more, then decided it would be better for his sanity if he ignored the whole incident.

He spun, turning his back on Seamus, the fireplace and the busty angel. A few steps farther, and he dropped into one of the plush chairs in the small sitting area. Moments later, Seamus settled into the chair opposite him. The king propped his chin on his folded hands and regarded Cody thoughtfully.

"You are troubled about something."

"I'm trying to figure out how to politely tell you to go to hell," he said.

Seamus reared back, startled.

"I came to a few realizations," Cody continued. "Actually, Kirit did, but that was only because I've been distracted. I had a little talk with one of the ambassadors, and he shared a very interesting story with me. Long-winded and convoluted, but interesting."

Seamus looked to one side. *Hah. He looks guilty.*

"Yeah, that's what I thought. So, care to offer a few explanations? Tell me, why have you virtually kept us prisoner here on what is technically supposed to be our honeymoon?"

The guilt slid away, to be replaced with a look much harder and a bit on the scary side. "Do you understand the place the dragons hold in my realm? And I'm not referring to their rank."

"I know you rely on them far too heavily," Cody said bluntly. "You have an entire army at your disposal, it's not necessary to make them dance attendance on you the way you do."

"I need them close," Seamus said. "They are more than my personal guard. We're tied together in ways a mere human could never understand."

"Good to know where I stand in your opinion."

Seamus closed his eyes briefly. "I didn't mean that as an insult. There is magic at work in our bonds, extremely old and very complicated magic. I don't believe even the dragons fully understand it themselves. Suffice it to say, their health and well-being are of a vital concern to me."

"If that were true, then you would have let Kirit go home!" Cody burst out. "Because he's been an unhappy, cranky, frustrated mess for the past couple of weeks."

"You do not understand."

"Oh, I believe I do." Cody glared at Seamus, fed up with being taken for an idiot. He was a lot smarter than the king was giving him credit for. "You think I don't know this whole mess was a test? You wanted to see if the hostile atmosphere of your precious court would send me running back to Earth. Well, I'm sorry to disappoint you, but it didn't work. I'm still here, and I have no intention of going anywhere. And if I have to break the nose of every stuffed-shirt imbecile here, I will do just that. So, take that bit of information and shove it up your—"

Seamus held up one hand. "I understand your point," he said. Cody wondered if he should be nervous at the annoyance in Seamus' voice. "There is no need to be vulgar."

Seamus fixed him with an icy stare. "I had to make certain. I cannot have my dragon becoming attached to someone who isn't worthy of his attentions. Kirit is, regrettably, not always the brightest dragon in Faerie. You also came along when he was feeling particularly vulnerable. I could not allow him to be taken advantage of."

Cody sputtered. "Kirit is *not* stupid. He's incredibly special, and if you can't see it, then you're blind in more ways than one. Do you have any idea how hard he had to work to get me here? I left my entire life for him!" He surged to his feet. This conversation required a more confident stance.

"For a far better one," Seamus pointed out. "I know precisely what you were doing on Earth for a living. You honestly want me to believe you would prefer the life of a whore to one of luxury at my palace?"

"In case it's escaped your attention, I hate your stupid palace. I'm here for Kirit, nothing else, so listen up, you pointy-eared, egotistical jerk," Cody said in a hard voice of his own. "I get that you're uber-powerful and could kill me with a pinkie, but Kirit is *my* dragon, and don't you forget it."

Seamus' mouth twitched, but otherwise his face remained impassive. Cody, on the other hand, had a brief 'oh, shit' moment when he realized he'd just yelled at the freaking *king of everything*. He went back over the entire conversation quickly and wondered just how much trouble he was in.

"You passed, in case you wondered," Seamus said. This time Cody was sure he was suppressing a smile. The earlier, darker emotions seemed gone now.

"Good for me. Look, butt out, will you? I'm keeping Kirit, and you don't really have much to say about it. So, we're going to pack up and leave, and you're going to let us."

"I find it very attractive when you act forceful."

Cody whirled in his seat, not having heard Kirit enter the room. His big dragon was standing in the doorway, shoulders reaching from one side of the opening to the other. Kirit ducked inside and came to stand behind Cody's chair.

"I am not pleased," Kirit stated with the solemn air of a pronouncement.

"Do I look like I give a damn?" Seamus said.

Kirit growled. The sound wasn't Kirit's sexy, irritated one, either. No, there was true anger in this one.

"Calm down," Cody advised. With Kirit's arrival, some of the edges of his own temper had smoothed out. Oh, he was still annoyed as hell, but he wasn't furious anymore. It was probably a good thing. Cody could only imagine how much trouble he would have been in if he'd hauled off and hit the king.

And here he'd been worried about *Kirit's* temper.

Kirit placed both hands on Cody's shoulders and offered a quick squeeze of encouragement. "I know you mean well, Seamus, but this is something in which you cannot interfere. Cody is my mate, and if you had made me choose between my two loyalties..." He shook his head. "You might not have liked the results."

That shocked Seamus, Cody could tell from the wide eyes and the flush in his pale cheeks. Seamus hadn't anticipated being told that Kirit would pick Cody over him. It gave Cody a weird, warm and fuzzy feeling, knowing where he ranked in Kirit's affections. That Kirit would be willing to choose him over someone he had called friend for centuries.

"Come, mate," Kirit said with another squeeze. "We are going home."

Cody paused for a moment to look at a surprisingly subdued Seamus. "I don't want Kirit to have to choose," he said softly. "But I'm not going to stand aside the way I have been. Kirit is important, yeah, but so am I." It was a hard-won realization, but Nyx had made his point the other night. The whole ogre incident had only confirmed it. Cody wasn't doing anyone any favors by pretending to be someone else. "Just leave us alone for a while, okay? We'll come back in..." he trailed off, looking at Kirit.

"At least a month," Kirit filled in. "I need time with my mate."

"Understood." Seamus stood, as well, and offered a quick nod in their direction. "For what it's worth, I apologize if my actions have caused you distress."

Cody shook his head. He took Kirit's hand and led the dragon from the room, not looking back. Seamus might have apologized, but Cody figured he would do it all over again just the same. The king still believed he had been right.

Seamus would have to learn his lesson about meddling the hard way. He'd been lucky this time, that Cody didn't hold a grudge. The next dragon mate might not be so understanding.

"I thought we were meeting in the courtyard," he teased gently.

"I couldn't wait. I had a servant begin packing our bags," Kirit said. "We can be home in a couple of hours."

Cody looked sideways at Kirit as they walked down the hall. "It's going to take longer than that," he corrected. "This time, I'm picking the horses."

Kirit threw back his head and laughed, the sound warming Cody from the inside out. He tugged the big dragon closer for a quick kiss. "Love you," he said softly.

"My Treasure," Kirit whispered back.

"Close enough," Cody said with a grin.

Chapter Twenty-Five

Cody hit the ground on all fours, trying desperately...nope, too late. He gagged and threw up onto the nearest patch of dirt. A leaf was thrust into his view, and Cody took it, shuddering. He used the piece of shrubbery to wipe his mouth. *I really wish Faerie had mouthwash.*

"I wanted horses," Cody complained. "Horses."

"The horses would take three days," Kirit pointed out with infuriating logic.

"And flying gets us here in hours, yeah, I know. But if we took the horses, I wouldn't be throwing up in the bushes."

"If we took the horses, your legs and butt would be sore for a week. And then you would be too sore for sex."

Sometimes I wonder about Kirit's priorities. Although, a week without sex wasn't exactly something Cody would have been thrilled about, either.

"I know, but I hate—"

When he saw Kirit doing his best puppy-dog impression, Cody stopped talking. The big guy shouldn't have been able to pull it off, but those eyes...

It was the same argument Kirit had used to get him up in the air again. It had just seemed more reasonable when Cody wasn't tasting bile in his mouth.

Kirit helped Cody to his feet and presented him with a flask of water. Cody gratefully rinsed out his mouth and finally began to survey their surroundings.

The landscape was stunning. They were perched on a small plateau, the mountains sloping down sharply beneath them and rising high above them. The space was maybe the size of a football field, bordered by trees and massive boulders. The air was crisp and fresh, the scent of pines creating a heady aroma. To the right, a narrow dirt path wound through the bushes, around an outcropping of rock, and up into the mountain.

"That way?" Cody asked, gesturing.

"Indeed." Kirit smiled, the expression so wide and happy that Cody had to return it. The dragon was thrilled to be home. Cody half expected him to begin bouncing in place.

"Come, mate," Kirit said, grabbing Cody's hand and tugging him towards the path.

"The bags—"

"I will return. I wish to show you my home."

Cody couldn't help but laugh at the excitement in Kirit's voice. He allowed the dragon to pull him along, through the trees and up, higher and higher. The path was narrow and clung terrifyingly close to the edge at times, winding around like a snake to keep from becoming too steep. Cody couldn't exactly tell time without a watch, but he figured they hiked for close to a half hour before the trail levelled off.

Cody was once again taken by surprise when he spied the entrance to the dragon caves — and there was no mistaking it for anything but the entrance. It looked more like the entrance to a temple than anything. Huge, wide stone steps were carved into the rock, large enough for at least two full-grown dragons to walk side-by-side. At the top, two intricately carved, massive pillars flanked the entrance, with more pillars inside. The arched top contained more carvings. Cody thought they were words, but if it wasn't a language he'd ever seen before.

It was the bottom of the stairs, though, that caught his attention. A pair of dragons guarded each side, the life-size carvings so realistic, he half expected them to move. Their front feet were braced up on a pedestal, wings outstretched, mouths open. Magic pulsed from them, saturating the air. It tingled along his skin and made his nose itch.

"Who are they?" Cody asked.

"The first." Kirit stopped and ran one hand lovingly down the flank of the dragon on the right. "Artemis and Sciota. All dragons can trace their line to them."

"What happened to them?"

"Sciota died in battle, many millennia ago. Without her mate, Artemis went into seclusion and was never seen again."

"Wow. That's…wait, there are female dragons?"

"Artemis was the only one. Dragons now are spawned by magic."

"So you don't have parents?"

"A father, technically, as a male dragon is needed to fertilize the eggs, although I have never met him, nor do I know who he was. But the eggs themselves are created by a spell, one only Seamus knows."

"Wow," Cody said again. "Wait. You could have kids?"

"Eventually, if the King desires it." Kirit smiled and quirked one eyebrow. "You do not wish to be a parent?"

"Not anytime soon, that's for damn sure. Come on, show me your cave." Cody decided it was time to change the subject. Talk of kids made his skin itch even worse than the magic.

They climbed the stairs, Kirit having to help Cody. The distance wasn't made for human legs.

"Is there another way into this place?" Cody huffed about halfway up. "Because I am not doing this on a regular basis."

"Yes, my mate. There is an entrance nearer to our caves that leads to a lovely little clearing. I can also take flight from one of my caves, as well. I rarely use the front entrance, but I wished to show it to you."

"Fair enough." Thank God, because this is worse than the doors at the palace.

They went past the pillars, into the huge entry hall. It stretched deep into the mountains, slightly smaller pillars marking tunnels on all sides. Cody counted at least eight before Kirit pulled him into one on the left. The tunnels themselves were surprisingly bright. The walls glowed with a dull light, and periodic holes in the ceiling allowed the sunlight to reach the cool stone. The feel of magic was even stronger in here — Cody was rapidly coming to recognize it. He only hoped he grew used to it, so the damned itching would stop.

He scratched at his nose and followed close behind Kirit. The tunnels wound and intersected and he was lost after about the second turn. Since it didn't sound like he would need to come back this way, Cody didn't bother trying to memorize the way.

They passed through a dim section of tunnel, around another corner, and hit a dead end. A large wooden door blocked their way, and Kirit put his hand on it, whispering something that Cody didn't understand. A dull light flared around the dragon's hand, and the door swung open silently.

"Cool," Cody said.

Kirit grinned, then pushed the door open the rest of the way.

Cody knew his mouth had dropped open, but damn. This was far, far better than he had expected. It was certainly unlike any cave he had ever seen before, or even imagined.

"Okay, I can live like this," he declared.

"Good. And I can change things to suit you. This is your home now, and I wish for you to be comfortable."

"Yeah, no problem there."

If not for the tunnels they had just exited, Cody would have sworn they were still in the palace. Almost every inch of the floor of the large room was covered in plush rugs. The walls were draped in tapestries and thick velvet curtains, all in shades of deep reds, purples, and blues. Bookshelves took up space along one wall, and the other two had open arches leading to other rooms. Most of the room was empty, but there was a low table in corner, and a seating area in another, made up of cushions and low couches. By the bookshelves sat a massive desk and another table, this one long, the top carved with scenes of dragons and knights.

"Very cool. What about food?" Because Cody didn't see anything even remotely resembling a kitchen.

"Ahh, there is a common room a few tunnels back, with a large firepit and storage. I will show you later. The bathing room is this way."

They went through the archway on the left, and Cody couldn't hold back a happy cry.

The ceiling was open to the sky in the middle, and despite being mostly underground, there was a flourishing rainforest inside. He could hear the trickling of water and traced it to a back corner, where a large pool bubbled. He tested it, and the water was nice and warm, almost hot. A stream ran from one end, down a slight slope, and out through a small opening in the side.

"This is fantastic," he said, breathing in the thick, humid air.

"One more room," Kirit said. "This one is special."

Cody took Kirit's hand again. They went back to the main room, and through the other arch. This one led to a small foyer-type space and another massive wooden door. Kirit opened it the same way as the first.

"Only the other dragons have seen this place," he said. "And Seamus, of course. But only certain people are ever granted entrance to a dragon's hoard."

Cody didn't quite know what to say to that, so he remained quiet.

They entered, and Cody had to blink a few times to clear his sight. The place was blinding, and not just because of the sun streaming through the back wall. The sun bounced off glittering piles of gold and gems, and it was enough to make spots dance in front of his eyes.

"Holy shit," he said in awe. It was like that damn Cave of Wonders from the animated *Aladdin* movie, only bigger. Gold bars and coins of different metals, emeralds and rubies, pearls and opals, sapphires and diamonds. It was incredible, and didn't quite look real to Cody.

Then the view caught his gaze, and he gasped again.

One wall was pretty much open, a low arch forming a half-circle in the stone. Beyond, the tops of the mountains gleamed with snow. Green fields butted up against the rock, flowers creating a splash of color. He took a step closer, utterly enthralled but the sight. They were above most of the peaks and there, on the horizon, he could make out the transparent shapes of the twin moons, only just visible in the daylight.

"Wow." He knew he was repeating himself, but what the heck did someone say to this?

It was a stark reminder that he had entered a different world. So much of life at the palace had been decadent, but familiar. This, though...this was completely alien.

And he loved it.

Cody turned to smile at his dragon. Kirit was watching him with eager eyes.

"Thank you," Cody said, moving closer to hug his dragon tightly. "Thank you so much for bringing me here. Into this world."

"I would have no one else," Kirit said, returning the embrace. They stood there for several long minutes, basking in the warmth of love and the heated rays of the sun. Then Kirit stepped back.

"May I..." He trailed off, looking uncertain. Cody chuckled.

"Go ahead, big guy. I know you've been going nuts."

Kirit's smile grew even larger. Cody moved back to give him room.

Raven had taken Cody aside early on and given him a little talk. Kirit, he said, and Nyx, to a lesser extent, were more dragon than human. While Raven and Chaos spent large amounts of time at court and were at home in their human forms, Kirit and Nyx were the opposite. They were happiest as dragons, and always had been. They had been known to spend weeks at a time without changing, and Cody would have to accept that. It wasn't something that could be helped.

Given space, Cody blinked against that familiar flash of light, the buzzing against his skin getting stronger, then fading.

"Damn, I'll never get used to that." The sight of Kirit's dragon form always took him by surprise. So big, so magical, yet with those same pale eyes looking out from the reptilian face. Cody lifted one hand and rubbed it on the long, narrow snout. The scales always took him by surprise, too, slightly scratchy but with a soft give to them.

Kirit huffed with pleasure, then waddled over to a nearby dragon-sized clear spot. He settled down, leaving the riches to pile around him. He spread his wings, wordlessly inviting Cody closer.

Cody eagerly accepted. He had found that he really like snuggling with a dragon.

First, though, he went and retrieved a pillow from the other room. Dragons might like lying on top of their treasures, but Cody found gemstones to be rather uncomfortable to sit on. The sharp edges poked his ass.

Pillow situated, Cody leaned back against his dragon. The sun was beginning to set, and the breeze coming through the opening was turning chilly, but the heat Kirit put out kept him nice and warm. They sat together in silence, watching the sunset turn the sky shades of light pink and burnt orange.

Kirit made a soft coo, the sound full of inquiry, and Cody snuggled closer into the sheltering warmth of scales and claws.

"Yeah," he said softly. "I'm glad I said yes to you."

Despite everything that had happened so far, and no matter what happened in the future, Cody would never regret saying yes to coming with Kirit. This new world may be strange at times, and intimidating at others, but having Kirit made any struggle worthwhile.

"I love you," he whispered, absently tracing along one hooked claw with his index finger.

Kirit rumbled back, the sound possessive and affection, saying everything that Cody could feel coming from the big creature.

It was amazing how much could be said without words.

They watched the sun vanish from view and the outline of the moons grow stronger. Cody's eyes were drooping, limbs heavy. Safe with his dragon, he let himself drift off to sleep.

Epilogue

"What is it, Majesty?"

Seamus sighed. With precise movements, he re-folded the letter from one of his guards on the outskirts of the city.

"Ellar is dead," he announced.

"Who killed him?"

Seamus quirked his mouth in amusement — or as much amusement as he could muster at the moment, anyway. "It doesn't escape my notice that you asked 'who killed him', not 'how did he die'."

Desmond shrugged. "Your nephew was, regrettably, a thoroughly dislikeable person."

"True. In answer to your question, I don't know. They found his body on the road to Faring Pass, just north of Malea. I should be sorry. I don't actually have that many relatives left."

"He was becoming a problem," Desmond replied calmly. "It would have come to this sooner or later."

It always surprised Seamus that his perfect courtier could be so pragmatic about violence. But then, Desmond was pragmatic about *everything*. His meticulous and practical nature made him the ideal steward. And the ideal confidante. Desmond was the only person in the entire palace that Seamus felt he could be brutally honest with.

"At least this way," Desmond continued, "you don't have to deal with him yourself. I, for one, am grateful that someone beat you to the punch."

"You've been spending time with Cody," Seamus observed with a smile.

"I like him. He brings a sense of change. I do hope Kirit doesn't keep them sequestered in the mountains for too long. Cody's presence is good for the rest of the court."

"They have become complacent lately," Seamus admitted.

He had enjoyed seeing the nobility at a loss. They held too much power these days—Seamus had to navigate the morass carefully. He welcomed anything that shook them up and took their attention away from his actions.

He should probably see about fixing the power balance, but there was always too much else to do.

Desmond paused, frowning in thought. Seamus waited patiently, knowing the man would speak up eventually.

Either that, or he would hover until Seamus yelled, *then* he would say what was on his mind. They'd been together many centuries—they had a system.

"Our new human isn't the only thing that will bring change in the coming days."

Seamus froze in the act of shuffling the disorganized piles of paper—he lived by the theory that if he moved them around, he could give the appearance of working without actually doing any work.

"What have you seen?" he asked.

"I don't know. There is...something. It is infuriatingly vague yet."

Desmond's voice held a familiar note of frustration. Seamus only heard that tone when they were discussing Desmond's slight precognition abilities. It was a dying talent among the Fae — few possessed any form of the Sight once so common to their people.

Unfortunately for Desmond, the ability he had inherited from his mother was more annoying than anything. If the power was any weaker, he wouldn't be able to foresee at all. Any stronger, and it would be infinitely more useful. As things stood, his poor steward only received hazy pictures and impressions, enough for a glimpse and no more. It left the normally even-tempered man irritable and snarly.

"You'll decipher it eventually." Seamus had every confidence in Desmond, who was nothing if not tenacious. He could, in fact, give the Draak lessons. From past experience, Seamus knew the man would poke and prod at the information until he made sense of it.

"I simply hope I do so in time," Desmond replied.

Seamus groaned. "Oh, no, that isn't ominous at all."

Some days, he really hated being the one in charge. Most days, come to think of it. The role of king was rarely a fun one.

"Contact Kirit, please," he said, changing the subject. No sense dwelling on Desmond's words until he could do something about them.

"Shall I call him back to the palace?"

"No, just let Kirit know his problem has been solved. He won't be pleased. He was having happy thoughts of maiming."

"I think he was going to go straight to dismemberment," Desmond said wryly, already scribbling the note in his perfect penmanship. "I'll let him know he's been thwarted. I am concerned, however, about allowing the Draak to scatter right now. Whatever I'm seeing, it will require their aid."

Seamus shook his head. "No, let him enjoy his new mate." Seamus scowled. "If you're correct, he deserves to do so while he still can."

About the Author

Born and raised in the middle of the Midwest, I have always been a dreamer. More often than not I could be found with my nose buried in a book (many of which I had to sneak past my parents). It wasn't long before I started trying my hand at writing more of the stories I loved. After years of penning tales that rarely left the hard drive of my computer, I discovered M/M romance. As with all genres, it wasn't long before my own characters started to take shape.

There is little I love more than wandering new places and, on occasion, entirely new worlds with my characters. They can range from cowboys to Victorian noblemen, accountants to shapeshifters, and everything in between. I write mainly m/m romance, usually with paranormal or fantasy elements. I willingly follow my characters wherever they decide to go, sometimes with unusual results. I have little control over their actions…any naughty behaviour is all their doing!

KM Mahoney loves to hear from readers. You can find her contact information, website details and author profile page at http://www.totallybound.com.

Totally Bound Publishing

www.ingramcontent.com/pod-product-compliance
Lightning Source LLC
Chambersburg PA
CBHW021521240626
47154CB00002B/731